HO-HO-
HOMICIDE

Books by Kaitlyn Dunnett

Kilt Dead

Scone Cold Dead

A Wee Christmas Homicide

The Corpse Wore Tartan

Scotched

Bagpipes, Brides, and Homicides

Vampires, Bones, and Treacle Scones

Ho-Ho-Homicide

Published by Kensington Publishing Corporation

HO-HO-
HOMICIDE

KAITLYN
DUNNETT

KENSINGTON BOOKS

KENSINGTON BOOKS are published by

Kensington Publishing Corp.
119 West 40th Street
New York, NY 10018

ISBN-13: 978-0-7582-9283-4

First Kensington Hardcover Edition: November 2014

Printed in the United States of America

For Amie, who will (I hope) get a kick out of All Things Mystical.

Chapter One

Liss MacCrimmon Ruskin emerged from the back room of Moosetookalook Scottish Emporium, where she'd been packing orders for shipment. A professional smile lit her face, and the words "Good morning. How may I help you?" were on the tip of her tongue. They never made it out of her mouth.

"Gina?"

The last person Liss expected to see at ten o'clock on a Wednesday morning in early November was her BFF from high school, Gina Snowe. They'd long since drifted apart. Gina hadn't even come to Liss's wedding. In the nearly five and a half years since, their only regular contact had been an occasional Christmas card.

"The one and only," Gina said.

She was a walking advertisement for the successful, high-profile businesswoman—power suit in a muted shade of red, perfectly manicured fingernails, exquisitely applied makeup, and light but expensive perfume. Liss didn't need to look down at Gina's feet to know she was wearing a designer brand of shoes with heels high enough to cause any ordinary woman to break an ankle. Not only could Gina walk in them, but she also thought they were comfortable!

In jeans and a loose pullover sweater, Liss felt decidedly underdressed.

They engaged in a brief hug. The gesture felt awkward, but it was a better alternative than air kissing. Liss retreated behind the sales counter as soon as Gina released her.

"This is a surprise."

"A good one, I hope. This place looks exactly as I remember it," Gina`added` as her gaze swept over the shop.

The shelves and tables were filled with Scottish-themed gift items, many of them imported from Scotland. Racks held ready-made kilts and tartan skirts. The walls were hung with colorful plaids and framed prints of heather-covered hills and rugged Highland peaks.

"It even smells the same."

"Lemon-scented furniture polish." Liss shoved a stray strand of dark brown hair behind her ear. "As the saying goes, if it ain't broke, don't fix it."

When Gina gave a toss of her head and laughed, Liss couldn't help but notice that her expertly styled black locks fell effortlessly back into place, not a single strand awry. Betsy Twining at the Clip and Curl, located in the back half of the building that housed the post office, couldn't have achieved such perfection if she'd had a month of Sundays in which to practice.

Liss eased herself onto the high wooden stool behind the sales counter and rested her elbows on its smooth, glossy surface. "What's up, Gina?"

"Up? Why should you think anything is *up?*"

"Oh, I don't know." Gina's "Little Miss Innocence" act didn't fool Liss for a second. The look in Gina's almond-shaped eyes was calculating rather than naive.

"Maybe because you're a hotshot lawyer in Chicago and I run what you'd probably call a mom-and-pop tourist trap in rural Maine? You didn't drop by to buy kilt hose or a thistle pin."

"We were good buddies once. Maybe I want to catch up with an old friend." Gina feigned interest in the small revolving display case on one end of the counter. It held an assortment of thistle jewelry, not only pins but also earrings, necklaces, and charms.

"That was half a lifetime ago," Liss reminded her. And even at seventeen, the two of them had never had a great deal in common. Just one thing, really. They'd each been deeply involved in extracurricular activities that nobody else in their high school understood or appreciated.

Back in the day, Gina had claimed they broadened each other's horizons. While Liss had spent all her spare time at Scottish festivals, entering, and usually winning, dance competitions, Gina had been on the beauty pageant circuit. She'd earned enough scholarship money to put herself through college and law school.

Gina batted the display case, setting it whirling. "Okay. Okay. I have an agenda. So, sue me!"

"I'm listening." With one hand, Liss stopped the spin, but she didn't take her eyes off Gina's face.

"I need a favor." The admission didn't sit well. Gina snapped out her next words, impatient and out of sorts. "Get something to write on. Knowing you, you'll want to take notes."

Liss's clipboard was on the open shelf beneath the sales counter. Without comment, she extracted it and fished a felt-tip pen out of the cracked mug she used to hold pens, pencils, and markers. Holding it poised, she waited, curious to learn what had happened to shake the cool-as-a-cucumber composure of Ms. Gina Snowe.

"I'm here," Gina said, "to offer you and Dan an all-expenses-paid week's vacation in an idyllic location."

At the word *vacation,* Liss felt her interest quicken. She doodled a palm tree on the yellow, college-ruled page. "Define *idyllic.*"

"Exactly your thing—rural, remote, and quiet."

Liss waved a hand toward the scene beyond the Emporium's display window. "Take a look outside. Moosetookalook already offers me all that and more." The village had a population of just over a thousand and was located in the scenic Western Maine mountains. It was close, but not *too* close, to several major ski areas.

Gina didn't bother to turn around. Instead she leaned in. "Here's the thing, Liss. I came to Maine to inspect a Christmas tree farm I inherited from a great-uncle. The original plan was to stop by your place for a visit, maybe even try to persuade you and Dan to join me for a few days."

"Uh-huh." Liss took the part about the invitation with a grain of salt. It hadn't escaped her notice that the other woman hadn't once asked after Dan. For all Gina knew, Liss and Dan could have separated months ago. Or be encumbered by small children. Or have one on the way.

Still, the words *Christmas tree farm* struck a chord. Liss cherished fond memories of the annual pilgrimage to find the perfect Christmas tree. When she was a girl, she and her parents had tromped all over a local farmer's fields. When they finally agreed on one, her father had always let her help cut it down with a handsaw. Beside her first doodle, Liss drew a tiny Christmas tree.

"I no sooner arrived," Gina went on, "intending to stay for two weeks, than I was called back to Chicago. I'm needed there to handle a major criminal case. I don't know when I'm going to be able to return to Maine."

Gina's plight didn't spark Liss's sympathy, not when Gina was highly paid to be at her clients' beck and call. "I'm not sure I understand the problem. Reschedule your stay."

"One issue to do with the property is time-sensitive."

"Meaning?"

"It's a *Christmas* tree farm. I need to know if there's any chance to make money off the place this year. If you and Dan will spend a little time there in my stead—just a week—you can evaluate its potential for me."

"We don't know anything about trees." Liss's protest was automatic, but she had to admit that her curiosity was piqued.

"You know how to make a success of a small business."

"Sure. Work ten-hour days, seven days a week. I don't have time to—"

Gina cut her off. "Some of the Christmas trees are Scotch pines. You can bring back as many boughs as you like to decorate the Emporium for the holidays."

"That's your best argument? You're slipping, Counselor. And isn't Scotch pine the variety that stinks to high heaven?"

"You're thinking of white spruce," Gina shot back, "and the branches smell bad only if you crush the needles."

"Been reading up on the subject, have you?" Quietly amused, Liss couldn't resist a bit more "needling."

"Come on, Liss. Be a sport and help out an old pal."

With a sigh, Liss abandoned the clipboard, hopped off her stool, and headed for the stockroom, leaving Gina to follow. "I wasn't kidding about the ten-hour days, Gina. The Emporium, especially the online and mail-order side of the business, keeps me plenty busy, and Dan—"

Gina caught her arm. "I'll make it worth your while. I'll pay you for your time, *and* I'll pay the salary of someone to keep this place open while you're gone." Liss turned to face her. "Seems to me that if you two are working as hard as you say, you *need* a vacation."

"Gina, I can't take money for—"

"Call it a birthday present, then."

Liss winced. She'd celebrated her thirty-fourth a few weeks earlier. By her thirty-fifth, she had a pretty big decision to make, one she'd been brooding about lately.

As if she sensed Liss was wavering, Gina abruptly changed tactics. "Think of the romantic possibilities," she argued, drawing Liss back into the main room of the shop. "You and Dan all alone—no interruptions by family or friends. Face it, Liss. You live in a fishbowl here."

When she'd hauled Liss to the front window, Gina came to a stop. A passing neighbor—Stu Burroughs from Stu's Ski Shop, on his way to the post office to pick up his mail—peered in at them and waved.

"Everybody in Moosetookalook knows everybody else's business. Wouldn't it be nice to get away for a bit to a place where *nobody* knows your name?"

There *were* some things she and Dan needed to talk about, Liss thought. And there was no question that they could do with a short vacation. From one heartbeat to the next, she came to a decision. "What do you want us to do?"

Liss retrieved her clipboard from the counter and scribbled down details as fast as Gina could rattle them off. As she wrote, her mind worked even more furiously. An hour later, Gina was on her way to the airport and Liss had committed herself . . . and Dan . . . to spending a week on a Christmas tree farm.

Now all she had to do was convince her overworked husband that he needed a vacation.

Liss stood in the doorway of what had once been an old carriage house. She told herself she was planning her strategy, but the honest truth was that she was taking advantage of an opportunity to admire the man she'd married.

Dan Ruskin was not movie-star handsome, nor was he athlete muscular. But he had a certain strength, both of character and in his person. That was what had drawn Liss to him even before they fell in love. He was, in the simplest terms, a nice guy.

That was not to say that they always agreed. Or that he was never irritated with her. But he accepted her as she was. He didn't try to change her. And when she was a bit too impulsive and committed them to something without running it by him first, he usually went along with it.

Usually.

Dan had begun using the carriage house as a wood-working shop as soon as he bought the house behind which it was situated. When his custom woodwork started to sell well, he'd built onto the back, doubling the size of his work space. The long, narrow room contained nearly a dozen large pieces of equipment—saws, sanders, and who knew what all. An elaborate filtration system kept down the amount of sawdust in the air and dissipated the fumes from varnish and other smelly substances. A propane-fueled heater warmed the place in winter.

Dan worked at the far end of the shop, securing Styrofoam corners onto one of his custom-made jigsaw-puzzle tables with stretch wrap and strapping tape. When a lock of sandy brown hair fell over his eyes as he worked, he absentmindedly shoved it out of his way. Liss supposed she'd have to remind him to get a haircut. Dan never bothered with to-do lists of his own.

She must have made some small sound. She had no idea how he could hear it with stereo speakers blaring, but he glanced up, smiled when he saw her, reached over to flick a switch, and cut off Gordon Lightfoot just as the gales of November slashed the doomed freighter *Edmund Fitzgerald*. Sometimes Dan listened to folk music, sometimes hard rock, and sometimes classical, but he never worked to the sound of skirling bagpipes. That was the one passion he and Liss did not share.

"Sorry to interrupt," Liss said when silence had descended.

"I'm almost finished for the day. All I have left to do is get this box ready for UPS to pick up in the morning."

Liss threaded her way through the shop until she was near enough to see his muscles flex beneath his sweatshirt as he wrestled the heavy wooden table and its equally well-wrapped detached legs into a reinforced cardboard carton for the trip to California or Florida or New Jersey. He'd dispatched jigsaw-puzzle tables to almost every state in the country, and only the prohibitive cost of international shipping had discouraged potential buyers from as far away as England and Australia.

"I had a surprise visitor today," Liss began, plunging into a full confession of what she'd agreed to do.

She'd barely finished before Dan shook his head. "I can't take a week off. I've got six more orders waiting to be filled."

"You *always* have orders waiting to be filled. You made more than fifty jigsaw-puzzle tables last year."

Dan didn't look up from sealing the carton.

"You *know* you need a break. That's why you raised your prices six months ago. You were hoping that would result in fewer orders." The plan had backfired. Even *more* people had preordered custom-made jigsaw-puzzle tables. "Dan, are you listening to me? The world will not come to an end if we go away for a few days of R & R."

"I can't just drop everything. Besides, what if Dad needs me? Or Sam?"

When they'd first been married, Dan had been working three jobs—at Ruskin Construction with his brother Sam; at The Spruces, the hotel his father owned; and as a woodworker, making boxes, clocks, and other small items in his spare time. Within a year of the wedding, he'd opened his retail storefront. Little had he known then that one of his offerings, the jigsaw-puzzle table, would become so popular that it would end up being his only product.

Both the credit and the blame for his success went to Liss. She had been the one who'd designed his Web page. Soon after, people from all over the United States and Canada had started ordering his tables. He'd stumbled upon a niche market lucrative enough to allow him to earn a living supplying it . . . so long as he was willing to work straight-out seven days a week, twelve months a year.

Hands on hips, Liss glared at her husband. "You have an overdeveloped sense of responsibility, Dan Ruskin. Right now, *I'm* the one who needs you."

At last she had his full attention. "You've *got* me, babe," he said with a grin and a glint in his eyes.

When he reached for her, she danced away, holding one hand in front of her in the traditional "halt" position. "Stop right there, mister. I'm trying to hold a rational discussion here."

"Oh, come on. Use your womanly wiles to seduce me into doing your bidding. Please?" This time he caught her and tugged her close for a kiss.

Dan Ruskin was a seriously good kisser. He was also six-foot-two to her five-foot-nine, broad shouldered to her slender, and she was crazy about him. For a brief interlude, Liss had a hard time remembering why she'd come looking for him.

"Rational," she repeated when they came up for air. The firmest tone of voice she could manage wouldn't have convinced a cat to roll in catnip, but Dan released her, anyway, and went back to his packing.

"Give it your best shot," he invited her.

Liss leaned back against one of Dan's worktables, arms crossed in front of her chest. "You and I have both been working straight-out ever since we got back from our honeymoon. No time off for good behavior. We *need* a vacation, and the timing is perfect. We're past leaf-peeper season, and it's too early for the pre-Christmas rush. I can close up shop for a week without losing much in the way of walk-in business. If we both set up 'out of office' e-mail responses, any new online customers will know when we'll be back and can plan accordingly. They'll still be able to send in orders."

"It's not a good idea to be unavailable. Customers expect fast service when they spend their hard-earned cash."

"Customers have to wait for the order to be filled, anyway. Seriously, Dan. Give me one good reason why we can't take a week's vacation. It's not like I want to go to Hawaii or Australia or Sri Lanka. Gina's Christmas tree farm is in New Boston. We'll be only a couple of hours away from home. If there's an emergency, we can hop in the car and come straight back."

"What would constitute an emergency?"

She came close to answering with a flip "Serious injury or death." In the nick of time, she realized that she might be tempting fate to joke about such a thing. It had been a long while since she'd last encountered sudden death—a little over five years, on a Halloween she'd never forget—but for several years before that she'd had an alarming tendency to stumble into murder investigations. She sincerely hoped she wouldn't have to deal with *any* sort of crime ever again.

"What if there's a crisis at the Emporium?" Dan asked.

"There won't be. I told you. I'll close it for the duration." She'd already countered Gina's original offer with the proposal that her old friend pay a cat-and-house sitter rather than a sales clerk. Liss had a certain young relative in mind for the job, one who was currently squirreling away every penny he could earn into a college fund.

"My shop, then."

"*Your* shop?" Liss couldn't help but smile. Dan was

running out of excuses. "It's a co-op now. Or have you forgotten?"

When he'd switched over to making nothing but jigsaw-puzzle tables, Dan's inventory of handcrafted wooden objects had shrunk to almost nothing. He'd solved the lack-of-stock problem by turning his storefront, Carrabassett County Wood Crafts, into a cooperative venture with other local craftspeople. They had pooled their resources, as well as the products they created, and had hired a full-time employee to run the place.

"I haven't forgotten. But what if—"

"If Maud can't handle anything that comes up, she shouldn't be working for you." Maud Dennison, the co-op's sales clerk and bookkeeper, was a retired teacher who'd found she didn't like having so much time on her hands. Since she'd capably managed obstreperous seventh graders for forty-plus years, Liss knew she could handle anything that came along.

"I don't see how we can close up and go away without a care in the world," Dan grumbled as he walked the heavy box onto a dolly and trundled it toward the door. There was only one more step to go—print a mailing label and assembly instructions and attach those to the carton.

Liss trailed after him, gaining confidence with every step. "It's easy. In my case, all I have to do is put a sign on the door. It isn't as if the Emporium is ever swamped with customers."

"You get a lot more walk-ins than you used to. So does Carrabassett County Wood Crafts. So does everyone in town."

"Victims of our own success," Liss agreed.

Where once she and the other local business owners

had taken every Sunday and Monday off, now they usually stayed open seven days a week. The Moosetookalook Small Business Association had become so adept at promoting the unique gift shops surrounding the village square as a shopping mecca that tour buses had them on their regular routes and groups of retirees booked blocks of rooms at The Spruces just to be able to enjoy the experience. Seasonal festivities drew good crowds, too, which meant that volunteering on behalf of the MSBA took up even more of Liss and Dan's dwindling supply of free time.

"I can't see how we'll manage, Liss," Dan said. "Tell Gina to hire someone to evaluate her property."

She threw her hands in the air. "She hired *me*. And she gave me a blank check to use to hire a cat sitter."

"Send it back." The box in position, he turned to face her.

Liss sent him her best exasperated glare. "If you really can't see your way clear to go, I'll take on the job without you. I gave my word to Gina that I'd evaluate the place for her. I don't break my promises."

Dan looked thoughtful. "How about this? You drive over there, take a quick look at the place, and come back the same day." He opened the door and gestured for her to exit first.

"I'm *going* for a week," she said as she swept past him. "Even if you don't need a break from routine, I do. So, I'm leaving on Friday—two days from now." She looked back at him over her shoulder. "Are you coming with me or not?"

The challenge in her voice made him scowl. He locked up, then stood there, staring at the back of their house and what could be seen of the street between it and the building next door.

Progress, Liss thought. After a moment, she went back to him and eased herself in under his arm. She planted a quick kiss on his cheek.

Darkness came early at this time of year. The pale glow of streetlamps illuminated not only the sidewalk and street but also a section of the town square, where a bandstand and merry-go-round held pride of place, along with a monument to the Civil War dead. As Liss watched, a woman appeared on one of the paths that wound through the green. Liss recognized her as soon as the light struck her pale hair—Sherri Campbell on her way home, crossing from the police station in the municipal building to her apartment above Carrabassett County Wood Crafts.

Sherri must be on the two-to-ten shift, Liss thought, *and taking a supper break to spend a little time with Pete and the kids.* There were two of them, Sherri's teenage son, Adam Willett, and the couple's four-year-old daughter, Amber.

Liss took a deep breath. "We could use an opportunity to talk about . . . things."

Dan said nothing, but she could feel his arm tense where it draped across her shoulders.

"I think I'll go look over what's in my closet." Liss slipped away from him. "I need to decide what to take with me. November weather is always tricky to pack for."

He waited until she reached the back door of the house before he spoke. "You'd best pick out clothes for me, too."

"Did you hear Liss and Dan are taking a vacation?" Sherri Campbell handed two heavy-laden plates to her husband and grabbed the other two herself. "They're leaving tomorrow."

"Yeah, Dan told me."

Pete deftly deposited his own supper on the table and slid the other plate into Sherri's place while she served Adam and Amber. The little girl's eyes lit up when she saw the mound of mashed potatoes. Sherri couldn't help but grin as she sat down and reached for the salt. Before their daughter ate a single bite, she would shape those spuds into the signature landscape from *Close Encounters of the Third Kind*. Young as Amber was, Sherri doubted she had understood much of the rest of that movie, but she had definitely got the part with the potatoes.

"He's not exactly enthusiastic about it." As Pete settled into his chair, it creaked under his weight. He was built like a linebacker, solid and square, but what had been chunky when they met had begun to waver on the edge of overweight.

Sherri needed a moment to switch out of Mommy mode. "Dan isn't? Why not?"

"Maybe he thinks Gina Snowe has a lot of nerve expecting them to drop everything to do her a favor."

"She always was something of a queen bee." Sherri ate mechanically, taking an occasional sip of Moxie, a beverage she'd only recently rediscovered. Her thoughts drifted back to the last time she'd run into Liss's friend Gina. It had not been a pleasant encounter.

Why she'd decided to attend her tenth high school reunion, Sherri would never know. Maybe because she'd had Pete as her escort, and Liss and Dan were with them? She should have known better. Ten years hadn't been enough time for the cattier members of the class to sheath their claws. Gina Snowe wasn't the worst of the lot, but she'd been ready and willing to repeat what she knew about Sherri and the mistakes she'd made when she was younger. That most of what she'd said was true only made it worse. Sherri had dropped out of school and left town halfway through their senior year. She'd taken up with some pretty unsavory characters during her years away from Moosetookalook. She'd returned with Adam but without a husband, adding one more "sin" to the list.

That was all a long time ago, she reminded herself as she looked around the table at husband, son, and daughter. She'd built a new life for herself since then.

At the time of that tenth reunion, Sherri recalled, she'd barely taken the first steps toward a tentative friendship with Liss MacCrimmon. The bond between them had strengthened in the months and years that followed. These days, with Sherri married to Pete and Liss to Dan, Sherri was closer to Liss than Gina had ever been. While it might be petty to think in terms of a rivalry of BFFs, the truth of the matter was that it *did* make Sherri feel better to know that Liss thought highly of her.

And it wasn't only Liss who liked and respected her, either. Sherri was certain no one in their small town had forgotten her past, but she also knew that, in the present, she was well regarded by the community she served as chief of police of the Moosetookalook Police Department.

The subject of Dan and Liss's "vacation" didn't come up again that evening, but Sherri did find herself thinking about her friend while she watched Amber at play after supper. Once Adam had gone off to his own room to do homework, the little girl reveled in having her parents all to herself.

"Come on, pumpkin," Pete crooned. "Show me what you can do with that pencil." He was trying to teach her to print her name.

They sat side by side on the carpet, dark heads bent over the oversize drawing pad between them. Amber already resembled her father far more than her petite, blond mother. Measurements taken by her pediatrician indicated she was going to be tall, close to Pete's five-foot-ten. She would tower over Sherri by the time she finished growing, and would probably end up being taller than Adam, too.

"She's only four, Pete."

"But she's the smartest little rug rat in the entire world. Look at that. That's an *A*."

It looked like three random lines to Sherri, but she hadn't the heart to burst Pete's bubble. Instead, from her perch on the sofa, she continued to watch the interaction between father and daughter.

There were a lot of smart little rug rats around, Sherri mused. She wondered if Liss and Dan were thinking of adding one of their own to the mix. Maybe there was more to their vacation than simply doing a favor for Gina Snowe.

Sherri was not the only one in their circle of friends and family to have been pregnant during the last few years. Sandy and Zara Kalishnakof, who owned and operated Dance Central, had two young children, both carrottops like Zara. And Mary Ruskin Winchester, Liss's sister-in-law, was currently expecting her sixth child. Liss, though, had never even hinted that she might want a child of her own.

Later, after Adam and Amber had been tucked into

their beds, Sherri broached the subject with Pete. "Has Dan ever said anything to you about starting a family?"

"None of our business, hon." Pete avoided meeting her eyes by pretending to be fascinated by the late-night news on TV.

Sherri wasn't buying it. He knew something. He just wasn't saying.

But he was also right. It was none of their business.

Frowning, Liss consulted the map Gina had drawn for her. "I can't make heads or tails of this. We're going to have to stop in town and ask directions."

They had driven some 140 miles, all the way from Moosetookalook to New Boston, the town in which the tree farm was located. Getting there had seemed simple enough at the outset, but now that they were in the immediate vicinity, the road signs and landmarks did not match up with Gina's squiggles.

Their truck did not come equipped with GPS. Dan considered these devices to be a waste of money, and in general, Liss agreed with him. None of them functioned well in rural areas, and she'd heard that on long trips they tended to choose the route with the lowest mileage, ignoring the fact that it would inevitably take the driver into the center of every major city along the way. Paper maps worked much better when it came to avoiding traffic jams and other delays. Usually.

Dan grumbled, but eventually he complied with his wife's suggestion. He pulled into the parking lot of a small grocery store. He hailed the first shopper they saw, an elderly man loading overflowing reusable canvas shopping bags into the trunk of his car.

"We're looking for Simeon Snowe's place," Dan said. "Can you tell us how to find it?"

"Nobody lives there." The old-timer had a vague look in his pale, rheumy eyes. "Hasn't been a going concern for some time."

"Yes, we know," Liss called across the cab of the truck. She smiled encouragingly. "The new owner asked us to take a look at the place for her."

"Then she shoulda told you how to get there." He opened his driver's side door and eased himself into the car. Without so much as another glance in their direction, he started the engine and drove away.

"Taciturn old cuss," Dan muttered.

"At least he confirmed that the place exists," Liss said brightly. "We'll have to find someone else to tell us how to get there."

The grocery store—the New Boston Food City—was bigger than the High Street Market in Moosetookalook, but not by much. Of the three checkout lanes at the front, only one was open.

The clerk was a teenager with a ring through her nose. She'd never heard of Simeon Snowe. Her customer, a jeans-clad woman in her midtwenties, who was busily piling cans, bottles, and bags of frozen food on the counter, didn't recognize the name, either, but she offered a practical suggestion—ask at the town office.

Following her directions, they drove to the New Boston municipal building, a one-story clapboard structure that looked as if it had originally been built for some other purpose. *A real estate office,* Liss thought. *Or maybe*—she sniffed the air as they entered the building—*a take-out pizza place.*

"Help you?" asked a sour-faced older woman seated

at one of several desks separated from the entrance by a wide wooden counter.

"Can you tell us where to find the farm belonging to the late Simeon Snowe?" Liss asked.

The woman rose slowly, as if she suffered from arthritis, and shuffled up to her side of the barrier. She appeared to be well past the usual retirement age and stared at them through thick glasses. "What's your business there?" she demanded.

The rude manner in which she asked the question took Liss aback and left her momentarily speechless. Dan stepped up to fill the void.

"We're here on behalf of the new owner, Gina Snowe." He leaned in, as if intent upon sharing a confidence, and added his best smile. "Ms. Snowe paid a brief visit to the farm herself a few days ago, but she was unexpectedly called away on business. She asked us to finish up her evaluation of the place. She drew a map for my wife here, but we're having a little trouble finding the landmarks."

The attempt at boyish charm fell flat. The woman looked even more suspicious of their motives. "We don't generally give out that sort of information," she said in a snippy voice. "I'll have to fetch the town manager." With that, she stomped off toward the back of the building, now moving at a surprisingly fast clip for someone who, only moments earlier, had looked as if she needed a cane.

Liss glanced down at herself. She'd worn jeans and a bulky sweater for the drive. Dan was similarly dressed. "Do we *look* like people who are planning to break in and rob the place?"

"She's right to be cautious. After all, we're strangers in town."

"Most folks aren't so standoffish."

"That old guy at the grocery store wasn't inclined to be helpful," he reminded her.

The New Boston town manager, a middle-aged man in shirtsleeves and an unknotted tie, emerged from the rear of the town office before Liss could reply. He smiled at them in that particularly insincere way politicians had perfected and shook hands with Dan in a hearty manner.

"Steve Wilton," he said. "Call me Steve. Bea here tells me you're looking for the Snowe Christmas tree farm. Imagine that! Am I to gather that the estate has finally been settled?"

"Apparently." Dan's tone was dry as he introduced himself and Liss. He explained again about the map.

"A map, you say? Let's have a look."

Liss handed it over. It was proof, she supposed, that they had the right to request directions to the farm.

Ten minutes later, they were back in the truck and headed west. It turned out that their destination was some seven miles distant from the center of New Boston, just short of the town line. Curious, Liss dug out the most recent edition of *The Maine Atlas and Gazetteer.* New Boston had a population of 4,980. That was almost five times the size of Moosetookalook. Even so, the Snowe farm was well away from any neighboring houses.

It started to spit snow the moment Dan turned off a two-lane country road into a long winding driveway. Sunset was at least an hour away, but the sky had already turned an ominous gray, which made everything look dark and dreary. To make matters worse, overgrown rows of evergreens planted on either side of the narrow way formed a high, nearly impenetrable hedge.

Liss began to feel uneasy as she peered at the thickly

intertwined branches. "All we need are a few thorns and I'll be wondering if we're about to stumble onto Sleeping Beauty's castle," she muttered under her breath.

"Hold on!"

That was all the warning she had before Dan slammed on the brakes.

Liss's seat belt tightened, pressing hard against her chest and lap. Fortunately, Dan had not been going very fast. They didn't hit anything, and the air bags did not deploy.

When she looked out through the windshield, Liss half expected to see a deer blocking their way, but what had caused their precipitous stop was not an animal. A heavy chain had been stretched across the driveway. Dan opened his door and got out of the truck. While he unhooked the barrier, Liss squinted to read the words on the sign attached to the links.

The message was *not* WELCOME TO VACATIONLAND.

It said: PRIVATE PROPERTY. TRESPASSERS WILL BE SHOT.

Chapter Two

After passing through the barrier and driving another eighth of a mile, still walled in by the evergreen hedge, they emerged into a large square parking area. Frost heaves had left the surface uneven. In spots the blacktop had entirely crumbled away. The farmhouse to their left was very plain, with a sagging front porch that extended the width of the building. The peeling white paint on the clapboard siding made it look even more dilapidated.

Dan brought the pickup truck to a stop in front of the large freestanding Quonset hut situated on the far side of the parking area from the house, the only other building in sight. "Huh," he said, staring at it. "You don't see many of those anymore."

Like the house, the galvanized-steel structure had seen better days. What remained of the murky late afternoon daylight revealed more rust than shine.

"You don't see many of those, period," Liss agreed.

Traditionally, outbuildings on Maine farms were built of wood. More often than not, they were also connected to the house, thus saving the farmer the trouble of going outdoors on a cold winter day to feed his livestock or milk his cows or collect a few eggs.

"It's a very convenient design, ideal for providing extra work space."

There was something in Dan's voice that had Liss narrowing her eyes. "If you're thinking of putting one of those ugly things in our backyard, you can forget about it."

He chuckled but got out of the truck for a closer look. By the time Liss hopped down from her side of the cab, he was examining the padlock on the Quonset hut's door. "Did Gina give you a key to this?"

Liss shook her head. "Only the one for the house, but I imagine there are other keys inside. If not, the caretaker will have one. I—" She broke off as for the first time, she noticed what lay down the hill beyond the Quonset hut. "Wow."

"Yeah. Have some Christmas trees." Dan rattled the padlock one last time, then let it go and came to stand beside her.

They were on a high point of land—no real surprise, since they'd been climbing steadily ever since they left the road—and the view was awe inspiring.

"How many do you think there are?" Liss asked.

"Must be thousands of them."

The trees stretched out in ragged rows, filling field after field—acres of land. Liss couldn't help but be impressed by all the work that had gone into planting them.

"It looks more like a wilderness than a crop to me, but we can't tell much from here." Dan cast a wary glance toward the sky. What had been only the occasional wet snowflake had turned into a fine but steady mist, the kind that could morph into sleet in a heartbeat. "We'd better get ourselves and our stuff into the house."

For a moment longer, Liss contemplated the vista before her, picturing it in bright sunlight with snow sparkling on the evergreen boughs. On a day like that, she imagined the trees would look exactly like a scene from a holiday greeting card.

They unloaded their luggage from the back of the pickup and braved the rickety porch. In contrast, the key Gina had given to Liss slid smoothly into the lock. The front door swung open on well-oiled hinges. When Liss flicked a switch, light flooded the entryway to show her one closed door straight ahead of her and another to her right. On her left there was a narrow hallway that ran the length of the house. She found a second light switch, which illuminated two closed doors along the hallway and another, also closed, at the end.

"According to Gina, there's a bathroom down that way," Liss said, "and there's a second bath upstairs. The kitchen, with the thermostat, is through here." She opened the door to her right and entered the first of two medium-size rooms connected by an archway. Both were haphazardly furnished with overstuffed chairs, end tables, and lamps. In the front room, a sofa faced a television set that appeared to be at least twenty years old.

Dan followed right behind her with their bags. When he put them down on the hardwood floor, the thump sounded ominously loud in the stillness of the deserted house.

Liss headed for the archway. "Gina told me that a caretaker looks after the place. Andy Dutton. He stocked the place with food and other necessities in advance of her arrival, but she didn't get a chance to meet him before she had to leave. Apparently, they've communicated only by e-mail. She couldn't tell me anything about him."

She continued on into the kitchen. It was larger than either of the other two rooms. It was also noisier. An ancient refrigerator hummed unevenly, the sound underscored by the slow rhythmic drip of a leaky faucet. A plain pine table with four mismatched wooden chairs occupied the center of the room. Against one wall was an electric stove, which appeared to be of the same vintage as the refrigerator. Cabinets and counter space were in generous supply, and everything had been freshly scrubbed. The faint scent of bleach still hung in the chilly air.

Dan went to check the thermostat. "It's set at fifty-five," he said and turned it up to seventy.

From the cellar below, Liss heard the rumble of an oil furnace firing up.

Dan cocked his head. "No explosions. Always a good sign."

"Pessimist!"

"Just being cautious. It's an old house. I'm going to check the smoke alarms to make sure all the batteries are still good."

While he did that, Liss turned her attention to assessing their supplies. The refrigerator, as promised, contained the essentials—bread, milk, eggs, cheese, cold cuts, iceberg lettuce, locally grown tomatoes, carrots, and even a package of ground round with a sell-by date that had not yet passed. Liss found condiments in the cupboards, as well as an interesting assortment of snack foods, which made her wonder how old Andy Dutton was—not that she had any objection to junk food, even at the advanced age of thirty-four. Potatoes, onions, and apples filled their respective bins.

"How about burgers for supper, with mashed potatoes and carrots and a salad?" she asked Dan after she unearthed a cast-iron frying pan.

"Fine with me, but I think you should phone Gina first. I have a feeling there's something she left out of her briefing."

Liss glanced over her shoulder. "Why? And what have you got there?"

"Magazines. They were stacked on an end table in the middle room." He frowned as he rifled through them. "Not one of these has a date more recent than seven years ago. When did Snowe die?"

"Gina didn't say."

"*How* did he die?"

"Don't give me that look! I don't know any details. I assumed his death was recent and from old age. She said he was her great-uncle, so he must have been her grandfather's brother." She faltered as the significance of the seven years sank in. "Surely you don't think . . . ?"

"Seven years, Liss." He waved an old issue of *Sports Illustrated* at her. "Isn't that the standard length of time it takes to have a missing person declared legally dead?"

"Well, yes. I guess so. In novels, anyway. I don't know about real life. Surely there's some other explanation."

"Better call your old pal Gina and find out what it is. Tell her to level with you, or we're out of here."

Resigned, Liss fished the cell phone out of her purse and punched in Gina's number.

As it rang, she wondered why it hadn't occurred to her to find out more about her friend's uncle before she and Dan left Moosetookalook. Although she'd known Gina since they were girls, she'd never met Simeon Snowe. It would have been perfectly natural to ask a few questions. Liss had an uneasy feeling she was going to regret her oversight.

Gina answered on the third ring. She didn't sound surprised to be hearing from Liss so soon.

"So, what's the story?" Liss asked when she'd explained why she'd called.

Gina told her.

"Well?" Dan asked when Liss disconnected the call.

"You were right. This place has been sitting empty for the past seven years because the Snowes had to wait to claim it until Simeon could be declared dead by the courts."

"Please don't tell me they think he was murdered."

"That's the good news. Gina says he just went missing one day. The official verdict is that he met with an accident somewhere on the fifty or so acres that make up this tree farm. The rest of the family didn't even know he'd disappeared for quite a while after the fact. He wasn't close to any of them, even though he left a will that gave everything he owned to his nephew, Gina's father."

"He died last year," Dan remarked.

"Right. So, since Gina was *his* sole heir, once every i was dotted and every t was crossed, she ended up owning this place."

"Lucky her."

Liss slipped her arm through his. "Lucky *us*. Pack your paranoia away, Dan. This new information changes nothing. We still need a vacation. You *know* we do. *Most* people take a couple of weeks off every year."

"Not most people I know."

"Workaholic!" But she smiled up at him when she said it.

It had warmed up enough that she could remove her jacket and hang it on one of the pegs next to the back door. While she made supper, Dan dropped the subject of Simeon Snowe's mysterious disappearance, but Liss was not at all surprised when he brought it up again during the meal.

"It would have been nice if Gina had filled you in about her uncle's vanishing act *before* we came here."

"Does it really make any difference? You know as well as I do that people of all ages get lost in the Maine woods." It happened with alarming regularity. "Besides, since Simeon was Gina's great-uncle, he would have been getting on in years. He probably suffered from Alzheimer's. That would certainly explain how he came to wander off, never to be seen again. He simply wasn't able to find his own way home."

"I suppose you're right," Dan said. "Still, it's odd that no trace of him was ever found."

Liss sent him an exasperated look. "Oh, come on. You know how often hunters stumble over decades-old remains. Stories like that are on the news all the time, especially during deer season." She exaggerated, but not by much.

Dan put down his fork, his supper only half eaten. "With our luck, *we'll* be the ones to find what's left of Simeon Snowe."

Liss's stomach did a little flip at the thought. She forced herself to chew and swallow. After a brief silence, she returned to the subject of Snowe's disappearance. "I don't remember hearing anything about a missing-person search in New Boston when it was happening. Do you?"

He shook his head. "That would have been the year you came back to Moosetookalook. When I wasn't working, I was trying to think of ways to get you into bed. Catching the evening news wasn't a priority."

She made a face at him. "Stalking me, were you? I can't say I noticed. I was spending all my time trying to make a go of the Emporium without Aunt Margaret around to help."

"And you were still recovering from your surgery and going through physical therapy, as well as getting used to being back in Moosetookalook after ten years away." Dan pointed his fork at her. "And I did not stalk you. I was endlessly patient and gentlemanly."

A smile on her face, Liss resumed eating. With a sense of surprise, she realized that it had been a long time since she'd given any thought to the days *before* her return to Maine. Once, she'd earned her living as a professional Scottish dancer. It hadn't been her idea to quit. A severe knee injury and a subsequent partial knee replacement had decided her fate for her. But whatever regrets she'd had at the time about the abrupt end of her career, she had no complaints now. Liss liked the way her life had turned out.

After supper, they retired to the living room. The old television set had stopped receiving current programming the day digital replaced analog, but it still worked. Fortunately, so did the VHS player attached to it. Liss found a copy of *Romancing the Stone,* a movie she'd always liked, in the collection of tapes stowed in the cabinet beneath.

"Odd choice for a crusty old bachelor to own," she remarked as she inserted it in the slot. She turned to the sofa to find Dan frowning. "What? We can watch something else if you don't—"

"It's not the movie. Without cable, I'm going to miss seeing the Pats game on Sunday. I can probably listen to it on the radio in the truck, but it won't be the same."

"Can't you watch it on your cell phone?"

"Not without paying for it."

That ended that discussion. Dan's frugal Yankee heritage trumped even his love of football.

"I'll make it up to you," Liss promised as the FBI warning ended and the movie began.

"Yeah?" He brightened noticeably.

"I can think of quite a few interesting ways to pass all the extra free time we'll have on our hands this week."

Snuggled together on the sofa, Liss tried to keep her attention on Dan or, by default, on the movie. Unfortunately, her unruly thoughts kept circling back to the mysterious disappearance of Gina's great-uncle.

Focus on your vacation, she ordered herself. Simeon Snowe had wandered off, died of exposure or maybe a heart attack. Natural causes. Search parties had failed to find his body. That was sad, of course, but it did *not* mean that there was a mystery to be solved at the Christmas tree farm. She needn't give Simeon Snowe's disappearance another thought.

As an added precaution, Liss slid one hand over the arm of the sofa to knock twice, very softly, on the hard wooden surface of the oak end table.

From the bedroom window on the upper floor, Liss looked out over field after field filled with evergreen trees. The view wasn't quite the Christmas card she'd been imagining. The bright morning sun emphasized the wild, overgrown appearance of the entire plantation, the inevitable result of years of neglect. The most discordant note was sounded by one particularly undisciplined tangle of trees. She couldn't say why the sight made her so uncomfortable, but as she continued to stare at it, an involuntary shudder racked her entire body.

"Are you cold?" Dan had finished dressing while she'd been gawking at the view.

"It *is* chilly here by the window," Liss replied, hedging. She told herself she'd shivered. That was *all* it had been. No sensible person put stock in premonitions of disaster.

"Then come away from there." His was the voice of reason. "We'll go down and fix ourselves a hearty breakfast and then go out and inspect the premises."

"Isn't it wonderful what amazing sex and a good night's sleep can do for someone?" Liss teased him. "You *almost* sound as if you're ready to relax and enjoy our vacation."

He laughed. "Let's just say I'm resigned."

"Good. Then *you* start the breakfast." He had once worked a summer job as a short-order cook and could do things with eggs that Liss only dreamed of. "I'll be down in a minute. I want to change into a heavier sweater."

It didn't take long to trade her lightweight cardigan for a cable-knit pullover. All their clothes were still in their suitcases. Liss had started to unpack the night before, only to discover that there was no room in the closet or the bureau drawers.

The master bedroom, like the rooms downstairs, had been recently vacuumed and dusted, but no one had thought to clean out Simeon Snowe's possessions. She'd opened one drawer to find neatly folded boxers and undershirts. Another was filled with socks and an assortment of wide, bright-colored suspenders.

Liss left the bedroom and hurried downstairs. The lone light fixture far overhead flickered ominously as she descended.

"That stairwell gives me the creeps," she told Dan when she joined him in the kitchen.

"Why?" He already had bacon frying in the cast-iron pan.

"If that bulb had burned out while I was on the stairs, I'd have been left in pitch blackness." The doors at the top and the bottom shut out any other source of light.

"Since when are you scared of the dark?"

"I'm not. I—" She broke off, unable to explain what she felt to herself, let alone to Dan. "You know what? I'm going to let you do *all* the cooking this morning. I need to find a spot with enough floor space to do my stretches."

"My hard labor will cost you," Dan warned.

After she paid him with a kiss, Liss headed back through the middle and front rooms to the small entrance hallway just inside the front door. The previous night she and Dan had discovered that the downstairs rooms went around in a circle, but she hadn't taken a close look at any of them besides the kitchen and the room with the television. What she needed was a space big enough to accommodate her daily exercise routine. Liss wasn't a fanatic about her workouts, but she knew from past experience that if she skipped more than a day or two, her knee would start to bother her. It was easier to keep limber with regular exercise than deal with the stiffness and pain. As a side benefit, all that stretching also kept the rest of her body in shape.

The first door along the narrow hallway opened into a tiny downstairs bedroom, barely big enough to hold a double bed and a dresser. The far side of the bed sat only inches away from the wall. It was made up, complete with a lovely wedding ring quilt on top. Curious, Liss took a peek inside one of the dresser drawers. Aside from a pretty lace-trimmed sachet, it was empty. Liss lifted the sachet to her nose and was rewarded with the faint scent of lavender.

Moving on, she passed the second door, knowing it led to the downstairs bath, to enter the small room at the end. This one had been set up as an office. The computer sitting on a small wooden desk had been outdated even before Simeon Snowe's disappearance. Its bulky monitor was a dead giveaway. So was the box of Zip disks sitting beside it. Liss intended to take a look at Snowe's business records later, in case there was something in them that would be helpful to Gina, but at present she had other things on her mind.

As a place for her to exercise, Snowe's office was as hopeless as every other room in the house. There was no clear space on the floor big enough for her to run through the combination of physical therapy, dance, and aerobics she'd devised for herself.

Liss sighed aloud. She'd been spoiled. Having a dance studio within a few yards of her house meant she'd gotten into the habit of running next door before work every day. While Zara warmed up, preparing to teach her first class, Liss ran through her routine, making use of the floor mats, the barre, and the big mirrors that lined one wall. After a quick shower, a glass of orange juice, and a slice of whole-wheat toast, she'd be raring to go, ready for whatever her day at the Emporium might bring.

The smell of frying bacon tickled her nose, reminding her that she was on vacation. What the heck! She could miss a few days of exercises, so long as she didn't skip the stretches that kept her knee from getting stiff. She smiled to herself. It was *good* to take a break from her routine. Besides, at thirty-four, she was way too young to turn into an old stick-in-the-mud.

The office boasted a second door. This one opened into a confined space with shelves lining one of the remaining walls and more doors filling the other two. Liss had opened the one to her right the previous night. On the far side, a steep flight of stairs descended into the basement. From the smell of damp earth that had wafted up it, she'd been able to tell that the cellar had a dirt floor, a feature common in this part of rural Maine. Liss had no desire to explore that part of the premises. Dan could do it and report to Gina on the condition of the furnace and water heater. She supposed there was a pump down there, too, to draw water into the house from the well. The Christmas tree farm was too far out in the country to be able to tap into a New Boston water main.

Liss chose door number two and stepped through into the middle room. She wondered if at one time it had been a dining room.

Hearing her footsteps, Dan called out that breakfast was almost ready.

They were still enjoying their leisurely meal when Liss heard the distant roar of a motorcycle. When it grew steadily louder, she glanced at her watch.

"That must be the caretaker, Andy Dutton. When I

talked to Gina last night, she said he'd be over this morning to show us around the property."

She couldn't see all of the parking area from the kitchen door, which opened onto a small porch at the side of the house. Dan was already heading for the living room, where the front windows offered a better view. Liss caught up with him in time to see a motorcycle pop out of the top of the driveway. For a moment, it appeared to be on a collision course with Dan's truck. The rider brought the noisy machine to an even louder stop mere inches away from disaster.

"Irresponsible fool!" Seething, Dan started toward the front door.

"He didn't hit anything!" Liss called after her husband. "For all you know, he skidded on a patch of black ice and careened out of control." Liss caught Dan's sleeve. "Give him the benefit of the doubt, okay?"

She held on until he nodded. Only then did she release him and open the door.

Their visitor had dismounted and was striding toward the porch. Clad in a bulky leather jacket and baggy jeans, the short, stocky rider wore a helmet with a face shield that prevented Liss from glimpsing any of the features beneath. Gina, she remembered, had called him "the kid next door." He had the gait of a young person, too, and given the evidence of his food choices, he was probably somewhere between eighteen and twenty-five. As for the "next door" designation, that was relative. As far as Liss had been able to tell from the map, the nearest house to Simeon Snowe's Christmas tree farm was at least a half mile distant.

"Andy Dutton?" she asked when the new arrival reached the porch steps.

"That's me." The voice was gruff. "You Mr. and Mrs. Ruskin?" With an abrupt movement, Andy shoved the visor to the top of the helmet, revealing a pale, plain, square face dominated by a snub nose and dark brown eyes.

"That's right." Liss pasted on her best shopkeeper's smile. "Please, call us Liss and Dan. Come on in and have a cup of coffee with us."

She got only a grunt for an answer.

Liss puzzled over Simeon Snowe's neighbor all the way back to the kitchen. There was something decidedly odd about Andy Dutton, but she couldn't put her finger on what it was.

"Thanks so much for picking up supplies," Liss said as she reached into the cupboard for another coffee mug. "Do we owe you anything for the groceries?"

"Ms. Snowe took care of it."

The voice, less muffled now, was still husky. Liss turned, mug and coffeepot in hand, and nearly dropped both. The helmet was off, setting masses of dark brown hair tumbling free. Andy Dutton was not a young man at all. She was, very obviously so when she went on to remove her jacket, of the female persuasion. A sweater patterned with tiny snowmen hugged every curve.

Well, Liss thought, *that'll teach me to jump to conclusions.*

"So, Andy," she said when the three of them were settled at the table with full mugs steaming merrily in front of them, "how long have you been looking after the house?"

"Ever since they figured out that old man Snowe wasn't coming back."

Andy wrapped both hands around the coffee mug for

a moment before taking the first sip. The temperature outside had dropped by some twenty degrees overnight, and it was only now starting to warm up again. She must have had a chilly ride, Liss thought, even if it had been a short one. The valley where the Christmas tree farm was located was one of those "usual cold spots" meteorologists liked to talk about during their weather forecasts.

"I used to work for him part-time when I was still in school," Andy volunteered. "He took on seasonal help for planting and again when it was time to ship the trees. We used to cut and net about a thousand of those suckers every year."

"Where did he sell them?"

"New York City mostly. Those folks will pay top dollar for a nice Christmas tree." She shook her head as if to say, "Damn fools!" and took another swallow of coffee.

"I suppose there's no hope of shipping trees this year."

"Too late in the season. They have to go out in October."

"So early?"

Until then, Dan had left all the talking to Liss. Now he tipped back in his chair and regarded Andy through half-closed eyes. "Seems to me that places that sell Christmas trees don't open until after Thanksgiving."

"But they have to have their stock ready to go beforehand. Takes time to get it there. Most states have their own regulations about what crosses their borders, too." Suddenly, Andy grinned, showing very large white teeth. "Got to keep those invasive species out of the ecosystem."

What she said made sense. Liss knew full well what a mess milfoil was causing in some of Maine's lakes. That particular invasive plant had been introduced from the hulls of out-of-state boats. Having learned that lesson, Maine no longer let campers bring in untreated out-of-state firewood. According to the news reports she'd heard, that was how the Asian long-horned beetle, a nasty piece of work if there ever was one, had taken over Ohio.

Since Andy had been given an opening, she cheerfully supplied, in much more detail than Liss either needed or wanted, a list of bugs that posed potential threats to Maine trees, Christmas and otherwise.

"I had no idea there were so many," Liss murmured when Andy finally ran out of pests.

"Did Snowe ever do any local business?" Dan asked before she could launch into a new lecture.

"Are you talking about a cut-your-own setup?" Andy had polished off the last drop of her coffee and left the table to rinse out her mug. "He always used to say it wasn't worth the hassle. Truth is, he didn't much like dealing with people."

Liss collected the rest of the dishes and dumped them in the sink, promising herself that she'd wash them later. "What about this year? Is there any part of the tree farm that *could* be opened up to folks who want to harvest their own Christmas tree? I remember doing that when I was a little girl. It was great fun."

"Have you taken a look at the trees yet?" Andy asked.

"Just a quick gander," Dan told her.

"Most of them are already way too big to sell. A tree gets much over seven feet tall and it won't fit into your average living room."

"*Most* are too big?" Liss seized on that. "But not all?"

Andy shrugged. "It takes ten years to grow a proper Christmas tree. Mr. Snowe planted seedlings ten years ago."

"Did he plant a crop nine years ago? Eight?" Liss asked.

"He put in seedlings from the nursery every year. But he hasn't been around to prune them. He didn't do much by way of shaping his trees, but you have to do a little. Otherwise they don't look the way people expect Christmas trees to look." Using both hands, she sketched the classic triangular outline in the air.

"That sounds like a lot of work," Liss said.

"Can be, especially when there's only one person doing it."

Liss regarded Andy with undisguised curiosity. Was she imagining it, or was the young woman suddenly avoiding eye contact? "Have you done any pruning since Snowe disappeared?"

Andy shrugged. "A little. To keep my hand in."

"So there could be, say, a few hundred trees available to sell, should the new owner open up a cut-your-own operation?"

Another shrug was her answer, accompanied by a scowl.

Dan sent Liss a speaking glance over Andy's head. Liss was pretty sure they were both wondering the same thing—why had this young woman in the leather jacket, Christmas sweater, and baggy jeans done work she'd had no hope of being paid for?

Liss had learned the hard way that it was a mistake to accept anyone at face value. Far too often, new acquaintances hid their true natures behind smiles and platitudes. Nine times out of ten, there was no harm in that. But the tenth? That was the one that caused all the trouble. By the same token, jumping to conclusions about someone's guilt was also a bad plan.

"Let's get this show on the road," she said, snagging

her coat off the peg by the door. "I'm ready for the grand tour."

At the Quonset hut, Andy produced her own key for the padlock. Although the top and sides of the hut were made of metal, both ends were wood and both, as it turned out, contained doors. "The one on the other end is a modified garage door," Andy explained as she flicked the switch to turn on the overhead lights.

The interior was dusty with disuse and crammed full of equipment, everything from a John Deere tractor to two odd-looking contraptions with hand cranks that had been mounted on sturdy wooden tables.

"What the heck are those?" Liss asked. They were made of metal and put her in mind of the rings lions jump through in a circus, even though they were way too wide to qualify as hoops.

"Netters," Andy said. "You use them to put netting around a tree so it can be shipped in less space. You've probably seen netted Christmas trees on the roofs of cars." She bestowed a fond pat on the nearest of the contraptions. "We used to have three of these, but the police confiscated the other one."

Liss turned to stare at her. "The police," she echoed. "Why?"

"Because of the dead guy." Andy paused in the act of brushing a cobweb off the shelf where several large chain saws were stored. She glanced over her shoulder, taking in the bemused expression on Liss's face and the consternation on Dan's. She blinked once, slowly, before turning to face them. "Guess you hadn't heard about that, huh?"

"Guess not." Dan's tone of voice was deceptively calm. The look he sent Liss warned her that there was going to be another long-distance phone call to Gina the minute they got back to the house.

"Who is this 'dead guy' you're talking about?" Liss asked. "Not Mr. Snowe?"

"Of course not. Old man Snowe vanished completely. The dead guy turned up in New York City. The customer went to unload his trees and found the body, netted neat as you please, smack-dab in the middle of a stack of Scotch pine."

Chapter Three

How on earth do you respond to a statement like that? Liss didn't even try.

The mental image that formed in her mind was macabre enough to strike her as funny when, at the same time, she knew the situation wasn't amusing at all. It was horrible. She avoided looking at Dan and made a little hand gesture to Andy, sufficient to encourage the young woman to go on with her story.

"Well, as soon as the dead guy turned up, the police got called in. They wanted to know how he got there. And who killed him. Because he'd been shot, you see. Murdered."

"Of course he was," Dan said in a low, tight voice.

Liss ignored him. "So the police came here." It wasn't a question. They'd have to pay a visit to the farm because the victim had been found among Snowe's trees. Odds were good that he'd been put through one of Snowe's netting machines. "What did Mr. Snowe have to say about it?"

"He couldn't say anything. The place was deserted by the time anyone came to investigate."

Now it was Liss's turn to blink. "*That's* when Snowe disappeared?"

Andy nodded.

"And you're *certain* it wasn't Mr. Snowe who went through the netter?" Dan asked.

"Positive." When he looked skeptical, Andy gave a derisive snort. "You think folks would have spent weeks searching the woods for him if it had been?"

"Good point," he conceded.

"So who *was* the dead man?" Liss asked.

"Nobody's ever said. Maybe they still don't know. I guess you'll have to ask the cops." Andy's expression brightened. "While you're at it, can you ask them if we can have the netter back?"

We? Liss found the pronoun telling. "If it's evidence, they'll want to hang on to it."

Not that it mattered. She was not about to talk to the police.

Her gaze returned to the two remaining netters, and her imagination, fueled by a steady diet of crime novels and a few firsthand encounters with murder, took flight in spite of her best intentions. Just how big a man, she wondered, had the victim been? A dead body would be deadweight. How had the killer gotten him onto one of those netter tables and through the hoop, never mind why? It seemed an insane thing to do, and pretty pointless, too, since the body was bound to be discovered eventually.

Maybe that was the point. Maybe someone had tried to frame Simeon Snowe for murder, assuming he wasn't the guilty party. He'd run off, hadn't he?

"Let me see if I've got this straight," Dan said. "A man was murdered and put through one of Simeon Snowe's netters and shipped to New York with a load of trees?"

"Right." Andy rested one haunch against the edge of a netter table, arms folded across her ample breasts.

"And right before the body was found, Snowe disappeared, never to be seen again?"

"You got it." Andy grinned. "And didn't that cause some excitement around here. The cops went over this place with a fine-tooth comb."

"I'll bet." The tone of Dan's muttered response warned Liss that his patience was wearing thin. Given their past experiences, he was not happy to have encountered yet another mysterious death.

Neither was she, Liss told herself, but she couldn't seem to hold back another question. "What persuaded the police to take the netter?" There had to have been something—fingerprints, maybe, or bloodstains. Her stomach twisted at the thought.

"Beats me," Andy said.

"I don't suppose they told you anything," Liss conceded.

Andy shrugged and looked a trifle sheepish. "Well, to tell you the truth, they barely talked to me at all. My mom got on her high horse about them badgering a kid. She wouldn't let me come near this place while the search was going on, either."

Liss studied their young guide's face. "How old were you when all this was happening?"

"Old enough to have been working for Mr. Snowe every afternoon after school and every weekend."

Dan had heard enough. "Time to see the trees." He held the door open until they went through. From the Quonset hut, they headed down a gentle slope, their boots crunching on a thin crust of snow.

Dan's longer strides soon put him in the lead. The day was warming up nicely, but the mixed precipitation overnight had left icy patches. Liss hung back, both to make sure of her footing and to give herself another chance to question Andy.

"You must have known Mr. Snowe very well. Could *he* have—"

"Not a chance! He wasn't easy to get along with, but he wasn't the sort to kill anybody, either!"

"Why did he run off, then?"

Andy scowled. "Who said he did?" She stepped over a chuckhole.

"You're right. His niece told us he wandered away from home and got lost." The timing could have been a coincidence, although Liss had her doubts. "Was Snowe getting on in years?"

This suggestion seemed to bother Andy even more than the possibility that her former employer might have murdered someone. "He wasn't *that* old. He still got around pretty good."

"His mind was sharp?"

"Sharp as his tongue." Andy gave a rueful laugh, as if she was remembering some particular incident. If she was, she didn't share it.

They'd caught up with Dan, who'd waited for them at the end of the plantation. Seeing the stormy expression on his face, Liss hesitated, but she had to ask one last question. "Do you think Mr. Snowe might have been murdered, too?"

Andy opened her mouth and closed it again, shook her head as if to clear her thoughts, then mumbled, "Guess he could have been."

Dan glared at his wife. "Gina *definitely* has some explaining to do."

"She may not know anything about this," Liss argued. "And even if she does, that doesn't change the fact that I agreed to evaluate this place for her." But she held both hands up, as if in surrender. "No more talk of murder. I promise. Come on, Andy. Show us the rest of the Christmas tree farm."

Although Dan did not look happy, he kept his thoughts to himself as Andy led them in among the trees. From a distance, they hadn't looked nearly so tall.

"I wonder if there's any way to market community trees to towns and cities?" Liss murmured.

Andy was quick to squelch that notion. "Municipalities don't pay for trees. They expect people to donate them."

"Bummer."

"Mr. Snowe used to plant about twelve hundred seedlings every year, half balsam fir and half Scotch pine, with a few blue spruce for variety. The spruces are more expensive, but some people really like the way they're shaped."

"Which variety are these?" Liss reached out to touch the nearest bough.

"Scotch pine," Andy said.

And that, Liss thought, inhaling deeply, was why the scent put her in mind of the rosin dancers stepped in to give their shoes traction on stage. Rosin was made from pine sap.

"Like I already told you," Andy continued as they left one field and entered the next, "it takes ten or eleven years for a tree to get big enough to sell."

In the second field, the trees were significantly smaller and were, Liss thought, mostly balsams.

"Mr. Snowe sold a whole year's crop at a time. Of course, some trees die off in the course of a decade, so he'd end up harvesting around a thousand a year."

"A thousand trees," Liss said, marveling. It seemed an astonishingly large number for an old man and a girl to cut down, net, and ship. Then she remembered something Andy had said earlier. "You mentioned that he hired extra help. Did his seasonal workers live around here?"

"Liss." There was a warning note in Dan's voice.

"I'm not trying to solve a murder," she insisted. "I'm curious about the details of operating the Christmas tree farm. For Gina, remember?"

"Uh-huh."

She couldn't fault him for his skepticism, but neither could she think how she'd be of any use solving a seven-year-old cold case, even if she wanted to get involved. Which she didn't. Not at all.

Andy's brows knit together, puzzled by their exchange of words. She gave each of them a curious look before she answered Liss's question. "He hired different people different years. Some local, some not. No one person every year. Except me."

"And that last year? Who did he hire then?"

"It was more than seven years ago. How am I supposed to remember?"

Liss was willing to bet that the police had those names. *None of your concern,* she reminded herself and forced her attention back to the matter at hand.

"The tree farm covers about fifty acres, right?"

Andy nodded. "The year after Mr. Snowe cut down a section, he'd leave it fallow, then replant the year after that."

"What do you do for irrigation?" Dan asked, interested in spite of himself.

Andy shrugged. "Trees don't need anything but natural rainfall most years, but there's a stream along the property line. He pumped water out of that a few times. If you want to walk the whole fifty acres, I can show it to you. It kind of winds around the perimeter."

"I'd rather inspect the parts that were planted most recently." Liss hadn't completely given up on the idea that there might be a few trees of a proper size to sell locally. "How far from the house are those fields?"

The first one, planted ten years earlier, turned out to be near at hand. It also showed evidence of having been pruned. Andy admitted that was her doing. The fields from eight and nine years back were a long hike along the overgrown remnant of a logging road.

"We used this route to remove the cut trees from the property," Andy explained. "Did the netting on the spot. Stacked the trees on pallets so the shipper could drive right up to them and load the cargo into his truck."

"What company did the shipping?"

Andy gave Liss a name, but it meant nothing to her. She didn't suppose it mattered. Gina wouldn't be likely to use the firm again.

They walked in silence for a bit, wending their way back toward the house. Andy stopped when they came to a field in which the trees were the smallest Liss had yet seen.

"This is the section Mr. Snowe put in seven years ago, the spring before he disappeared."

There was something odd about the field in front of her, but it took a moment for Liss to figure out what it was. The trees in the other sections had all been planted in rows. The open spaces between them, roughly a mowing deck in width, formed paths that were clearly discernible despite underbrush and overgrown branches.

"Why on earth are these trees planted so close together?" As they'd grown, their branches had intertwined until they were tangled into what appeared to be one impenetrable mass.

"No idea." Andy shrugged. "He'd tell me where to dig holes, and I'd dig."

Frowning, Liss glanced toward the house. Had it been this field she'd noticed from the bedroom window, the one that had left her feeling so unsettled? It had to be.

Looking at the mess in front of her, she wondered again if Snowe's mind had been deteriorating during the months before he disappeared. Andy had said he was still sharp, but since he'd lived alone out here, his only regular visitor a teenage girl, it was possible that he had drifted slowly into senility without anyone noticing.

Andy headed home as soon as they finished their tour of the Christmas tree farm. By the time the sound of her motorcycle faded away, Dan was lobbying for Liss to phone Gina.

"In a minute," Liss said, slipping out of her coat. "There's something else I need to check on first."

Grumbling under his breath, he followed her upstairs. Liss went straight to the bedroom window and stared out at the tree farm. She'd been right.

"Dan? Come and take a look at this."

After a moment, he came up beside her, slinging one arm around her shoulders. "What am I supposed to be looking at besides a heck of a lot of Christmas trees?"

"That last field Simeon Snowe planted before he disappeared." Liss pointed. "It's the one—"

She broke off as his grip abruptly tightened. "The one where the trees are all planted too close together. It's like a hedge or a . . . well, damn!"

The proverbial lightbulb had come on, just as it had for Liss.

"You see it, too?"

"Snowe *must* have been losing his mind."

"That's what I thought, too, until I realized how much clearheaded planning it would take to put together something that complex."

The trees were so overgrown that the design was difficult to make out, even from above. It had been impossible to spot at ground level. But once Liss had realized what she was looking at, the entire field resolved itself into a pattern that was not in the least random, only inexplicable. Simeon Snowe had used his last batch of twelve hundred seedlings to create a maze.

"Hit the speaker button," Dan reminded her when Liss finally made her call to Gina. They'd already talked about how they'd handle the conversation. Dan had promised to listen and not weigh in too often.

"I don't know anything about any dead man in a shipment of trees," Gina insisted when Liss repeated Andy's astonishing revelation.

"Did your father, do you think?"

"If he did, he never mentioned it to me, and he certainly would have if Uncle Simeon had been suspected of murdering a man. I expect Andy was confused. Or exaggerating. How extraordinary that all this time I thought she was a young man."

"So did I, at first. Can you tell us anything more about your great-uncle?" Liss asked.

"Not a lot. He wasn't close to the rest of the family."

"How old was he?"

After a long pause, Gina said, "About the same age as my father, I think. He was my grandfather's much younger half brother, so he'd have been in his midfifties at the time he disappeared."

"Not exactly senile, then," Dan said.

"Of course not." Gina sounded offended.

Liss glanced at Dan, eyebrows raised. "Ah, Gina, if he didn't just get confused and wander off, get lost, and die of exposure, then the most logical reason for him to go missing at that particular point in time is that he had something to do with the murder."

"Nonsense."

Liss waited.

A deep sigh came over the airways. "I suppose, since you're already there, that it would be a good idea for you to contact the local police. Find out what's what. After all, you're good at that sort of thing."

"And you're a criminal attorney, Gina," Dan said. "Surely you have contacts with law enforcement in both Maine and New York."

"But you two are on the spot. It makes better sense for you to ask questions face-to-face with the local constabulary."

"Gina, I—"

"Look, Liss, I really have to go." She sounded impatient. "I know it's Saturday, but I still have tons of research to do for this trial that starts on Monday. I'll be in touch. Ta!"

"In other words," Dan said as dead air followed the click of a disconnect, "don't call us. We'll call you."

"Don't hold your breath."

"So why are you smiling?"

"Remember the movie we watched last night? Ralph, the character Danny DeVito plays in *Romancing the Stone,* gets left behind when his cousin is escaping by boat. The cousin—"

"Ira. The cousin's name is Ira."

"Right. Ira shouts across the water that he'll come back for Ralph, and Ralph wants to know when."

"Soon. Very Soon." Dan sounded no more convincing than Ira had.

"Exactly. For some strange reason, when Gina promised to be in touch, I immediately thought of Ira."

Her sarcastic tone had Dan giving a short bark of laughter, but he quickly sobered. "Liss, I don't like the way Gina's manipulating us. We're under no obligation to play detective for her. You've already found out what she wanted to know—that it's too late to ship trees this year. Send her that information in an e-mail and we're done. We can go home this afternoon."

"No, we can't. I haven't had a chance to go through her great-uncle's business records yet. And there's a possibility that Andy could open this place for Gina this year as a cut-your-own operation. Since we have to stay on long enough to look into those things, we may as well do as she asks and talk to the police."

"Let Gina hire an accountant and a private detective for those jobs. She can afford it."

"There *is* one other reason to stay on." Liss stepped closer to her husband and ran both palms up the front of his shirt. "We came here for a mini-vacation. Remember? I'd really like to stay a little longer, Dan. Think how nice it would be to relax, just the two of us. Seems to me you were all for that plan only a few hours ago."

Her hands climbed to his face and then into his thick sandy brown hair, sifting through the curls.

"This morning I didn't know there had been a murder."

"Neither did I." She tugged his head down so she could plant a smacking kiss on his lips.

"So you won't have any trouble staying out of police business?"

"A visit to the police station does not constitute meddling in murder! Besides, it's Mr. Snowe's disappearance Gina wants to know more about, not the man in the netter."

"Are you sure about that?"

She grimaced and released him. "No. But what harm will it do to ask a few questions? You can't tell me you're not curious, too."

"Maybe a little," Dan admitted.

Elated, she grabbed his hand and tugged him after her. "Come on, then. Let's get it over with."

"Why do I let you talk me into these things?"

It was a rhetorical question, but she answered it, anyway. "Because you love me."

"I do, don't I?" He helped her into her coat. "Okay. Here's the revised plan. We go into town. You ask your questions. Then we do nothing else for the rest of the weekend but enjoy each other's company."

"And on Monday?"

"On Monday we decide whether we want to stay longer or head home."

"Fair enough. And we have lunch in town while we're there." The noon hour was almost upon them.

"Done."

During the drive into New Boston, Liss gave herself a little lecture. No matter how strange the events of seven years ago, she was not, absolutely not, going to be tempted to investigate beyond a few questions at the local police department. She'd keep her focus on the two goals she'd set before leaving Moosetookalook. While here, they'd enjoy a well-deserved vacation. They would also settle a very personal matter once and for all—the question of whether or not to have a baby.

Liss stole a sideways glance at her husband. She knew what she wanted, but Dan's thoughts about having children were a mystery to her. Did he secretly yearn for offspring? Was he waiting for her to speak before expressing his wish for a son to carry on the family name and the family businesses? Or did his silence on the subject mean he lacked any particular desire for sons or daughters of his own? Liss wished she could discover the answers to those questions without coming right out and asking. If he was bound and determined to father a child, she'd just as soon he never found out that her own feelings about motherhood were, at best, ambivalent.

"How long have we been here?" Liss asked without opening her eyes. She hadn't thought to bring a book with her. Within five minutes of taking a seat in the small, stuffy lobby of the police station, she'd been bored silly. She'd have napped if the chairs weren't so uncomfortable.

She heard the slide of fabric as Dan shoved up his sleeve to take a look at his watch. "Half an hour, give or take."

She shifted in the hard plastic chair, trying unsuccessfully to find a more comfortable position. She'd thought, when they told the receptionist they wanted to talk to the chief about Simeon Snowe, that they'd be ushered in to see him fairly quickly. Instead, they'd been left to cool their heels. The uniformed officer seated at a desk on the other side of a glass partition looked up from his paperwork from time to time to glance their way, but no one spoke to them after that first brief exchange.

"How do you want to handle this?" Dan asked when she opened her eyes, yawned, and stretched. "Obviously, the chief's in no hurry to be accommodating, and strictly speaking, he has no reason to tell us anything."

Liss sighed. "I know." The police in general were notorious for keeping information close to their chests, and here in New Boston she and Dan didn't know anyone on the police force or in the local county sheriff's department. "I guess we play it by ear."

At last, a short, wiry man emerged from a back room. "Wyatt Purvey, chief of police," he said in a low, whispery voice that went oddly with the position of authority he held. "How can I help you?" He ignored Liss and offered his hand to Dan.

"Dan Ruskin," Dan replied, shaking it. "This is my wife, Liss. We're staying out at the Snowe farm for a few days at the request of the new owner."

"And he would be?"

"*She* would be Ms. Gina Snowe of Chicago."

"We have a few questions on her behalf." Liss cut in, annoyed by Purvey's attitude. He hadn't looked directly at her once, almost as if he wanted to pretend she didn't exist.

Forced to acknowledge her, Purvey presented Liss with a poker face. "Yes?" he hissed, the word nearly inaudible.

"It seems one of the netters used in Simeon Snowe's Christmas tree business was confiscated by the police. His niece hopes to reopen and was wondering when she might have it back." It had been Andy Dutton who'd wanted it returned, not Gina, but Liss was sure Gina would have agreed if only Liss had remembered to mention it to her.

Purvey blinked cold little fish eyes. "I think it unlikely that will happen."

"Why not?"

He hesitated.

Dan, a look of resignation on his face, jumped in with an "innocent" remark of his own. "Miss Dutton, who worked with Mr. Snowe, told us some preposterous story about a murdered man."

Purvey shifted so that he no longer had to look at Liss. "Miss . . . ? Oh, that would be young Andy? That girl."

The way the police chief shook his head made his opinion of Andy crystal clear. She was a "foolish young thing," not to be taken seriously. "Do you have me pigeonholed, too?" Liss wanted to ask him. No doubt she was already filed under "pushy female who doesn't know her place."

His chauvinistic attitude made her bristle, but she held her tongue. It was obvious Dan would have more luck getting answers than she would.

"Did she get that wrong?" he asked Chief Purvey, still feigning ignorance. "Are you saying that no one died?"

"Oh, there was a body, right enough. But it was no one from around here." The implication was that since the man had been from away, his death was of no importance.

"Where was he from?" Dan asked.

"I don't think the state boys ever did find out. Or his name, either."

"How . . . odd," Liss murmured. Purvey ignored her.

"So you're telling us that we can't get the netter back, because it might still be needed as evidence?" Dan did a good job of looking confused.

"That's exactly right. Sorry I couldn't be more help." Purvey started to retreat in the direction of his office. "Now, if you'll excuse me, I—"

"What about Simeon Snowe?" Liss blurted out her question so loudly that both the New Boston police officer and the receptionist turned to stare at her from behind the glass partition.

Purvey's expression did not change, and the volume of his voice continued to be set on low. "What about him?"

"What do you think happened to him? Did he take off because he was a suspect in the other man's death?"

"That's not for me to say."

"But—"

Dan cleared his throat. "Chief Purvey, I think Ms. Snowe has reason to be concerned. Even if her uncle was not involved in the crime, a man appears to have been murdered on her property. As Snowe's heir, she might even be liable for damages."

Liss wondered if Gina had thought of that and decided she likely had. After all, she was a lawyer.

Purvey's unrevealing features seemed to become blanker still. "You think someone might sue her at this late date?"

A strange rustling sound issued from his throat as he retreated through the door that led to the inner sanctum of the police station. Liss thought it might be a laugh. Whatever it was, it was all the answer he intended to give them.

"I don't think he knows any more than he's saying," she murmured when the automatic lock clicked closed behind him. "Not about the dead man, at any rate. The state police would have taken charge of the murder investigation, and they probably took over the disappearance of Simeon Snowe, as well." It made sense that they'd assume the two cases were somehow connected.

"I think you're right," Dan said. "So, that's that. Questions asked. Duty's done." He took her arm in a firm grip and steered her outside.

Liss had just settled herself in the passenger seat of Dan's truck when the uniformed police officer they'd last seen doing paperwork emerged from the building. He appeared to be in his late thirties, a good ten years younger than his boss. When he spotted them, a frown creased his brow. After a fractional hesitation, he headed their way. Although Dan didn't look pleased by the delay, he waited beside the open driver's side door for the other man to reach him.

Liss stayed put. She'd have had to climb over the gearshift to get close to the two men, an awkward maneuver at best, but if she inclined her body a bit in Dan's direction, she'd be in earshot of whatever they said to each other.

"I overheard what you asked the chief," the policeman said.

By squinting, Liss could make out the name on the metal tag on the officer's jacket—Michael Jennings.

"Is there really a chance the tree farm will reopen?" Jennings asked.

"A chance," Dan conceded. "Is your interest personal or professional?"

"Both. My brother used to pick up work there sometimes. He . . . well, he had a hard time of it when his National Guard unit was sent to Afghanistan. It would be a godsend to have even a few more seasonal jobs open up in this area."

Liss leaned farther across the driver's seat, anxious not to miss a word of the exchange and hoping for a better look at Jennings's face. "Can you tell us any more than your boss did about this murder?" she asked. "Is it true that no one has been able to identify the victim?"

Jennings bent forward and nodded at her, both in greeting and in answer to her question. "The way I hear it, they've tried everything, even face recognition software. Nothing came up a match except the trace of dried blood on Snowe's netter."

"And no one local knew who the man was?"

"If they did, they didn't admit to it. The state troopers had us show his picture around, and it was printed in the local biweekly newspaper."

"A photograph?"

"That's what I saw."

"If it was taken after he was dead, he wouldn't have been looking his best."

"I beg your pardon?" Her comment had him backing away from the truck.

"I'm not a ghoul," she called after him. "Honest. I'm just trying to understand what happened. For the new owner."

Jennings didn't look convinced. Neither did Dan. After a moment's consideration, the officer circled in front of the truck to Liss's window. Dan got in on his side and started the engine so she could lower it.

"I suppose there's no harm in your knowing what little I can tell you. No one from local law enforcement ever saw the body, and the investigators from New York didn't release many details, except to say that he died here."

"Was Simeon Snowe suspected of killing him?"

"I imagine he was, but as far as I know, there was nothing except that netter to link him to the crime." Jennings's eyes were a soft green and fringed by lashes a woman would kill for. Liss could see the sincerity in them when he added, "I don't know anyone around here who believes Snowe was a cold-blooded murderer."

"How did you discover he'd gone missing?"

"When we got word of this body being found and the police in New York discovered that the shipment of trees had come from the Snowe farm, I was sent out there to talk to Snowe. No one was around. The house was all closed up and quiet. Not abandoned. More like Snowe had gone into town to run errands. I waited around for a bit. Left and came back. After the fourth try, I started asking around among the neighbors. No one had seen him for at least a week. That's when I sent out a BOLO for his truck."

Liss nodded. She'd heard Sherri use the term. It meant "Be on the lookout." "The thought must have crossed your mind that he might be guilty and had run off."

"It crossed the minds of the New York police. They got a warrant to search the house, but it didn't look like he'd taken anything with him. Clothes and such were all there. There had been no withdrawals from his bank account. No new charges on his credit cards. Later we found someone who'd seen him in town as late as the day before I started looking for him, but after that, nothing."

"Did his truck ever turn up?"

Liss hid a smile when Dan asked the question. In spite of his reservations, he was intrigued by the mystery. Who wouldn't be?

Jennings grimaced. "Yeah. Right on his own back forty. But Snowe himself? We never found a trace of him."

"Maybe he was abducted by aliens," Liss murmured.

She expected her facetious remark would make Jennings smile. Instead, he just shook his head. "You aren't the first to suggest that." At her look of astonishment, he tried to backpedal. "It wasn't a widespread notion! Heck, it wasn't even the only suggestion our local fortune-teller came up with."

"You have a psychic working with the New Boston PD?"

Color crept from beneath Jennings's collar into his face. "Rowena's not a psychic. She owns the occult shop down on Commercial Street. Rowena Luckenbill. She's something of a local character. A harmless eccentric, I guess you'd say."

"I'm surprised to hear there's an occult shop in a place the size of New Boston." The retailer in Liss was intrigued by the notion.

"I don't understand it myself," Jennings admitted. "The place is filled with peculiar-smelling herbs hanging from the ceiling, and books on spells and the lost city of Atlantis and crop circles and such. But Rowena's been in business for over a decade, so I guess all that weird stuff must sell to somebody."

"Crop circles?" Struck by a sudden thought, Liss spoke more to herself than to the police officer. "I wonder if she knows anything about mazes."

"I'm afraid I can't answer that one," Jennings said.

"No. No, of course not." Liss sent a bright smile his way. "Thank you so much for taking the time to talk to us."

"No problem." Looking relieved that they had no more questions, he touched the rim of his cap in farewell.

"Does it occur to you," Dan asked as they watched Jennings pull out of the parking lot, "that Gina might have had an ulterior motive for having us talk to the police?"

"She's in Chicago. We're here."

Dan made no attempt to back out of their parking space. "She's a lawyer, Liss. There's no way she didn't already know all the ins and outs of Snowe's estate, including the fact that he disappeared right after a murder."

"So asking us to come to New Boston was a ploy to get us interested enough in the case to investigate her uncle's disappearance and John Doe's death?"

"To get *you* to investigate. Why not?" His hands clenched the steering wheel. "She knows you've tracked down killers in the past. And that you have an uncanny ability to spot things the police have missed."

"I'm not sure Gina is that devious," Liss said in a mild voice, "but if that was her plan, then it failed. I have no interest in sticking my nose into something that's none of my business."

"No inclination to solve a mystery when it falls right into your lap? Are you sure about that? You were asking plenty of questions just now."

"That was just idle curiosity. The rest of our time here is for you and me." She grinned at him. "Think of this as our second honeymoon."

Dan visibly relaxed. He released his death grip on the wheel. "Good. Let's go find someplace to have lunch."

Chapter Four

They ended up in a small coffee, soup, and sandwich shop tucked away on a side street near the police station. Madison's contained only a half dozen two-person tables. At the far end of the restaurant, next to a pair of commercial coffee grinders, a series of large bins held more than a dozen coffee bean selections. The smell of the place was heavenly.

The menu was limited to "offerings of the day," scrawled on an old-fashioned chalkboard to the left of the sales counter. The soups available were corn chowder and tomato, and customers could select either a BLT or a hot pastrami sandwich on rye. There were also two salad choices, both guaranteed to be "fresh-made."

"I haven't had a Waldorf salad in ages," Liss declared when she'd read through this short list. "Apples and walnuts. Yum."

Dan went with the pastrami.

They had to wait to order while a woman paid for a pound of breakfast blend. As they made their way to a table, another customer crossed their path, this one carrying a pound bag of unground coffee beans. Liss could hear the cheerful sound they made bumping against each other inside the brown paper sack.

They had plenty of seating choices. Only one table was already occupied. The coffee section, on the other hand, continued to attract a steady stream of customers.

Once they were settled, their coats and gloves removed in the welcome warmth of the café and Liss's bulky purse, the one she always took with her on trips, safely stowed on the floor between her feet, Liss felt herself begin to relax. She sat facing the plate-glass window at the front of the café, with a superb view of all the foot traffic that passed by. There was a bench in front of it for the convenience of those who wanted to sit and sip their coffee in the fresh air. On this chilly November afternoon, it was unoccupied.

"We're on vacation," Liss announced. "No more Snowe business until Monday, at the earliest."

Dan grinned. "With one exception."

Liss cocked her head and waited, unable to guess what he meant.

"I saw your face when Officer Jennings mentioned that the occult shop had books on crop circles, and I definitely heard you ask if this Rowena character might know something about mazes."

"Sheesh. No pulling the wool over your eyes, is there?"

"If you want to spend a little of our vacation time learning more about mazes, it's okay with me."

"I can probably find almost as much information online."

"I know you better than that, Liss. You'd much rather read a book on the subject."

"You're being awfully accommodating."

"Maybe I'm curious myself." He chuckled. "I can still

remember the first time I heard the word *maze*. One Halloween when I was a kid, maybe ten or eleven years old, my folks announced they were taking us to visit a corn maze. I couldn't figure out what they were talking about until we got there, because in my head, I was spelling the word m-a-i-z-e."

Liss laughed. "The Indian word for *corn*. How redundant. No wonder you were confused."

On the other side of the window, a man in a well-cut gray overcoat stopped beside the bench Liss had noticed earlier and tethered his dog to it. She couldn't hear what he said to the animal, but his body language conveyed the meaning. When he bent forward and used his index finger to point, the golden retriever obediently sat. As soon as the man turned his back, the dog was right back up again. A moment later it was looking through the window at Liss, its nose pressed flat against the pane. Liss stifled a laugh, causing Dan to turn in his chair to see what had tickled her fancy.

"Afternoon, Harlan," a woman's voice called out from behind the counter. The cook, Liss presumed, since the young man who'd taken their order was a baritone.

"Afternoon, Miranda," the new arrival called back. He headed for the coffee bins.

"How are you and Jonas today?"

Jonas, Liss presumed, was that beautiful golden retriever.

"Just fine. Thanks."

The acoustics in the café were excellent. Both parties spoke in normal tones, but Liss could hear every syllable with crystal clarity. She quickly reviewed what she and Dan had said to each other while they'd been sitting at the table and breathed a sigh of relief once she was sure they hadn't touched on anything too personal. Nor had they mentioned murder or missing persons.

Warning herself to stick to neutral topics while they ate, she glanced again at the window. A woman and a little girl had stopped to pet the dog. The golden retriever danced with pleasure over the head rub. Once the child and her mother continued on their way, Jonas returned to staring forlornly into the coffee shop. A few minutes later the scene was repeated with a new cast when a young man of college age paused to make much of the dog.

New Boston might be five times bigger than Moosetookalook, Liss thought, but it was still a small town. It wouldn't surprise her at all to learn that half the population knew that the golden retriever named Jonas belonged to a man named Harlan.

A voice Liss recognized as belonging to the previously invisible Miranda spoke right at her elbow, startling her. "Haven't seen you folks in here before. You new in town?"

"We're visiting for a few days," Dan answered.

"Let me guess. You're the couple staying out to the Snowe place." From the tray that held their order, she off-loaded plates and steaming mugs of coffee. Her plain, pleasant face wore a hopeful expression in anticipation of learning something from them that would be worth passing on to other customers.

"That's pretty good guessing," Dan said.

"Might have been helped along a bit by the fact that the town manager stopped in for coffee on his way home last night. Did I hear you mention a maze?"

Liss saw no reason to keep their discovery a secret and reasoned that people who had known Simeon Snowe might have some idea why he'd planted such a thing in the first place. She described what she'd seen from the upstairs window of Snowe's house.

"Well, I'll be!" Miranda exclaimed. "If that don't beat all."

"So, you had no idea it was there?"

"Now, how would I? I've never set foot on the Snowe farm in my life."

"But you must have met Mr. Snowe. I bet you know everybody in town."

"Most," Miranda conceded, looking pleased that Liss had noticed. "I guess you heard what happened out to his place some years back."

Liss glanced at Dan. Having insisted that she wasn't interested in cold cases, she hesitated to encourage their chatty waitress to talk about the murder or the disappearance, but it wasn't as if she'd set out to interrogate the woman. "From what we've been told, quite a few things happened."

Miranda's eyes gleamed. "Oh, honey, it was a circus out there. The police practically lived there for weeks after they found that body in New York." She leaned in close and lowered her voice to what she probably believed was a whisper. "Never did find out who killed him."

Liss couldn't resist. "What do you think happened to Simeon Snowe?"

"No idea. Of course, I make it a practice to mind my own business. Nobody likes a gossip, you know."

On that note, she left them alone to enjoy their lunch, but she'd no sooner disappeared into the kitchen than the man in the gray overcoat—the dog's owner—sidled up to their table. He had a bag of freshly ground coffee in one hand and an apologetic expression on his lean, age-lined face.

"I couldn't help overhearing that you're staying out at Simeon Snowe's farm."

Dan had his mouth full of pastrami, so Liss answered. "That's right. We're evaluating the Christmas tree business for the new owner. Did you know the late Mr. Snowe?"

"In fact, I did. We often crossed paths." His lips curved into a reminiscent smile. "I guess you'd say we shared a common interest."

From the look of the man—casually but expensively dressed, dignified demeanor, somewhere in his late six-ties—he was probably retired from a business or profession. Given the entertainment options in a town of this size, Liss was pretty sure that the "common interest" he'd shared with Simeon Snowe was membership in the Elks Club or maybe in the local Masonic lodge.

"Such a shame to let those fields go wild," the man continued. "I hope the new owner plans to do something constructive with the property."

A sudden suspicion had Liss frowning. "You aren't in real estate, are you?"

The implied criticism in her tone surprised a laugh out of him. "Once upon a time I was a chiropractor, but I'm retired now. Harlan Woolgar, at your service."

Following a leisurely lunch that was not interrupted again after Mr. Woolgar and his dog departed, Dan drove two blocks to Commercial Street and found a convenient parking space right across from All Things Mystical. Liss studied the storefront through the windshield of the truck with a vague sense of disappointment.

"What's wrong?" Dan asked.

"I guess I expected the place to look like the Magic Box. You know, from *Buffy the Vampire Slayer*."

Instead, at this distance, the storefront might have been that of a boutique or a bookstore. Two large display windows flanked a door that was painted bright red. One held an assortment of jewelry and charms, artfully arranged on tables and stands draped with black velvet and on a manikin dressed in a colorful caftan. The second window was full of books. From Liss's vantage point, they appeared to be a jumble of old and new titles, although she perked up when she spotted a mortar and pestle on top of one of the stacks. And were those clay pots and jars in various sizes and shapes? Any herbalist worth her salt would use such containers to store potions and hand-rolled pills.

"This section of town has a nice mix of offices and small businesses," Dan remarked, "though our town square has a better one."

Liss followed his gaze to a dress-shop window. Winter coats were already on sale. Tasteful lettering on a nearby door announced that the premises belonged to a "painless" dentist. Liss's survey of her surroundings came to a sudden stop when she caught sight of a sign that read DANCE-EX in large brightly colored letters.

"Well, well," she said aloud. Only a few hours earlier, she'd been ready to abandon all hope of keeping up with her daily exercises. The cramped confines of the old farmhouse had defeated her. But now, if they did decide to stay the week in New Boston, she had a solution to her dilemma—a dance and exercise studio only seven miles from the farm.

A half dozen young girls came out of the building in a rush, all laughing and talking. Most of them were lugging tote bags of one sort or another, but one carried an old-fashioned hatbox with a wrist strap. That sight brought a nostalgic smile to Liss's face.

"Are we planning to sit here all day?" Dan inquired.

"No, but do you see that sign? If we do stay beyond the weekend, I'll want a decent workout. That looks like the perfect place to get one."

"*Are* we going to stay?"

"Not if you don't want to, but I'm still in favor of taking some time for the two of us. You know . . . relax. Goof off."

"Except for the occasional exercise class? Go ahead." Dan made a shooing motion. "Find out if they accept walk-ins, just in case we stay on." His tender smile told her that was more and more likely. "I'll wait here."

She leaned across the seat to kiss him on the cheek, then hopped out of the truck.

At some point in its history, the dance studio had been a retail store with a small display window to one side of the door. A red velvet curtain shielded the interior from gawking passersby and served as a backdrop for three neatly lettered signs. One announced an upcoming ballet recital. The second was a list of the classes offered by the studio. Liss was impressed by the variety of choices. Dance-Ex instructors taught the standards—ballet, tap, and ballroom—but there were also lessons in yoga, aerobics, rhythmic gymnastics, and something called "advanced stretching."

The third sign was tucked away in a corner, smaller than the other two. PRIVATE LESSONS AVAILABLE it read. SURPRISE YOUR WIFE OR SWEETHEART. LEARN YOUR WAY AROUND THE DANCE FLOOR. THEN SHOW HER A NIGHT SHE'LL NEVER FORGET.

What a sweet idea, Liss thought, although she couldn't

imagine that the offer had many takers. Learning ballroom dancing would not be high on the to-do list of most of the men she knew.

The door to the studio opened directly into a large room. A barre was attached to one wall. Mirrors covered the one opposite. Windows filled the third. The curtains were open to reveal a small parking lot at the rear of the building. The layout was pretty much what Liss would have found in hundreds of small dance studios across the country. A bit out of the ordinary were the half dozen colorful mats spread out across the floor. Ditto the rolling cart piled high with assorted weights and other exercise paraphernalia. A second cart held the balls, hoops, clubs, and colorful ribbons used in rhythmic gymnastics.

"Hello!" Liss called. "Anyone here?"

The mirrored wall was bisected by a single door. A tall, athletic-looking woman with short blond hair emerged through the beaded curtain that hung across it. Liss caught only a glimpse of the narrow corridor behind her, but she could guess what else was there. On one side would be an office, a bathroom, and maybe a small storage room. Perhaps even a minuscule kitchen. A large room for the little girls to change in—street clothes to leotards and back again—would take up the space on the other side of the hallway. It would be furnished with benches to sit on while they tied the ribbons on their toe shoes, and if this was a really classy place, there might be lockers in which the students could stow their personal belongings while they attended class.

Although her own focus had always been on Scottish dancing, Liss had taken her share of lessons in other disciplines. Fond memories of her first ballet teacher, Miss

Winona, had her greeting the blonde with more warmth than she usually extended to strangers.

"Sorry to barge in," Liss said, "but I couldn't resist when I saw your sign. Perhaps you know my good friend Zara Kalishnakof? She and her husband own Dance Central in Moosetookalook. The three of us worked together for years in a Scottish dance troupe called—"

"Is there something I can do for you?" the woman interrupted. She wasn't rude so much as impatient, an impression reinforced when she glanced at her watch.

Liss kept her friendly smile in place. The blonde probably had another class coming in and had been counting on the time between sessions to prepare. Or maybe she'd been trying to grab a bite to eat. As someone who ran a one-person business herself, Liss could sympathize.

"Sorry. I'll get to the point. I'm in this area for a week, and I was hoping I could participate in a few of your classes while I am here. You know how it is," she added with a little laugh. "Got to keep the old muscles toned."

"I charge thirty dollars for an hour-long session in any discipline," the woman said. "If you need workout clothing or shoes, I can sell them to you."

"Great. Do you have a schedule of classes?"

"Follow me." The second glance at her watch was as unsubtle as the first. She had a long, fast stride. Liss had to scurry to keep up with her.

The office was exactly where Liss expected it would be. From the top drawer of a file cabinet, the blonde extracted a sheet of paper and handed it over.

"Is this you?" Liss indicated the name printed at the top of the page. "Juliette Cressy?"

"That's right. Did you say you were here for a week? My usual minimum commitment is six sessions, paid in advance, but I suppose I can make an exception for you if you agree to sign up for five."

"That's reasonable, assuming there's something on this list that appeals to me."

The longer Liss spent with Juliette, the less inclined she was to bother being pleasant herself. The other woman's brusque manner wasn't only off-putting but catching, too.

More than ever, Liss missed Dance Central. Zara and Sandy had instituted a pay-as-you-go policy, collecting the money before the start of each class. If a student missed one, because she was sick or for some other reason, she didn't have to pay. Liss herself used the facilities for free. She'd tried to pay when Dance Central first opened, but Zara had insisted that having her company bright and early every morning was worth more to her than money.

Dance-Ex offered a greater variety of classes than Dance Central did, but Liss couldn't help but notice that there were no trademarked names among them. If you were looking for Jazzercise, dancercise, Zumba, or the like, you were flat out of luck in New Boston. Dance-Ex was strictly generic.

Liss shifted her gaze from the list to Juliette, taking in the other woman's height and generous bosom. It was doubtful she'd ever been a professional ballerina. "What's your background?" she asked.

"Does it matter? If you sign up, you'll get a workout, and that's what you're interested in, right?" Juliette's impatience had become a palpable force in the small office. Whatever she had scheduled, it was clearly much more important than luring in a new customer, especially one interested only in the short term.

"I'm looking for something each morning for the next week, but not too early." Liss studied the page in her hand again. "I'm on vacation, you see. Besides, I'll have to drive into town from the old Snowe place. I know it's not all that far, but—"

She broke off when the dance instructor made a startled sound. Her head shot up, but she was already too late to catch a glimpse of Juliette's expression. The other woman had turned away, giving Liss nothing to look at but her back.

"Did you know Simeon Snowe?" Liss asked.

"No. Not at all. Never met the man." But the tension in Juliette's shoulders was impossible to miss.

"I suppose everyone in New Boston heard about it when he disappeared."

Juliette's voice dripped ice. "Of course. The consensus of opinion was that a bear got him."

Liss considered asking Juliette if she knew anything about the man in the netter, but decided against it. "How long have you had this dance studio?" she asked instead.

"Eleven years."

When Juliette turned, the light from the overhead fixture fell fully on her face. She was older than Liss had first thought, nearer to forty than thirty. Beneath those hard, cold eyes were the beginnings of crow's-feet.

With an impatient gesture, Juliette indicated the sheet of paper Liss had been studying. "Why don't you take that list home with you? If you decide to join a class, show up at the first session with a check for a hundred and fifty dollars in hand."

Liss allowed the other woman to herd her back through the beaded curtain but balked at being shoved out the front door, even after Juliette opened it as wide as it would go and, despite the cold air that billowed in, seemed prepared to leave it open until Liss left the premises.

"I'll be here on Monday at ten for the aerobics class," Liss told her, deliberately lingering on the threshold.

"Good choice. See you then."

Still dawdling, driven to be provoking in response to Juliette's attitude, Liss finally took one slow step in the direction of the street. She pulled back sharply as a young woman rushed into the studio, nearly bowling her over in the process. There would have been a nasty collision if Liss hadn't stepped aside in the nick of time.

"Oops! My bad!" said the newcomer.

"No harm done," Liss assured her, but the other woman, a brunette barely out of her teens, had already shifted her attention to Juliette.

"Sorry I'm late, boss. I got held up at home. It won't happen again. I swear. Cross my heart and hope to die."

Liss hovered for a moment longer, wondering why the young woman was so agitated. She might be late, but no students had arrived yet for the next class.

The door closed with a decisive thump, shutting the two dance instructors in and Liss out. A distinctive click followed—a dead bolt being engaged. As Liss turned her steps toward Dan's truck, she glanced again at the paper Juliette Cressy had given her. There were no classes scheduled on Saturdays after advanced ballet from one to two, the session that had just finished up when she and Dan arrived on the scene.

Juliette probably gave lessons to her instructors, Liss

decided. She'd have to teach them the routines she choreographed for use in their classes. Given what little Liss had seen of the woman, she'd be a hard taskmaster, reason enough for her employees to be nervous around her.

From the opposite side of the street, Liss heard the driver's side door of the truck open and shut as Dan got out. He'd been watching for her. That knowledge, and the welcome sight of him striding toward her, erased every other thought from Liss's mind. She tucked the class schedule into her shoulder bag and quickened her pace so that they met on the sidewalk in front of All Things Mystical.

"Welcome to the wonderful world of the strange and fantastic!"

The moment Liss and Dan stepped into her shop, Rowena Luckenbill swooped down on them, her gauzy, flowing garments aflutter and beads and bangles clanking with her every movement. The loose clothing obscured the shape of her body, but nothing could disguise Rowena's height. She had several inches on Liss, and Liss usually towered over every other woman in the room.

They grew them big in New Boston, Liss thought. Juliette Cressy was even taller than Rowena Luckenbill. Unlike Juliette, Rowena was pink-cheeked and smiling. Her sparkling blue eyes danced with barely suppressed delight. She was also somewhat older than the dance instructor. Short, fluffy snow-white hair formed a halo around her head, and close up, she smelled faintly of lavender.

She hovered at first, eager to be of assistance. "Anything you're looking for, I can find," she offered. "I know exactly where all my bits and bobs are shelved."

"We're just browsing," Liss insisted and then felt guilty when she saw the disappointment on Rowena's face. The poor woman probably didn't get all that many customers. It was cruel to deprive her of an opportunity to extol the virtues of dried herbs and magic potions.

There were plenty of both in evidence. As Officer Jennings had warned them, odd-looking clumps of vegetation, none of which Liss could name, hung from the ceiling above the sales counter. Behind it, several shelves held glass jars filled with leaves, berries, and a few other substances Liss decided she would prefer *not* to identify. She was pretty sure one of them contained a mandrake root. Creepy!

Her gaze shifted to the sales counter itself. Incongruously, a large stuffed toy cat had been placed next to the cash register. If it had been black, she'd have seen the connection. The pairing of black cats with witches and spells had been a cliché for centuries. But this faux feline was clearly a Scottish Fold. The breed was instantly recognizable because the ears were, well, folded over. She reached out, curious, to search for a price tag and yelped in surprise when the cat opened its eyes. They stared at each other for a long, fraught moment. Then the cat yawned and went back to sleep.

Behind her, Liss heard Dan chuckle. Flushed with embarrassment, she turned to glare at him, but he'd already gone back to inspecting the contents of a bookcase on the far side of the showroom.

"I didn't think it was real," she muttered in her own defense.

"This is Gozer." On a wave of lavender, Rowena Luckenbill floated to Liss's side and extended a hand to scratch the animal behind one of his peculiar ears.

"Guard cat?"

Rowena gave a snort of laughter. "Not hardly."

Having bonded over the cat, Liss introduced herself as the proprietor of Moosetookalook Scottish Emporium. "I'm always interested in seeing how other small businesses catering to a niche market manage. Do you get much walk-in business, or do you rely on Internet sales?"

"I've established a decent-size local clientele," Rowena told her. "Early on I promoted the business by doing readings."

"Tarot cards?" One of Rowena's display cases showed off some of the more colorful artwork used on this classic fortune-telling tool.

"Oh, yes. I'm also proficient with a crystal ball, and I read palms. And, of course, I offer Ouija boards for sale." She made a vague gesture that drew Liss's attention to the whole of her shop.

Every shelf, every nook and cranny, was stuffed with oddities ranging from the whimsical to the disturbingly occult. Role-playing games were stacked alongside books on herbs, magic, witchcraft, and alien abductions. A nearby cabinet held DVDs of the complete seasons of *Bewitched*, *Sabrina, the Teenage Witch*, and *Charmed*, together with almost every movie featuring witches that Liss had ever heard of—everything from *The Witches of Eastwick* to *Practical Magic*.

Another of Rowena's glass display cases contained very old books, their leather covers dark with age. Liss's eyes widened as she stared at the gold lettering on one of them. The title was unfamiliar to her, but she knew that this was a grimoire—a *serious* book of spells. Such things had been the foundation of more than one paranormal thriller.

It's a good thing I'm not superstitious, Liss thought. But she found herself edging away from the display.

Rowena had retreated behind her sales counter, but her bright-eyed gaze darted back and forth between Liss and Dan with the same avid interest a robin gave to a promising worm. She stroked the cat and asked, "Wouldn't you like to know what the future holds?"

"I'd rather be surprised," Liss answered. "But maybe you can help us with something. Do you know anything about mazes?"

The question sounded almost mundane in these surroundings, but it seemed to surprise the proprietor of All Things Mystical. "Well, that's a first. Folks usually want to know about astral projection or whether or not I'll sell them a love potion."

"We came across one," Liss said. "A maze."

She glanced at Dan. Booklets were mixed in with thicker volumes in the bookcase he was examining. He was methodically pulling out each one to check the title, but she knew he was also aware of what was going on around him and he was close enough to hear what she and Rowena said to each other.

"A maze," Rowena repeated. "Do you mean here in New Boston? How odd. I didn't think anyone in these parts had the know-how to create that sort of landscaping. Or the money to waste on it."

"This isn't an ordinary maze."

Rowena chuckled. "Define *ordinary.*"

"Hampton Court," Liss said at once. She'd seen photos of the maze at that royal palace. It was a major British tourist attraction and featured neatly trimmed hedges and wide, easy-to-walk passages.

"And I presume you aren't talking about a corn

maze—something someone made in a field for Halloween."

Liss shook her head. "Not exactly."

Dan came up beside her, holding a thick black booklet in one hand. "Found one," he announced and handed over *Mazes: Ancient & Modern* by Robert Field.

"Cash or charge?" Rowena asked as Dan reached for his wallet.

"Cash."

Completing the transaction did not take long. Dan was ready to leave as soon as Rowena tucked the receipt into the bag with his purchase, but Liss knew they weren't going to make their escape until she'd satisfied the other woman's curiosity. She didn't bother waiting to be asked.

"We're staying at Simeon Snowe's Christmas tree farm at the request of his heir," she said. "Ms. Snowe wanted us to assess whether or not the business is still viable."

Rowena sucked in a startled breath. Liss thought she started to cross herself, but her hand stopped partway through the gesture, fingers grasping one of the three long strings of beads she wore around her neck. "That's where the maze is?" she asked in a hushed voice.

Liss nodded. "When we took a look around the property earlier today, there was something odd about the section where Mr. Snowe planted his last crop. It took a while to figure out what it was, but from the second floor of his house, you can see that the trees form a maze."

"Well, for goodness' sake! Did you go inside? I've always wanted to explore a real maze. It must have been fascinating."

"We didn't even locate the entrance."

"Were you acquainted with Simeon Snowe?" Dan asked.

Rowena hesitated. "I knew him."

"Any idea why he'd plant a maze?" Liss asked.

"I wouldn't have taken him for the fanciful sort. Then again, I wouldn't have thought he'd take off without telling anyone, either." Liss heard the deep sadness in Rowena's voice and noticed the faraway look that came into her eyes.

"We've been told he wandered off and got lost," Dan said.

Abruptly, Rowena shook off her melancholy and gave a derisive snort. "Highly unlikely."

"Perhaps he met with an accident and couldn't get back to the house," Liss suggested.

"Well, it hardly matters now," Rowena declared. "If he could have come back, he would have. He's dead and gone, and those left behind have to move on. The great mandala, eh?"

Liss didn't understand the reference, but she nodded, anyway, sorry to have caused the other woman even momentary distress. Absently, she scratched Gozer behind one of his uniquely Scottish Fold ears. After a moment, the cat responded with a rumbling purr. The soothing sound made her realize that she'd been missing Lumpkin and Glenora, even though she'd been away from them only for a single day.

"I'm guessing you have a cat of your own," Rowena said.

Liss nodded. "Two of them. Lumpkin is a Maine Coon. And Glenora—well, she'd fit right in with the decor and theme of your shop. Her fur is solid black. Not even a trace of any other color."

"Unusual names." Rowena's eyes twinkled.

Belatedly catching on, Liss laughed. "Gozer? From the first *Ghostbusters* movie?"

"That's right. One of the demons. Seemed appropriate at the time. He was a holy terror as a kitten."

Dan, who had been amusing himself by flipping through a book on the healing power of crystals, just shook his head.

The more they talked, the more Liss found herself liking Rowena Luckenbill. Officer Jennings had called her a "harmless eccentric," and she supposed that was accurate as far as it went, especially given the rather bizarre stock Rowena carried. But the older woman had a solid, down-to-earth side, too. The term "crazy like a fox" came to mind. Liss had a sneaking suspicion that Rowena wore outfits that put one in mind of a gypsy fortune-teller for the same reason Liss's aunt Margaret had always dressed in tartan skirts accessorized with clan crest jewelry when she worked at Moosetookalook Scottish Emporium.

"Perhaps you'd like to see our maze." The impulsive invitation surprised all three of them.

"Ah, Liss, I'm not sure that's a good idea." Dan sent Rowena an apologetic look. "It's not our property, after all."

"I quite understand." If Rowena was disappointed, she didn't show it, but after a moment she murmured, "What a pity we can't ask Simeon to give me permission to view it."

"And while we're at it, ask him why he planted a maze in the first place," Liss agreed.

A wicked gleam came into Rowena's bright blue eyes. "I don't do séances, but there may be another way to get answers."

Liss didn't trust that smooth segue. "Really? How?"

"First you must ask how much."

Liss's eyebrows shot up. *Crazy as a fox, all right.* "Okay. How much?"

"Forty-five dollars, plus tax." She had that figure right on the tip of her tongue.

Liss fought a grin. "A little steep, don't you think?"

Rowena waved away the complaint with a careless gesture of one hand. "A paltry sum."

"What does it buy?" Dan admired a good sales pitch as much as anyone. As president of the Moosetookalook Small Business Association, he'd heard quite a few.

With a dramatic flourish and a jangling of bracelets, Rowena Luckenbill reached beneath the sales counter and came out with a large sparkly crystal ball. "Ask Madame Rowena to gaze into the depths," she intoned in a low, sepulchral voice, "and all will be revealed. Madame Rowena sees all and tells all."

Chapter Five

_____

"Are you *sure* you don't want to buy some time with that crystal ball?" Dan teased his wife when they were back in the truck.

"I'd have more faith in a séance," Liss said with a laugh. "Quite a character, isn't she?"

"An interesting woman," Dan agreed, "but I wonder if she really manages to make a living catering to such a limited clientele."

"I expect she does, probably the same way I do, with online and mail order sales to take up the slack. So, what do you want to do next? Shall we explore New Boston or head back to the farm?"

The truck's engine came to life with a roar. "What else do you think this burg has to offer? Theater? Museums? Fenway Park?" He pulled out of their parking spot and continued along Commercial Street until he had to stop for a red light.

Liss gave a snort of laughter and pointed to a sign at the intersection. "There you go. Fenway Park. One mile."

Unlike the famous original in old Boston, this Fenway Park was a small picnic area with a Little League field and a playground. At the moment it was deserted.

"Well, that was exciting," Dan said as he headed back toward the main road. "What next?"

"Let's find a supermarket," Liss suggested. "I feel like cooking something substantial for supper, and I need a main course." She also wanted to pick up a few odds and ends Andy hadn't thought to supply.

Dan drove to the same small grocery store they'd stopped at the previous day. Once inside, they separated. Liss sought the meat department. Dan headed for the beer aisle.

"Meats" consisted of one large refrigerated case at the back of the store. A woman, small and stooped with age, stood blocking the whole of it, her back to Liss. She appeared to be weighing the relative merits of two packages of pork chops. Liss slowed her steps, intending to wait until the other woman made her decision and moved on. She changed her mind when she was close enough to recognize the meat customer as the sour-faced clerk from the town office.

Unable to resist, Liss called out to her, using her cheeriest voice. "Hello. How nice to see you again. Bea, isn't it?"

This friendly sally did not go over well. Bea barely topped the five-foot mark, but if she felt at a disadvantage because of her height or small stature, she didn't let on. When she turned to square off against the much younger, much taller Liss, her stance was rigid and a forbidding scowl darkened her features.

"That's Mrs. Purvey to you, missy."

"I . . . I beg your pardon," Liss stammered. "We met yesterday. My husband and I—"

"I know who you are. And I know what you're up to, too." Beatrice Purvey got right in Liss's face, even though she had to go up on tiptoe to do it. "You've got a lot of nerve! This is a nice little town. You've got no right to go stirring things up again!"

"I didn't—"

"Next thing you know, you'll be saying that New Boston has a drug problem or some other terrible big city trouble. I'll have you know that this town has very little crime. Our chief of police knows how to deal with the wrong sort of people."

"He seems very . . . efficient," Liss blurted.

Mrs. Purvey's hands clenched so tightly on the packages of meat that Liss feared for the shrink-wrap and Styrofoam.

"I assure you, my husband and I mean no insult to your hometown."

Truthfully, Liss couldn't think what she or Dan might have said or done to give that impression, or to whom, but an apology seemed the safest way to go. They were already attracting the attention of other shoppers. Feeling the heat creep into her face, Liss considered making a run for cover.

Woman up, she told herself. Besides, her insatiable curiosity demanded that she find out exactly how she'd managed to earn Mrs. Purvey's wrath.

Lowering her voice, she adopted a soothing tone. "I have nothing against New Boston, Mrs. Purvey. Dan and I came here to do a favor for the woman who inherited Mr. Snowe's estate. Ms. Snowe hopes to reopen the Christmas tree business." She told the little white lie without a qualm, reasoning that she fully intended to convince Gina to make it true. "That's good, right? It will mean more jobs for local workers and more tax revenue for the town."

Mrs. Purvey resisted the effort at conciliation. If anything, she became more implacable. "You came here to snoop. You think I don't know who you are, but I do. I read the newspapers every day and have since I was a girl. I remember what the reports said about those goings-on down to Moosetookalook a few years back."

For a moment, Liss could think of nothing to say. The woman must have a memory like an elephant. Her part in those cases had been played down in the press. Even when she'd been able to assist the police in solving a crime, her name had rarely appeared in print in connection with the capture of a criminal. Besides, in that context, how could Mrs. Purvey possibly think it was a *bad* thing for Liss to have been involved? Didn't everyone want murderers brought to justice?

"Mrs. Purvey, I . . . oh!" Belatedly, the penny dropped. "Are you related to the chief of police?"

"I'm his mother." Her bosom swelled with pride.

Now the elderly woman's accusations made a convoluted sort of sense. There had been time since Liss and Dan visited the PD that morning for Bea Purvey to hear of it and put the worst possible interpretation on that turn of events. She assumed that they'd come to town to dig up dirt on local law enforcement.

Liss could follow Bea's train of thought easily enough, now that she knew the older woman had been reading newspaper accounts as far back as the first time Liss became involved in the investigation of a murder. She'd had no choice in the matter on that occasion. The state police officer in charge of the case had been an absolute jackass, and he'd been convinced that *she* was the killer.

There had been a time or two since when Liss had found evidence that honest, capable officers had missed.

She'd never set out to make the police look incompetent, but it was entirely possible that Beatrice Purvey had gleaned that impression from the accounts she'd read in the local press.

One look at Bea's set features warned Liss that it would be an uphill battle to change her mind. Clearly she'd convinced herself that Liss was a threat to her son. Overprotective parents weren't known for their ability to listen to reason.

She considered and rejected a variety of responses, everything from asking why Mrs. Purvey thought her son might have something to hide to telling her to contact the chief of police of Moosetookalook, Liss's best pal, Sherri Campbell, for a character reference.

"Well, missy? Don't just stand there with your mouth hanging open." She tossed one of the packages of pork chops back into the meat case. "If you have something to say, then say it." The other package landed in her shopping cart with a plop.

"I can only give you my word, Mrs. Purvey, that I did not come to New Boston to cause trouble." Although Beatrice Purvey already knew the basic facts from overhearing what Liss and Dan had told the town manager, Liss repeated them, anyway. She ended by emphasizing the fact that Gina Snowe was a lawyer with a practice in Chicago. "She'd be here in person to evaluate her property if she didn't have an unbreakable commitment there. An important criminal case, as I understand it."

Mrs. Purvey did not look impressed. "Why did she send you? Why not a relative?"

"We're old friends. Gina Snowe is originally from Fallstown. My husband and I both went to high school with her."

Mrs. Purvey huffed out a breath and looked annoyed. "He was a strange man."

"Simeon Snowe?"

"Who else have we been talking about? He kept himself to himself, even more so than most folks do."

Liss breathed a little easier as the older woman's overt hostility faded into simple querulousness, but she was a trifle surprised at this assessment of Gina's uncle's character. It didn't mesh with the impression of Snowe she'd formed after talking to the man in the coffee shop and Officer Jennings and Rowena Luckenbill and Andy Dutton. Mrs. Purvey made Snowe sound overtly antisocial.

"He was a hard worker," Liss ventured. "He'd have to be to plant so many trees year after year."

"Christmas trees! I ask you, where's the sense in cutting down a live tree and putting up with all those messy needles when you can buy an artificial one that will last for decades?"

Liss wasn't about to get involved in that debate. Mrs. Purvey already had enough reasons to dislike her. But it did occur to her that someone who worked in a town office would be in an ideal situation to hear about everything that went on within the municipality.

"Do you happen to know who Mr. Snowe hired to help him with the planting? His niece will be looking for local labor when it's time to put in the next crop."

"Only that Dutton girl." Mrs. Purvey made an odd little sound in her throat. "I wouldn't advise taking her on. Even her own mother despairs of her."

And yet another conflicting opinion. Liss wondered if there was anyone, aside from her own son, of whom Mrs. Purvey *did* approve.

"Andy seemed nice enough when we met her earlier today."

"Running around on a motorcycle? I ask you, what good can come of that sort of behavior?"

Liss thought about asking what *bad* it could cause, but Mrs. Purvey was still talking.

"I'm not supposed to know about it, of course, but Andrea Dutton had her share of run-ins with the law when she was younger."

What a nasty piece of work this woman is turning out to be, Liss thought. A quick glance from side to side relieved one concern. Although other shoppers browsed the shelves at a distance, no one was close enough to hear the chief of police's mother blacken Andy's name.

"That girl would have ended up in jail for sure if she hadn't been a minor at the time. But you didn't hear it from me." She mimed zipping her lips.

Liss had liked Mrs. Purvey better when she was defending her son. That the elderly woman would say such things to a stranger, especially one she clearly distrusted, cast doubt on her mental state and made Liss doubly anxious to get away from her.

"Don't worry, Mrs. Purvey," she said in the too-sweet voice she usually reserved for obnoxious salesmen. "I didn't listen to a word you said. In fact, as far as I'm concerned, I never even *met* you. You have a nice evening, now."

Eyes narrowed, as if she suspected that she'd been insulted but couldn't quite figure out how, the unpleasant old woman gave a curt nod of farewell, spun her shopping cart around, and wheeled it briskly away.

Liss drew in a deep, cleansing breath. She could just

imagine what Mrs. Purvey would have to say to her cronies about that awful Liss Ruskin.

Dan reappeared a few minutes later. Liss selected a thick steak for their supper. Dan dropped a six-pack of Geary's Pale Ale into the cart, then took a close look at her face. "What's wrong?"

Speaking in a soft voice, even though they had the aisle to themselves, she filled him in on her exchange with Beatrice Purvey.

"I guess she'd know if Andy was ever in trouble with the law," Dan said, "but why do you suppose she made such a point of telling you about it?"

"It certainly wasn't to do me a favor by putting us on our guard. She's not the sort of woman who does anything nice for anyone." She frowned. "But since she was so determined to dis Andy, I wonder why she didn't provide specifics?" Had the girl been caught shoplifting? Joyriding? Or had it been something more serious? In spite of the fact that her first impulse was to protest the younger woman's innocence, Liss couldn't help but wonder what the real story was.

As he so often did, Dan seemed to read her thoughts. "If it's a juvenile record, what does it matter? Let's face it. If Andy had wanted to rob the Snowe house or commit any other crime on Snowe's property, she's had seven years to accomplish it."

"You don't suppose *she* could have killed the guy in the netter? And then maybe Snowe, too, to cover up the first crime?"

Dan laughed. "I doubt it. She'd have been what? No more than fourteen or fifteen years old at the time."

Once again, Liss checked to make sure no one was showing any interest in the conversation of two people standing in front of the day's offerings of meat. A woman with a child in the basket of her shopping cart turned the corner and headed their way. Liss ducked into the cereal aisle. It was empty of other shoppers, but she continued to speak only loud enough for Dan to hear.

"Even at that age, I imagine Andy was a sturdy girl."

"And I'm sure she was questioned at the time."

"She said her mother intervened. Remember? Because she was a minor."

"A fifteen-year-old who kills someone is usually tried as an adult. I'm no expert, but if she already had a record of violent behavior, they'd have talked to her, protective mama or not."

Liss knew he was right, but Bea Purvey's insinuations had raised doubts. One continued to niggle at her. "Didn't it strike you as odd that Andy kept on tending Snowe's crop? Do you think she planned to steal some of Gina's trees and sell them herself?"

"The thought crossed my mind," Dan admitted, "but she didn't do all that much tending. Maybe she was hoping Snowe would come back."

After a detour to pick up a carton of skim milk, they headed for the checkout aisle. The same bored teenager who'd waited on them the previous day was working the cash register. She couldn't be more than a few years Andy's junior. Liss was tempted to ask her if she knew the older girl. If this were Moosetookalook, the clerk would be a gold mine of information.

Since they weren't in Moosetookalook anymore, Liss kept her question to herself.

*   *   *

In the time they'd been inside the grocery store, the sun had set. The parking lot was shrouded in murky half-light, the prelude to true darkness. The visibility was even worse where Dan had parked—off to one side and well away from the nearest streetlight.

Liss tugged on the passenger side door handle, but Dan hadn't yet pressed the unlock button on his key chain. She stretched her neck and rotated her shoulders while he finished securing their grocery bags in the back of the pickup. It had been a long day.

The soft thunk of the door unlatching had her reaching for the handle again, but before her fingers could connect, three things happened at once. Dan cried out. Liss heard an ominous thump. And the entire truck rocked as something heavy fell against it.

"Dan? Are you okay?" Her heart in her throat, she was already running toward him, circling the hood, the shortest route from her side of the truck to his.

"Watch your footing!"

Liss skidded to a stop, but her anxiety skyrocketed. That was pain she heard distorting Dan's voice. When she saw him lying on the ground next to the driver's side door, she ignored his warning and rushed to his side. Even before she knelt beside him, she could see that his right leg was twisted at an awkward angle, but it was his head he held clasped with both hands.

"How badly are you hurt?" She wanted to throw her arms around him, but she was afraid of doing more damage.

"Hit my head on the door." Dan sounded short of breath. "And I think my ankle is broken."

"Don't talk if it hurts to speak. You might have a broken rib." Liss fumbled in her purse for her cell phone to call for help.

Dan had lowered his hands, but he seemed to be having trouble focusing. "Slipped on something," he said. "Hit the side of the truck. Landed wrong."

In Liss's ear, the 9-1-1 operator asked for the nature of her emergency.

The glow from her cell phone was sufficient to verify that something was wrong with Dan's ankle, but Liss didn't have enough light to get a good look at his head. As soon as she'd relayed the pertinent information and responded to the operator's questions, she used her teeth to tug off one glove and ran the fingertips of that hand over Dan's scalp. It didn't take her long to find a tender spot. His grunt of pain put an end to the gentle exploration.

She'd kept a death grip on the phone with the other hand. Relief made her almost dizzy when the 9-1-1 operator assured her that an ambulance was on its way.

"Sit tight," the dispatcher said. "Five minutes, tops."

Liss relayed this news to Dan, hoping she sounded bracing. Inside she was terrified. She'd suffered a good crack on the head herself once and knew that head injuries were nothing to take lightly. That was why so many contact sports required helmets. And why wearing them was encouraged for skiers, bicyclists, and those who rode motorcycles. Right now she'd vote for adding anyone who was planning to get into a motor vehicle to that list.

"Lucky for me, I've got a hard head," Dan muttered.

Liss's attempt at a smile faltered and died. She didn't suppose it mattered. She doubted he could see the expression on her face in the gloaming.

"I slipped." Dan sounded stronger but very confused. "How could I have slipped? There's no ice."

"It's shady over here," Liss said, as if that explained it.

Except it didn't. The temperature had risen steadily all day. Any icy spots had long since melted, even those shielded from direct sunlight. And since the number on the thermometer hadn't yet dropped below freezing for the night, no new ice had had a chance to form.

Tentatively, Liss touched her fingertips to the ground. She moved the hand that wasn't still clutching her phone first one way and then the other. She froze when her thumb came in contact with a thick oily substance.

"It feels slick here," she said. "Maybe one of the cars that parked here earlier today had a leak in its oil tank."

"Just my luck. I probably stepped in the only slippery spot in the entire town."

"You always were a klutz," Liss said in an effort to cheer him up. "Oh, no, wait! That would be me."

This pitiful attempt to be funny won her a weak chuckle. Encouraged by his response, she squeezed his hand. Maybe he'd escaped a concussion, after all. She felt even more optimistic when she heard the distant wail of a siren.

"Don't move," she ordered and stood up to wave the ambulance over once it turned into the parking lot.

For the next hour and more, Liss was too busy to think beyond the next moment. First there were the mechanics of getting Dan loaded into the ambulance and transported to the nearest hospital. Then she had to deal with paperwork, all the while worrying about what the emergency room doctor might find. Fortunately, there were no patients ahead of Dan. His injuries received immediate attention.

As soon as Liss finished filling out forms, a helpful nurse directed her to the exam rooms. She heard Dan's voice from the far end of a short corridor.

"Concussion? How can I have a concussion? I wasn't knocked out."

"You don't have to lose consciousness to have a concussion, Mr. Ruskin." From the tone of voice alone, Liss could tell that the emergency room doctor was rapidly losing patience with his patient.

She entered the small exam room before the debate could escalate. Although she sympathized with her husband's desire to leave the hospital, she wasn't about to let him take any chances with his health.

"Save the arguments, Dan. You're not going anywhere."

"Liss, I'm fine. Really. Nothing's wrong with me except for a little headache."

"And a fractured ankle," the doctor said in a dry voice. He was a middle-aged man with deep bags under his eyes, but he had an air of competence about him that Liss found reassuring. "He'll need a cast."

"Fine. Put me in plaster. But then I'm out of here. She'll drive." His attempt at a careless nod in Liss's direction had him grimacing in pain.

Not going to happen, Liss thought.

"Your skull came in abrupt, hard contact with the side of your truck," the doctor said. "I strongly advise that you stay overnight for observation."

"I don't see why I—"

Liss cut him off. "Not thinking clearly is a symptom of concussion, right?"

The doctor's lips twitched, but otherwise he betrayed

not a hint of amusement. "That is correct, Mrs. Ruskin. As I've already told your husband, concussions are tricky things. Some people recover completely in a couple of hours. Others still feel the effects a month later. In some very rare instances, there is permanent brain damage. You can't be too careful with something like this. That's why I'd like to keep Mr. Ruskin here until tomorrow. You can come and get him in the morning, or I can arrange for a cot and you can stay in his room with him."

"I'll stay." Liss spoke without hesitation, settling the matter before Dan could get another word in.

While he went off to have the cast put on his ankle, Liss located the hospital cafeteria. There would be no steak dinner tonight, and now that her worst fears had been assuaged, she was aware of the first pangs of hunger.

The food offered for sale was much more varied than she'd expected. There was a cook on duty, who, according to a sign on the wall, would be happy to whip up anything on the health-conscious menu. The smell of garlic, onions, and green peppers sautéing in olive oil tempted Liss to order the stir-fried chicken, but she decided not to risk it. Dan wasn't out of the woods yet, and worry had a tendency to unsettle her stomach. A bowl of homemade vegetable soup struck her as the safest and most comforting choice under the circumstances. She carried it and a slice of crusty bread to a corner table.

When she had finished eating, she glanced at her watch. The nurse had told her it would be an hour before they'd have Dan installed in a room. She'd managed to kill only fifteen minutes. After she bused her bowl and ordered a cup of tea, she fished in her purse for her iPad mini. The hospital had Wi-Fi. She used it to connect to WebMD.

What she read about concussions both alarmed and re-assured her. The advice given online echoed what she'd been told a few years back and what the emergency room doctor had verified. For the next little while, Dan should get plenty of rest. If he tried to do too much too soon, he could make his condition worse. On the other hand, if he behaved himself, there was no reason why he shouldn't make a full recovery. She'd have to keep an eye on him, that was all—ride herd on his tendency to overdo.

On the lined, five-by-seven tablet she also carried in her bag, Liss made a list of the symptoms she'd need to watch for. Most made sense, given a hit on the head—headache, blurry vision, dizziness, problems with balance. A few were less obvious and therefore more alarming. She'd have to take Dan to their own doctor pronto if he showed an extreme sensitivity to light or became more emotional than usual.

Easily upset or angered, she read. *Sad. Nervous or anxious.* Who wouldn't be after whacking his head on a metal truck door?

She uncapped her felt-tip pen and wrote another note to herself. *Don't overreact.*

Easier to diagnose would be Dan's sleep habits. If he slept more than usual, less than usual, or had trouble falling asleep, she would be sure to notice. In the normal way of things, he was regular as clockwork, drifting quickly into slumber when it was time to sleep and wak-ing up a minute or so before the alarm clock went off in the morning.

The cats provided a handy backup. On the rare occasions when Liss and Dan decided to sleep in, Lumpkin and Glenora had their own methods for convincing the humans in their lives to get up and refill their food bowls. Thinking of the two family felines made Liss wonder how they were getting along with their cat sitter. Most people she knew would have put their pets in a kennel for the week, but she and Dan were too soft-hearted. If the cats couldn't have their people around, the least they deserved was to stay in their own digs for the duration.

It would be comforting to have a cat in her lap right now, she thought. Something soft to stroke. The rhythmic, calming sound of a purr.

She smiled at the fancy as she glanced around her. Neither Lumpkin nor Glenora would be calm or comforting in this setting. Glenora would hide under the table, wary of strangers. Lumpkin would bite an ankle or two on his way to help himself to any food left unguarded.

She went back to enumerating the list of symptoms.

Changes in sex drive came next.

That one ought to be easy to spot. Liss smiled to herself as she added it.

When she next glanced at the clock on the screen, three-quarters of an hour had gone by. She put the iPad, tablet, and pen away and stood. With any luck, Dan would have been assigned to a room by now. She'd go there and wait for him.

It came as a pleasant surprise to discover that all the rooms in this small rural hospital were private. They didn't have that awful hospital smell, either. She was also impressed by the staff. While a nurse was getting

Dan settled, the doctor who'd examined him took her aside to give her an update.

"I expect to approve your husband's release from the hospital in the morning," he told her, "but I strongly advise against making the three-hour drive back to Moosetookalook right away. I've been there a time or two. The entire distance is on winding, bumpy rural roads. Wait until the worst of the aftereffects—the splitting headache, the dizziness, and the nausea—have abated a bit."

It was good advice. Liss intended to follow it.

After he had been installed in his hospital bed and an orderly had set up a cot for Liss, Dan continued to grumble about having to stay overnight. Liss ignored his complaints. Before long, he exhausted himself. When his breathing evened out and Liss was sure he slept, she retreated into the tiny bathroom and, leaving her underwear in place, exchanged her slacks and blouse for a hospital bathrobe. The door to the corridor was left open for the convenience of the nurses. She had no intention of sleeping in the buff.

In the harsh overhead light of the bathroom, Liss couldn't help but notice an ugly grease stain on one knee of her good wool slacks. She stared at it, trying to think how it had gotten there. Then she remembered the feel of oil on her fingers as she knelt in the parking lot. Her brow furrowed. That was the only place this spot could have come from, and yet it didn't appear to be motor oil. It wasn't the right color. An oil leak from a car would have left a darker stain.

Cautiously, she lifted the fabric to her nose. The smell was elusive but somehow familiar. She sniffed again. It was definitely not motor oil. Nor was it any other petroleum product. But it had a distinctive aroma. After a moment, she identified it as a scent she'd encountered only a short time earlier right here in the hospital.

Olive oil.

Liss rubbed her forehead, where a dull throbbing had begun, trying to make sense of her discovery. Could she be mistaken about when she'd stained her clothing? Could she have come in contact with the olive oil during her supper break?

No, she thought. A stain in that location and of that size and shape could only be the result of kneeling in a substance, and the only time she'd been on her knees was in the parking lot.

It was the parking lot of a grocery store, she reminded herself. It was possible that some unlucky shopper had dropped a bottle of cooking oil.

She'd have liked to believe that theory, but it wouldn't stand up to close scrutiny. Break a bottle of olive oil and you'd have a lot more of it on the ground. There would be fragments of glass, too, although nowadays most cooking oil came in *plastic* bottles, which wouldn't have broken and spilled in the first place.

What Dan had slipped in hadn't been a puddle. It had been more like a slick.

Had someone *deliberately* poured olive oil on the ground beside the truck?

That explanation didn't make a lick of sense, but when there was no logical solution to a problem, then the illogical one that remained, no matter how unlikely it seemed, had to be the right answer. So quoth Sherlock Holmes, more or less.

Liss took a deep breath and reviewed the "facts" as she knew them.

The oily spot had not been there when she and Dan

went inside the grocery store. She was certain that Dan would have noticed it if it had been. He'd have stepped right in it when he got out of the truck.

Someone could have created the oil slick while they were doing their shopping.

It was right beside the driver's side door, in a spot where Dan would have to place his feet in order to climb into the truck.

That meant someone—person or persons unknown—had intended that he slip and fall and injure himself.

And that meant that the accident wasn't an accident at all.

Chapter Six

"This is insane," Liss whispered.

So was talking to herself.

She took her clothing with her from the bathroom into Dan's hospital room. He was still asleep. That relieved her mind. If he saw her face right now, he'd know something was wrong.

With great care to be quiet, she hung her slacks and blouse in the room's tiny closet, next to Dan's garments and her coat. Her hands were shaking, making the hangers rattle on the metal clothes bar. Once that small task had been accomplished, Liss didn't know what to do next. She didn't even know what to *think* next.

Why would anyone want to set a trap for Dan? Unless you counted Mrs. Purvey, they hadn't offended anyone since coming to New Boston. For a moment, Liss seriously considered the chief of police's mother as saboteur, but the notion was too far-fetched. Even with her vivid imagination Liss had trouble visualizing the elderly lady pouring olive oil on the pavement. Besides, how would she have known which vehicle belonged to Dan and Liss?

Liss sank into the room's only chair and stared at

nothing. She couldn't make sense of what had happened. She just knew that it *had*.

Think, she ordered herself. What did the person who set that trap hope to accomplish? A fall was a chancy way to murder someone. Dan might have been much more seriously injured than he was, perhaps killed, but even more easily, he might have done no more than lose his balance for an instant, escaping unscathed. Did the perpetrator care? Was the whole thing an impulsive prank? Or was there some specific motive behind the madness?

If the goal was to get them to leave town, it was a strange way to go about it. The result was the exact opposite. Because of Dan's concussion, they might have to stay longer than they'd intended.

When she realized she was clenching and unclenching her fists, Liss flexed her fingers, rotated her shoulders, and ordered herself not to tense up. It didn't help that the chair was singularly uncomfortable, but the only other place to sit was on the cot. Tempting as it was to crawl under the covers and pull them over her head, Liss knew she wouldn't be able to sleep until she had a handle on the situation.

Think. Reason it out.

What if the goal was to keep them away from the Snowe farmhouse overnight? Was someone searching the place even now? Liss gave a huff of frustration. If that was the case, there wasn't a darned thing she could do about it. She'd feel like a fool if she asked Chief Purvey to check on the property. He'd be certain she was imagining things. He'd probably be right.

Still, she liked that scenario better than the one in which someone tried to murder her husband.

Don't panic, she warned herself. *And don't get paranoid.* While it was true that one man with a connection to the Snowe Christmas tree farm had been murdered and another had disappeared, that did not mean that she and Dan had put themselves in danger by staying there!

Argue with herself as she might, Liss couldn't help but fret. Someone had caused Dan's fall. That was enough to make anyone worry. *Why* some unknown person had arranged his "accident" was only part of the puzzle. Discovering *who* was behind it had to be the key. Liss fished in her bag for the five-by-seven tablet and a pen. The culprit had to be someone they'd met since their arrival in New Boston.

Although they'd been in the area only since yesterday afternoon, they'd encountered a fair number of people. She listed them in the order of their appearance, starting with the crusty old gentleman in the parking lot of the grocery store. She didn't suspect him or the young woman who worked in the market or the woman who'd suggested they try asking for directions at the town office, but she jotted down their descriptions, anyway.

The next person on her list, and the first for whom she had a name, was Beatrice Purvey. Liss put a star by her name. She'd been at the store right before Dan fell. She'd had opportunity. She might even have had motive, depending on whether or not she really believed Liss's and Dan's questions could harm her son's reputation. It still seemed absurd to Liss that the mother of the chief of police would stoop to committing a crime, let alone one that was so impulsive and poorly planned, but she couldn't completely dismiss the possibility, especially after it occurred to her that Mrs. Purvey *might* know what Dan's truck looked like. She could have been watching from the window of the town office when they drove away on Friday afternoon.

The town manager was next on her list. Liss couldn't remember his name, but she knew it would be easy to find. New Boston undoubtedly had a town Web page. These days, even the smallest villages invested in their own domains. She resolved to search for it on her iPad just as soon as she finished writing down names.

The next few flowed easily from her pen: Andrea Dutton, Wyatt Purvey, and Michael Jennings. She didn't know the name of the receptionist at the police station, but the woman wasn't a likely suspect, either. No matter. Liss wrote "police receptionist" after Officer Jennings's name.

"Clerk in café and Cook in café," came next. Then she scratched out the last line and replaced it with "Miranda." That was what the man with the dog had called her. And he'd introduced himself as Harlan Woolgar. What a name! She wrote it down, too, and put Jonas—the dog's name—in parentheses.

Liss paused, her pen suspended above the tablet. Given the acoustics in the café, anyone who'd been there could have overheard what she and Dan said to each other, to Miranda, and to Harlan Woolgar. She hadn't paid any particular attention to the other patrons. She thought there had been two men seated at another table. And at least three people had come in to grind their own coffee beans. Liss couldn't recall anything about any of them, not even whether they'd been male or female. She was pretty sure there had been no other dogs.

Maybe it didn't matter. Maybe this was all a waste of time. Still, she forged ahead, adding the names Juliette

Cressy and Rowena Luckenbill. She couldn't identify the young woman she'd met going into the dance studio as she'd been coming out, but she put down a description—"young, brown hair, apologetic." She couldn't even recall that much about the other shoppers at the grocery store. The only one she'd paid attention to was Beatrice Purvey.

So, that was everyone. She counted—eight names.

Liss fired up her iPad and entered her favorite search engine. As she'd anticipated, the New Boston, Maine Web page provided the name of the town manager—Steven Wilton—and that of the woman at the PD. It turned out that her actual title was dispatcher. Her name was Philippa Crockett.

The coffee shop, Madison's, also had a Web site. Liss was not surprised to discover that Miranda's surname was Madison. It did not provide a name for the young man who was Miranda's employee.

Dance-Ex and All Things Mystical both had Web pages, but neither had been updated recently. Only Rowena's offered a bio page, and it was clear to Liss after reading only a few sentences that Rowena had made up the details, beginning with her claim to have been born on the planet Actuarius.

Frustrated, Liss typed in a new search string. Information on the seven-year-old murder and the missing persons case was sketchy. The few listings she did find led to newspaper archives that were available to view only if she wanted to subscribe or pay a fee or both. For the time being, she declined these offers. It seemed unlikely that she'd find any details in those articles that she did not already have. She'd do better by finding a way to go directly to the source—state police reports.

Liss exited the search engine and entered her e-mail program. For once she ignored the messages waiting to be read in favor of composing one of her own. It took considerable time to organize everything she wanted to say. Along the way, she changed her mind about asking for the inside scoop on the two cold cases. She'd have less to explain if she stuck to questions about the people on her list of suspects. Even so, she almost hit the delete key. She stopped herself in time and read over what she'd written one last time. Deciding it would have to do, she closed her eyes and hit SEND.

At once she felt better, as if a great weight had been lifted off her shoulders. She thought she might even be able to fall asleep now. A glance at the clock on the iPad had her hoping she could. At best, she'd get only four or five hours of sack time.

The Moosetookalook Police Department operated out of two small rooms in the municipal building: a waiting area and an office that contained a desk, several filing cabinets, and a closet-size holding cell. When Sherri Campbell had taken over as chief after Jeff Thibodeau's heart attack convinced him to opt for early retirement, she'd replaced the rumpsprung desk chair out of her own pocket. Little else had changed. The annual budget covered Sherri's salary and those of one other full-time officer and three part-timers. It did the department no good at all that Sherri's mother-in-law was a member of the board of selectmen. The town's coffers weren't just locked up tight. They were sealed with superglue.

As she always did when she logged on to the department's computer, Sherri gave silent thanks for federal grant money. Those funds, before they'd dried up, had paid for a badly needed upgrade in equipment. At her fingertips, she had the technology to search records from all sixteen Maine counties.

There was a downside, of course. She had to enter all her own reports into the system. When she worked the late shift, she often spent nearly the entire eight hours typing.

She took a break at three in the morning. After a good stretch, a few jumping jacks, and a minute or two of running in place, she refilled her coffee mug and checked her personal e-mail. She smiled when she saw that she had a message from Liss Ruskin. Her expression changed to one of concern as she read it.

The e-mail was short on explanation. In essence, Liss had sent her a list of names and wanted Sherri to check them out. She apparently thought one of them might have a police record.

"Oh, Liss," Sherri whispered. "What have you gotten yourself into this time?"

Unsure she wanted to know the answer to that question, Sherri printed the e-mail. When she'd finished entering the last of her official electronic paperwork, she read over the e-mail again.

It would have been a simple matter to open another program and type in the first of the names on Liss's list. Unfortunately, that would be "using department resources for a private purpose." Personally, she wouldn't fire one of her officers for running a check on his daughter's new boyfriend, but all these names? With no clear suspicion of wrongdoing? And in someone else's jurisdiction? Nope. Not worth losing her job over.

On the bright side, criminal records were available to

the general public online . . . for a fee. Whatever this list was, it had to be connected to the Snowe farm, since that was where Liss and Dan were staying. That being the case, Sherri saw no reason why Gina Snowe shouldn't reimburse her for the charges she was about to run up.

An hour later, Sherri sat back in her chair, uncertain whether to be relieved or worried. Nothing had popped up, not even an unpaid parking ticket. It appeared that the good citizens of New Boston, Maine, were all remarkably law-abiding.

At six, she went off duty. She shed her uniform the moment she got home, but it wasn't as easy to shake off the nagging conviction that Liss had run into more than she'd bargained for on her "vacation." Honestly! The woman had a positive talent for walking into trouble!

Quietly, since Pete and the kids were still asleep, Sherri fixed herself two slices of toast and a cup of hot cocoa. She knew she ought to try to nap for a few hours, but she was too keyed up to rest.

At seven, she picked up the phone and used speed dial to call Liss's cell phone. She was sent straight to voice mail.

Muttering to herself, Sherri booted up her laptop and checked for new messages. Nothing. She started to log off, then gave a resigned sigh and typed "Gina Snowe" into the search engine.

Ancient history aside, Sherri thought it a little odd that Gina had asked Liss to do such a big favor for her. She had family—her mother and at least a couple of cousins that Sherri knew of. And she could have let the matter ride until after the case she was working on in Chicago was wrapped up. Or hired someone—

She jumped a foot when Pete touched her shoulder.

She'd been so intent on reading what was on the small screen that she hadn't heard him come into the kitchen.

"Why are you checking up on Gina?" he asked.

Sherri handed him the printout of Liss's e-mail.

He read it while he waited for their single-cup coffee brewer to do its thing. "Any hits?"

"Not a blessed one. These people are pure as the driven snow. Even Gina. Pun intended."

"Maybe."

Her head, which had been drooping, shot up. "What do you know that I don't?"

"I recognize one of the names. I went through the criminal justice academy with a Mike Jennings."

"Same guy. It's got to be. He's on the New Boston PD. Tell me everything you know about him."

"Give me a minute. It was more than a dozen years ago." Pete sat and downed half the coffee in his mug before he began. "I don't remember much, but I do recall that he didn't trust his boss."

"That would be this Wyatt Purvey?"

Pete shrugged. "He didn't give me a name. Or if he did, I've forgotten it. To tell you the truth, Mike was pretty careful not to say anything specific, but I had the distinct impression that he thought the guy was dirty. He talked about being glad he'd landed a job in law enforcement in his hometown, but he was worried that he'd be working in a department where the chief might end up being investigated. If that happened, Mike could end up being tarred with the same brush."

"But it didn't happen. One of us would remember hearing about it if there had been a scandal in law enforcement in New Boston."

"Yeah. Seems likely. And if this Purvey is chief now,

chances are good he was chief back then, too, or at least on the force, him being a local and all."

Things didn't change much in small towns. They operated on the maxim "If it ain't broke, don't fix it." And sometimes they didn't bother fixing things that *were* broke. Sherri supposed that only proved another old saw: "Better the devil you know."

She and Pete sat in silence for a few minutes. The only sounds in the kitchen were the hum of the refrigerator and the occasional slurp as Pete drank more coffee.

"I'm too tired to think about this now," Sherri said.

She called Liss's number again and this time left a message.

Then she went to bed.

Dan was still protesting the decision to remain at the Snowe Christmas tree farm until his headache diminished when Liss parked the truck beside the Quonset hut. He'd been given crutches at the hospital and needed help getting down from the cab's high passenger seat. The walk to the house was a slow, painful process. He was visibly flagging by the time Liss got him into the house and installed in the downstairs bedroom. Moments after he lay down atop the covers, insisting all he was going to do was rest his eyes for a minute or two, he was out like a light.

"Sweet dreams," Liss whispered and went back outside to unload the groceries.

The paper sacks from the grocery store had spent the night in the bed of the truck, but the cold temperature had kept the contents from spoiling. After Liss had put away their purchases and checked on Dan once more, she methodically searched every room in the house. She couldn't spot anything that was out of place. If anyone had been inside while they were gone, they'd been extremely careful to leave no trace.

Paranoid much? Liss wanted to laugh at her own foolishness, but she wasn't able to talk herself into discounting any of the scary possibilities she'd come up with after discovering it was a puddle of olive oil Dan had stepped in.

He was still sleeping when she circled back to look in on him again.

The cot the hospital had provided for her had been hard and the blanket thin, but Liss had managed to snatch a few hours of rest. She'd get more later, she promised herself. At the moment, she was too wired to consider crawling into bed beside her husband. She returned to the kitchen and made herself a cup of chamomile tea instead. It was her aunt Margaret's sovereign remedy for a nervous disposition.

Once she was settled at the kitchen table with the hot beverage, Liss checked her e-mail. She was disappointed not to find an answer from Sherri. Then she remembered that her friend was working nights. She'd probably gone straight to bed when she got off shift at six.

On the table, next to Liss's purse, lay the bag from All Things Mystical. Liss fished out *Mazes: Ancient & Modern* and skimmed the first few pages while she sipped her tea. In her present restless mood, she found it difficult to focus on what she was reading. The need to do something—anything!—more active drove her to drain her cup, retrieve her tablet and pen, and climb the stairs to the second-floor bedroom. She was no artist, but she could make a passable sketch of her bird's-eye view of the maze. The result would be a rough map of the pathways.

She felt calmer when she had completed the drawing

and checked that item off her mental to-do list. She still didn't know why anyone would have wanted to hurt Dan. She didn't have *any* answers. But her self-confidence was back. She was smart and capable. With the map she'd drawn, she could see what route she'd need to follow to reach the center of the maze. It was all a matter of perspective. Given time enough, she'd also figure out what was going on in New Boston.

Liss hurried back downstairs, stopping only long enough to make sure Dan hadn't awakened before she returned to the kitchen. She checked her e-mail again. There was still no reply from Sherri. Although she thought it unlikely her friend would shell out for a long-distance phone call, she burrowed into her oversize purse for her cell phone to check. One glance at it had her groaning aloud. The hospital, while happy to provide Wi-Fi for laptops and e-readers, had insisted that all cell phones be turned off while on the premises. She'd forgotten to turn hers back on when Dan was released.

As soon as Liss listened to Sherri's voice-mail message, she returned the call.

A groggy voice answered.

"Sheesh, Sherri. I'm sorry. I forgot you'd be sleeping."

"It's okay. I'm awake now. Talk to me. What's going on there?"

Liss gave her the short version. "Dan had a bad fall. He's got a concussion and a broken ankle."

"Is he going to be okay?" To judge by the sounds coming over the phone, Sherri was out of bed and on her way to the kitchen.

"I've got my fingers crossed. The doctor was encouraging, but I have to keep a close eye on Dan for the next couple of days and make sure he doesn't overexert himself."

"No sex, huh?"

"Sherri!"

"Sorry. Blame it on caffeine deprivation."

Liss heard a refrigerator door open and close and the fizzing sound of a carbonated drink being opened. *Moxie for breakfast?* She grimaced.

"I appreciate what you're going through with the fracture," Sherri said. "When Adam broke his arm, that cast he had to wear made doing the smallest thing a huge challenge."

"Adam was *seven*."

"And your point is?"

Sherri's quip surprised a laugh out of Liss. Men *were* big babies when they were sick or injured.

The moment of levity past, Sherri was all business again. "I repeat, what's really going on there? Start with that list of names you sent me. They're squeaky clean. All of them."

"Even Andy Dutton? She's supposed to have a juvenile record."

"You didn't mention that in your e-mail." Liss heard the scratch of a pencil as Sherri wrote a note to herself. "I don't know if I'll be able to access it or not. What do you expect to find?"

"Honestly? I don't know. I'm grasping at straws."

Liss told Sherri the rest of it then—about the John Doe in the netter and Simeon Snowe's disappearance and the mysterious slick spot that had caused Dan's accident. She didn't identify the substance as olive oil. Even a good friend might find *that* a little far-fetched. But she didn't hold back any other relevant facts.

Somewhere during the narrative, Liss rose to her feet and started to roam. She wasn't quite pacing, but as jumpy as she felt, she found it necessary to *move*. By the time she finished telling her story, she had come to a halt in front of a window. Everything outside looked still and calm, almost picture perfect.

Dead silence reigned on the other end of the phone line. It stretched until Liss felt compelled to break it.

"Say *something*," she begged.

"You're sure there was nothing slippery on the ground next to the truck when you parked there?"

"I'm certain. I know it sounds crazy, but what if we did spook someone into trying to run us off?"

"Because you showed a perfectly natural curiosity about two old, unsolved cases?" Sherri sounded skeptical, and Liss couldn't blame her.

"Can you think of any other reason?" Liss rested her forehead against the cold windowpane and closed her eyes.

Instead of answering, Sherri asked another question, one Liss had already asked herself. "Why use such a chancy method to drive you away? If Dan had simply lost his balance for a moment, he wouldn't have been scared off, and anything more serious would only make you stay longer, as it has."

"My alternate theory was that someone wanted us out of the house for that one night." Liss turned away from the window. The kitchen snapped into focus, reassuringly ordinary and nonthreatening in appearance.

"Did you find any indication that anyone had been in the farmhouse while you were at the hospital?"

"No." Liss felt her frustration building again. "But, Sherri, I don't know what's *supposed* to be here."

Another silence descended.

"I'm not making this up."

"I didn't say you were. But facts are almost always subject to different interpretations."

Liss frowned at the phone. "Do you think I'm imagining some unknown enemy?"

Sherri's chuckle was oddly reassuring. "Knowing you? Hard to say. You've got good instincts. On the other hand, you've been going nonstop for a long time. You're overtired and stressed out. Your mind could be playing tricks on you."

"So now I'm nuts? Thanks a lot!"

"You're the most sane person I know. Let me do some checking on the two cold cases and on your juvenile delinquent and get back to you."

Liss had to be content with that.

"Son of a bitch!" Pete exclaimed. "Why the hell would somebody try to kill Dan?"

"Whoa! Who said they were trying to *kill* him?"

"*Hurt* him, then."

"Get him and Liss out of the way *temporarily*. Maybe. And that's only if we assume Liss hasn't been letting her imagination run wild."

"Liss is impulsive, sure, and she's been known to leap to the wrong conclusion a time or two, but she's not a flake. And she's always been good at noticing details. I'll put money on her instincts anytime."

They were in their apartment on Sunday evening, shortly before Sherri had to leave for work. As soon as the children were safely asleep, she'd filled him in on everything Liss had told her. In a second phone conversation late that afternoon, she'd been able to reassure her friend that there was nothing alarming in Andrea Dutton's past. She'd also passed on what she'd uncovered concerning John Doe and Simeon Snowe. There had been precious little to find, even stretching to the limit her authority to access confidential police reports.

"You're sure there was nothing in that juvie record?" Pete asked.

Sherri hadn't been able to share details with Liss, a civilian, but Pete was a fellow officer of the law, as well as her husband. "Some life of crime," she scoffed. "Andrea Dutton and a group of her friends raided an orchard. They'd been at a party where liquor was readily available and no one was asking to see an ID. Eight of them were caught pitching apples at each other out of open car windows."

Two cars had been racing side by side down a two-lane road when they were spotted by a deputy sheriff. The operators of both vehicles had been charged with driving to endanger. The passengers had been taken in for petty theft, vandalism, and littering.

"Andrea's parents bailed their daughter out, paid her fine, and that was the end of it . . . except in the minds and memory of one of New Boston's more upright citizens."

"Make that up*tight*." Pete's grin and the reminiscent gleam in his eyes told her he'd probably chucked a few stolen apples of his own back in the day.

"Most kids that age do stupid things," Sherri agreed. She certainly had. "And most luck out and never get caught. Did Liss ever tell you about the time she, uh, *borrowed* Moose Mayfield's truck?"

"Hey! Officer of the law here. I don't want to know."

"Trust me, the statute of limitations has long since

run out on that one. My point is that I was able to reassure Liss with a clear conscience. What Andrea did as a teenager was no big deal. She's unlikely to be the one who's out to get them. The problem is that no one else on that list seems a likely villain, either."

Sherri left Pete in the living room while she ducked into the kitchen to make herself a sandwich to take to work. She didn't come home for lunch when her meal break fell in the middle of the night. She was putting a package of cold cuts and a loaf of bread back into the refrigerator when Pete joined her. His lighthearted mood was conspicuous by its absence.

"*Somebody* killed that John Doe," he announced.

"True, but it wasn't necessarily anyone who's still living in New Boston."

"Maybe you should make a few calls to New York."

"I'm pushing my luck as it is." Sherri grabbed the paper sack containing her lunch, ready to head out, but she hesitated in the doorway to the living room. "Do you remember hearing anything about this murder or Snowe's disappearance at the time?"

Pete shook his head. "They must have kept the John Doe quiet. As for the missing man, looking for him would have been one search out of many."

Sherri nodded. Some missing persons turned up. Some didn't. Since Snowe hadn't disappeared from Carrabassett County, no one from around here had been involved in looking for him.

"What else did you tell Liss?" Pete asked.

"There wasn't much I *could* say. On the surface, it looks like she's making a mountain out of a molehill. I tried to be reassuring. After all, she and Dan are stuck there for at least a few more days. She shouldn't have to spend that time worrying about some unknown adversary and dreaming up worst-case scenarios."

Sherri lifted her uniform jacket off the coatrack. Pete, having followed her from the kitchen, helped her into it. He left his hands resting on her shoulders. "You've reassured her, and now you're the one who's worrying."

"She'll be fine. If that oil spill was real *and* deliberate, then the most logical motive was to get Dan and Liss out of the Snowe house long enough for someone to retrieve some kind of incriminating evidence. They got their chance. So, assuming they already found whatever it was they were looking for, there's no reason to go back and no reason to cause Liss and Dan any more trouble."

"A nice pat solution."

"Yeah. So why am I not buying it?"

"Because you don't believe in coincidences any more than Liss does. She's going to figure that the dead guy and the disappearance and Dan's fall are all connected somehow, and she's going to keep on asking questions. Questions make people nervous, especially people who have something to hide."

Sherri turned in his arms until she could see his face. "She'll be busy taking care of Dan. Maybe she won't have time to get into trouble."

Pete's skeptical expression was not reassuring. They both knew Liss MacCrimmon Ruskin way too well.

A glance at her watch reminded Sherri that she had to get moving, even though the PD was only across the town square from the apartment. It didn't set a good example when the chief was late relieving the officer on duty.

Pete's voice stopped her at the front door. "What do you *really* want to do?"

Sherri answered without stopping to think. "Provide Liss with backup." She frowned. Where had *that* come from? "With Dan laid up," she added, "she's on her own there."

"I just put in my last eight-to-four shift," Pete said. "I've got the next few days free."

"You think you should go to New Boston?"

"If there *is* a connection, we'll both feel better if I'm there. If there's nothing to it, I can still help Liss out. I'll bet Dan is hell to live with when he's under the weather."

"What about the kids? We can't leave them alone when I'm working nights."

"Then maybe it's time we did something nice for my mother. She's been after us to let Amber stay overnight at her house. How about we let her have Amber *and* Adam? In fact, if she agrees, you and I can both spend a few days in New Boston."

"I can't just take time off from work!"

"You're on night shift. You know it will be a cinch to find a part-timer willing to fill in for you. Besides, what's the point of being the chief of police if you can't pull rank once in a while?"

Chapter Seven

Over breakfast Monday morning, Liss couldn't stop yawning. Neither she nor Dan had slept well. He'd had a hard time finding a comfortable position for his ankle, and every time he'd thrashed about, the movement had woken her up. When she had slept, her dreams had not been restful. She retained vague memories of unidentified bodies and gigantic marching bottles of olive oil.

"You should have slept in the upstairs bedroom," Dan said when Liss fell prey to yet another jaw-popping yawn.

"I'd have been lonely up there."

"You'd have gotten a good night's sleep." He sounded grumpy, or maybe envious that she'd had a choice.

"No, I wouldn't. I'd have been too worried that you'd get up in the wee hours and fall trying to hobble to the downstairs bathroom."

"Hey! I managed it."

Liss sent him a skeptical look and took another sip of her coffee. She'd listened, holding her breath, while he'd stumbled around on his crutches. True, he hadn't fallen, but to judge by all the thumping and banging, it had been a near thing. She'd needed all the willpower she possessed to stay under the covers. She hadn't drawn an easy breath until he crawled back into bed beside her.

"How's the head today?" she asked.

"Not too bad." But he didn't meet her eyes.

"Uh-huh."

"It's still sore, okay?" The admission made him as grouchy as an old bear that had been awakened too early from hibernation.

"I'm not surprised. You whacked yourself a good one. Any dizziness?"

"No. And no double vision, either." He managed a weak smile. "Things are definitely getting better."

Liss swallowed the last of her coffee and began to clear the table, her mind on her list of "symptoms to watch for."

"What time is your class?" Dan asked.

She turned a blank stare his way, and he chuckled.

"Exercise class? In New Boston? The one you were so gung ho to sign up for on Saturday?"

Liss had forgotten all about it, what with the stay in the hospital and her worry over what had caused Dan to fall in the first place. She'd been only partially reassured by Sherri's follow-up call late the previous day. There was nothing in Andy Dutton's juvenile record to be concerned about, but that didn't mean the young woman was dealing honestly with them now. Liss was still charged with making recommendations to Gina about the future of the Christmas tree farm.

"So, are you going to class or not?"

"I didn't make a definite commitment. I'd just as soon stay here with you."

"I don't need a babysitter, Liss." For an instant, temper sparked in his molasses-brown eyes, but it was quickly replaced by contrition. "Sorry. I don't mean to snap at you. But for God's sake, stop treating me like I'm made of glass. You know you'll feel better if you give that knee of yours a workout."

"The knee is fine." This time she was the one who sounded testy.

Washing the few dishes they'd used for a breakfast of ham and eggs gave Liss time to think. The more time that passed, the harder it became to believe that anyone had been out to get them. She'd been stressed and over-wrought. She'd overreacted. Maybe someone *had* acci-dentally broken a bottle of olive oil and cleaned most of it up, leaving only that one slippery spot next to the truck. A random prank wasn't out of the question, ei-ther. And Dan was right. He didn't need her hovering over him every minute.

She rinsed soapy water off the last plate and placed it in the drying rack. "You're right," she admitted without turning around. "A workout would do me good."

"Where did you put that schedule of classes?"

"It's in my bag. I'll get—"

The thump of her heavy purse landing on the kitchen table cut her off. She'd set it on the floor beside her chair to make room for them to eat.

"Aerobics, right?" Paper rustled. "That class starts at ten o'clock. You've got plenty of time to get into your warm-up clothes and make the drive into town."

"Are you angling to get a glimpse of me in my leo-tard?" Liss kept her tone light, teasing him to cover up the fact that she didn't like leaving him on his own.

When she turned away from the sink, her misgivings

increased. Dan was hurting. She could tell by looking at him—the stiff way he sat, the stoic expression on his face. He'd closed his eyes against a spasm of pain.

How could she leave him alone? He could barely walk, and he was recovering from a concussion. Whether he thought he needed someone to look after him or not, she ought to stay right where she was to keep an eye on him.

Dan's eyes popped open. "I love the way you look in that leotard," he said. "Who wouldn't?" He made a production out of smacking his lips. "Skintight and formfitting. It's one of my favorite outfits."

His imitation of a dirty old man made her laugh in spite of herself. "Good to see you feeling so chipper, Grandpa."

"Come over here and I'll show you exactly how chipper I am." He patted his lap.

"Behave, or I'll lock you in your room."

She pulled out her own chair and sat.

Dan handed over the printed list of classes offered at Dance-Ex. "There's no reason not to go. I can manage on my own for a couple of hours. Besides, I need you to pick up new batteries for the smoke and carbon monoxide alarms. I noticed the day we got here that they haven't been changed since Snowe vanished. I meant to pick some up at the grocery store on Saturday, but I forgot."

Liss fished out her tablet and wrote "batteries" at the top of a blank page. "What size?"

"Nine volt."

"Anything else?"

He shook his head, wincing when the movement made his headache throb.

"Dan, are you sure?"

"I'll be *fine*. And I promise I won't do anything more strenuous than watch TV while you're gone. Cross my heart and hope to die." He made the appropriate gesture.

Liss wished he'd settled for a pinkie swear.

It will be good to have a short break from each other, she told herself. Besides, if she didn't go, Dan would wonder why. She was a creature of habit when it came to her exercise routine. Breaking her pattern would raise questions Liss didn't want to answer. She had no intention of worrying her husband by telling him about the olive oil in the parking lot or the scenarios she'd imagined after she realized what had caused his fall. If it turned out, as she hoped, that her fears were groundless, he'd never have to know a thing about them.

With a sigh, she stood. "I'm going. But you'd better behave yourself, Mister. Otherwise it's thirty lashes with a wet noodle."

She left him smiling and went to change her clothes. She still felt uneasy about going into town, but what alternative was there? She'd come straight back, and before she left, she'd make sure Dan's phone was right next to him on the sofa in case of an emergency.

Juliette Cressy looked surprised to see Liss walk into Dance-Ex. "Minimum of five sessions," she said, "paid in advance."

The none-to-subtle reminder was unnecessary. Liss had written Juliette a check before she left the Christmas tree farm. The dance and fitness instructor regarded it with suspicion but apparently decided that a bank in Fallstown was sufficiently "local" to allow her to accept it.

The other women in the class came in all shapes, sizes, ages, and levels of ability. There were ten of them in all. Liss recognized two. One was Rowena Luckenbill, although it took Liss a minute to realize that the statuesque female in the royal blue leotard and the woman who wore flowing, concealing gypsy-style garments in her occult shop were one and the same.

The second familiar face was that of the young brunette who'd nearly bowled Liss over on her first visit to Dance-Ex. When Liss introduced herself, the young woman supplied her name—Kitty Sloan—but they had no opportunity to talk further before class began.

Juliette was an adequate if uninspired teacher. She was also a hard taskmaster, exactly what Liss needed.

Kitty and a redhead who looked to be in her early twenties were the youngest members of the group. Both were fit enough to keep pace with Juliette. Liss held her own better than the others—all more mature ladies— but she got her money's worth out of the workout. Juliette didn't cut anyone any slack. When someone lagged behind or stopped to catch her breath, she shouted words of encouragement that sounded closer to taunts until the "shirker" rejoined the routine.

By the time the hour came to an end, Liss was drenched in sweat but full of energy and bonhomie. She was grateful for the towel Kitty handed her to wipe perspiration off her face, since she'd forgotten to bring one, and followed her chattering classmates into the changing room. Liss had worn jeans and a crewneck pullover over her exercise clothing on the drive into town, but she peeled off the leotard before donning those garments for the return journey.

"I guess you've all been taking aerobics together for some time," she said to Kitty, who was unself-consciously stripping down to bare skin.

"Some longer than others," said the brunette, reaching into a pink duffel bag to pull out a thong and a lacy bra. As she put them on, Liss couldn't help but notice that she had a hickey on one butt cheek.

She wasn't the only one who caught sight of it. The redhead hooted. "One of the boys get a little frisky?" she asked.

"Oh, ha-ha!" Kitty finished dressing, apparently accustomed to such good-natured teasing.

"Occupational hazard, right?"

"You should know, Josie," Kitty shot back.

The redhead turned to Liss. "Josie Underhill," she said. "It's nice to have someone else in the class who can keep up."

"Liss Ruskin. Nice to meet you."

The changing room had emptied rapidly. Liss supposed that Juliette's students had to hurry home or to work. Only Kitty remained by the time Liss was ready to leave. The young brunette sat on the bench, polishing off an energy bar. Together with a bottle of spring water, it had materialized from the depths of the pink duffel.

"Do you teach here, too?" Liss asked, remembering that Kitty had called Juliette "boss" when she'd arrived late at Dance-Ex on Saturday.

"Sometimes. Aerobics and gymnastics."

"No ballroom dancing?"

"Me?" Kitty gave a snort of laughter. "The only dance I'm any good at is the horizontal mambo."

"I enjoy that one myself," Liss quipped, "but I wouldn't want to teach it."

"Good one," Kitty said with a laugh. She was still chuckling when Liss collected her coat, waved good-bye, and left the changing room.

She paused in the doorway leading from the hallway into the studio, surprised to see Juliette and Rowena standing close together on the far side of the room, engaged in what appeared to be an intense discussion, if not an actual argument.

"Do what you like. You always do," Rowena said. But then she gave Juliette a quick hug before heading for the exit.

She and Liss crossed paths at the door to the street. "Hello again," Liss greeted her.

Rowena flashed a sunny smile. "Say, I meant to ask you, was that book on mazes any help with the one Simeon planted?"

"I haven't had a chance to do more than glance through it," Liss admitted.

"What about the maze itself? Have you explored it yet? I have to say I've been curious ever since you told me it existed. It's so fascinating to think that it's been there all this time and no one knew a thing about it."

They stepped out onto the sidewalk together.

"I expect I'll take a closer look at it soon."

She would, too, Liss promised herself after she told Rowena to have a nice day. But even before she'd crossed the street to the truck, her mind was preoccupied with other things, chief among them the need to get back to the house and make sure Dan was okay.

The first thing Liss saw when she pulled into the parking area at the Christmas tree farm was a New Boston police cruiser. She flung herself out of the truck and raced to the house. She burst in through the side door and stopped short at the sight of Wyatt Purvey, hat in hand, standing in the middle of the kitchen. To Liss's immense relief, Dan was seated at the table, his broken ankle propped up on a second chair and a glass of milk and a half-eaten sandwich in front of him.

He lifted an eyebrow at Liss's obvious panic but said only, "Chief Purvey got here a few minutes ago. He was about to tell me why he came."

Purvey's face was as unrevealing as it had been at the PD. He nodded at Liss, then once again pretended that she didn't exist and addressed Dan as if he were the only person in the room. "I heard about your accident, Mr. Ruskin."

"I'm not surprised," Dan said. "Word travels fast in small towns."

"The manager of the New Boston Food City has always been good about maintaining his parking lot."

Dan gave a short bark of laughter. "I'm not going to sue him, if that's what he's worried about."

"You can't blame him for being concerned, you being from away and all." Purvey's lips stretched into what he probably imagined was a smile.

In a young woman, Liss thought, a breathy voice like Purvey's might be thought sexy. Issuing from the mouth of an out-of-shape middle-aged man, it was both annoying and a little creepy.

"Didn't you tell me that the new owner is a lawyer?" Purvey asked.

"She is," Dan agreed. "I'm a custom woodworker myself, and my wife is the proprietor of Moosetookalook Scottish Emporium."

Purvey didn't even glance her way. If his mother had

told him about Liss's crime-solving exploits, he'd apparently chosen to discount them.

"Why are you so sure what happened to my husband *was* an accident?" she blurted.

She got Purvey's full attention with that question . . . and Dan's, too.

"I don't follow you, Ms. Ruskin," the chief of police whispered.

Dan's eyes narrowed, but he kept silent, letting Liss explain herself.

Oh, boy! Open mouth. Insert foot. She hadn't meant to say anything, but Purvey's attitude had annoyed her and she *was* short on sleep, not that any of that mattered. *Think fast, Liss!*

She struggled to look earnest and a trifle naive but stopped short of fluttering her eyelashes. "All I meant, Chief Purvey, was that there is *always* paperwork to fill out when there's been an accident, especially one that requires a trip to the hospital. Why, if two vehicles crashed into each other, you'd test the blood alcohol levels of both drivers. If a snowmobile hit a tree, you'd take the time to find out if it was a moose or a squirrel or a bunny rabbit running in front of the machine that caused it to veer off the trail. So, naturally, in a case like this, I'm sure you sent someone to the scene to inspect the ground around where our truck was parked."

"That hardly seemed necessary when your husband told the emergency room doctor that he slipped in a patch of motor oil. I saw no need to investigate."

"And yet you spoke to the manager of that Food City."

"He spoke to me. He assured me that he's sanded the

spot so no one else will slip. There's nothing for you to worry about on that score."

For a moment, Liss thought he might actually act out the cliché of patting the "little woman" on the head. His superior manner amounted to the same thing.

Purvey left a few minutes later. Liss closed and locked the door behind him and watched until he got into his police car and drove away. "He's gone," she reported.

"What was all that about?"

"Nothing, apparently." She watched her husband with wary eyes, uncertain how much information to volunteer.

"You were yanking his chain for the fun of it?"

"He yanked mine first. He was *ignoring* me."

As soon as the words were out, Liss felt foolish. Sleep deprivation was no excuse. She'd let her dislike of Wyatt Purvey goad her into doing exactly what she'd promised herself *not* to do—let Dan wonder if there had been something odd about his fall. The next thing she knew, he'd be pressuring her for answers, and she'd have to spill the beans and tell him she'd sent Sherri a list of suspects because she'd been convinced there was foul play involved. Of course, only a few hours ago, she'd decided there *hadn't* been any deliberate intent to harm Dan.

Purvey's visit confused the issue. Why had he *really* shown up on their doorstep this morning? His appearance at the Snowe farm was reason enough, she decided, to think that she might have been wrong to dismiss her earlier conclusions.

"Earth to Liss," Dan said.

She blinked, and he came into focus. He looked . . . amused.

"I almost feel sorry for Purvey," he said. "Bad enough

he has to put up with that mother of his. Now you're picking on him."

She was off the hook! Dan thought her reaction to Wyatt Purvey was funny. Annoying as that was, it was far better than the alternative. She wasn't going to be subjected to the third degree. She didn't have to worry Dan with her unsubstantiated theories and suspicions.

She gestured toward the remains of his lunch. "I don't suppose you made one of those sandwiches for me?"

"In fact, I did. It's in the fridge."

"You are a paragon among men."

"Of course I am. That's why you married me."

There followed an amicable half hour, enlivened by Liss's account of her aerobics class. Afterward, Dan let Liss persuade him to take a nap.

"You could join me," he suggested, but she shook her head.

"I'm going to tackle Simeon Snowe's office. I promised Gina I'd evaluate his business. While you rest, I'll spend a couple of hours going through his papers."

She needed a fresh cup of coffee to keep her awake, the second wind she'd gotten after her workout having long since blown out to sea. Snowe's ledgers provided her with statements of profit and loss at the tree farm. Another file yielded the names of seasonal workers, all of which she duly wrote down. But although Liss had an associate degree in business, bookkeeping had never been her favorite course. Going through Snowe's accounts was mind-numbing. Even his diary was dull. He'd used it to record dates of planting and pruning.

Eyes at half mast, she opened the final file drawer. For a moment, she perked up. It contained Snowe's personal records. Unfortunately, the insurance policies and the statements from checking and savings accounts were nearly as boring as the annual Christmas tree inventory. Receipts for prescription medicines yielded only one highlight. Simeon Snowe had suffered from high blood pressure and high cholesterol, but he'd also taken Viagra.

Simeon, you old devil you, Liss thought.

There were no photographs, no scrapbooks, no cards, and no letters. Liss supposed men weren't as likely as women to keep such things, but since Snowe had been quixotic enough to plant a maze, own a copy of *Romancing the Stone,* and take Viagra, she stubbornly held on to a glimmer of hope that something interesting might yet turn up.

A single sheet of paper was the only thing in the last manila folder at the back of the file drawer. Liss stared at it in disbelief. It was a handwritten poem. An incredibly bad poem. It did not improve when read aloud.

> *Mighty oak, thick and hard*
> *Wood for mast, quarterstaff, and yard.*
> *Cortland and McIntosh, both varieties to delight*
> *But some of the apples don't fall quite right.*
> *Rowan tree very pretty, but the berries aren't sweet.*
> *Balsam, pine, and spruce, those are the real treat.*
> *See what I have planted for you, my love?*
> *And how my plot is revealed from above?*

In the next line, "I am amazed" had been crossed out and "I am a maze" substituted, but the composition ended there, as if the author couldn't think of anything that would rhyme.

Liss wondered why Snowe hadn't torn up his pathetic attempt at versifying. Maybe he'd thought he could improve upon it before the trees in the maze grew high enough for anyone to recognize what it was.

She pondered that awhile. Six months after he'd planted it, at the time of his disappearance, it wouldn't have looked like much. It's only distinguishing feature would have been that the trees were smaller than those growing elsewhere on the farm.

Liss glanced at her watch. She hadn't been going over Snowe's records for as long as she'd thought, even though the two hours she'd spent on the project had felt like twenty. She had time to take a closer look at that maze. Sunset was more than an hour away.

Since Dan was still sleeping, she wrote him a note and stuck it on the front of the refrigerator with a magnet in the shape of a Christmas tree. Taking her coat off the peg inside the kitchen door, she slipped into it and added hat and gloves. Then, before she went outside, she rummaged in the kitchen "junk" drawer. There had to be something in there that would suit her purpose. Twist ties. Rubber bands. Yarn. Heck, she'd settle for an indelible marking pen.

"Ah! Perfect!" Triumphant, she seized a ball of twine that had been shoved to the back of the drawer, extracting it from the rest of the clutter. Her book on mazes had mentioned that the labyrinth of legend had actually been a maze. Using twine or string or yarn was a time-honored method of marking the way back to the entrance.

The afternoon was overcast, and the air had the smell of impending snow, but nothing had yet started to fall. Liss hurried across the parking area and down the hill into the trees.

Liss hoped to navigate Simeon Snowe's maze and

reach its center. From the upstairs bedroom she'd been able to make out a relatively empty space in the middle. Although it was undoubtedly clogged with underbrush and weeds, at least there were no seven-year-old Christmas trees growing there.

There would be no convenient bench to rest on, either, she thought as she reached the field. An authentic hedge maze usually featured such an amenity—a place to sit a spell before beginning the long trek home.

She had the sketch she'd made with her. In spite of what she'd told Rowena, she'd had time the evening before to study a few of the puzzle mazes pictured in *Mazes: Ancient & Modern*. Some of them existed *only* on paper. To solve them, it was necessary to avoid loops that circled back on themselves and dead end passages and figure out which was the true path to the center.

It took considerable time for Liss to find the entrance to Snowe's maze, but eventually she spotted a double-wide break between trees. She patted herself on the back for remembering to bring the twine. On crutches, Dan would be hard pressed to rescue her if she couldn't find her own way out.

She tied one end of her lifeline to the first tree, took a deep breath, and stepped inside. The trees brushed against her on every side. Having the sketch helped a little, but it was difficult to tell where the paths went. As she advanced, Liss slowly played out the twine. She thought she was doing well . . . until she stopped and looked behind her.

At ground level, these trees didn't look all that different from those on the rest of the plantation . . . except that they'd been planted closer together. A flutter of panic unsettled Liss's stomach when she realized she could no longer see the path she'd been following, let alone pick out the route back to the entrance.

"Don't be an ass," she whispered. "You've got the twine. You're not lost."

She was not by nature claustrophobic, but she could swear these trees were moving closer, cutting off her escape. They were tall enough to block her view of the world beyond the maze. She swallowed hard, uncomfortably aware that her heart was beating too fast and she'd broken out in a sweat.

Liss took another step forward. When her coat snagged on a branch, her breath came out in a ragged gasp. She glanced behind her again. The thin brown twine looked impossibly frail against a solid barrier of evergreen trees.

"Maybe I should have gone with bread crumbs," she said aloud. Big mistake. The tremor in her voice echoed the fine trembling of her limbs.

And then it started to snow. First there were only a few oversize wet flakes. Then they were falling faster and faster, until the twine vanished beneath the accumulation.

Liss gave a shaky laugh. Who was she to ignore a sign from above? She jerked on her lifeline, making it visible again.

She rewound the ball of twine as she went. It took only a few minutes to break out into the open, but that was a few minutes too long. The snow was coming down even harder, but she could see the house. Dan had turned the porch light on for her.

Although her panic now seemed foolish, nothing on earth could have persuaded her to go back inside that maze. She was almost running by the time she crested the rise behind the Quonset hut. The parking area was a sea of white, but she could see Dan standing at the front window, watching for her.

Liss toed off her snow-caked boots in the entry hall, shrugged out of her coat, and walked straight into Dan's open arms. "That was one of my stupider ideas," she whispered.

"You okay?"

"I am now."

After a brief affectionate interlude, they stood together by the window to watch the dooryard fill up with snow.

"I can't say I mind the idea of being snowed in with you," Dan admitted.

"You'll change your mind fast enough if we run out of food. Any idea how much snow we're supposed to get?"

"I used the weather app on your iPad. They're predicting six to eight inches by morning."

Not too bad, Liss thought, except that she was the only one able-bodied enough to wield a shovel and the Snowe farm had a *very* long driveway. "I guess I'd better phone Andy Dutton," she said aloud. "As caretaker, she must have made arrangements to keep the way in open."

"Either that or she swaps her motorcycle for a snowmobile." Dan didn't seem at all concerned, but Liss didn't like the idea of being cut off from the road. In an emergency, no one would be able to reach the house.

Gina had given her the Duttons' phone number. Liss located the slip of paper she'd written it on and retrieved her cell phone from the charger she'd left on the kitchen counter, carrying it back into the middle room and sinking into an overstuffed chair to punch in the digits. Someone picked up after two rings, but it wasn't Andy who answered. It was her mother.

"She's busy," Mrs. Dutton said. "She's got better things to do than be at the beck and call of strangers."

In the background, Liss could hear Andy's squawk of protest, quickly followed by her demand that her mother give her the phone. Mrs. Dutton hung up instead.

Seeing the incredulous look on his wife's face, Dan paused on his way to the downstairs bath. "What?"

"Nothing. I hope." Liss waited, flipping idly through one of the old magazines piled beside the chair. Less than two minutes later, her ringtone sounded.

"I can't talk but a minute," Andy said. "Sorry about my mom."

"One minute will do. Can you give me the name of someone who will come here in the morning and plow the driveway? If this snow keeps up, we're going to need digging out."

Andy laughed. "Already taken care of. I'll be over around eight, if that's okay."

"That's perfect. And a great relief. See you tomorrow."

It was only after Andy broke the connection that Liss realized the young woman didn't know Dan was laid up with a fractured ankle and a concussion.

Then again, maybe she *had* heard. Liss remembered what Dan had said to Chief Purvey, and it was true. If New Boston had anything akin to Moosetookalook's local grapevine, the news had been all over town before they'd even left the hospital.

One thought led to another, and she wondered why Andy's mother had set her mind against them. Beatrice Purvey, she recalled, had said that Mrs. Dutton "despaired of" her daughter. Did that mean Mrs. Purvey and Mrs. Dutton were friends? She wasn't about to ask. Besides, small town rumor mills being what they were, Mrs. Purvey could easily have heard stories about Andy's relationship with her mother from any number of sources.

Liss smiled to herself. Most mothers and daughters had issues. It went with the territory. She'd certainly had a few with her own mother when she was growing up, and more recently, too.

A line from that awful poem she'd found in Simeon Snowe's file drawer came back to her: *But some of the apples don't fall quite right.* She wondered if that was a variation on the saying "The apple doesn't fall far from the tree." As far as she knew, Snowe hadn't married or had children, but there were certainly hints of a lady friend. Maybe she had a child with whom she did not always see eye to eye.

The rhythmic clump of Dan's crutches pulled her back to the present.

"All set?" he asked, stopping beside her chair.

"We seem to be." By the time she had recounted her conversations with both mother and daughter, he was chuckling and she had forgotten all about Simeon Snowe's enigmatic poetry.

"You think that's funny, huh?"

"I think it's typical," Dan said.

"You won't be laughing so hard twenty years from now, when I've turned into my mom. Didn't anyone warn you that daughters become more and more like their mothers as they age?"

Dan made the sign to ward off evil but refused to take her warning seriously. "You're as different from Violet MacCrimmon as night and day."

"Thank you." Liss was glad he thought so, but she wasn't sure his confidence was justified.

Was this the opening she'd been waiting for? Fear of becoming like her mother *had* always been one of the reasons why she hesitated to embrace motherhood.

No, she thought. *Be honest.* The truth was that she'd never felt the slightest urge to give birth to a child of her own.

That was what "choice" was all about, wasn't it? A woman could have a dozen kids or none—her decision. But it was one she ought to share with her husband. Her partner. The designated father of any hypothetical offspring.

She opened her mouth to broach the subject and realized that Dan had gone on into the kitchen. The rattle and clang of cookware told her he wasn't waiting for her to start supper.

We'll talk this evening, she promised herself and went to help with the meal. Dan was a top-notch sandwich maker and was not bad at throwing together a few simple dishes, but he was a sloppy cook. It was far easier for her to take over the prep work than it was to clean up after him.

Chapter Eight

Liss's evening didn't go quite as she'd hoped. The storm exacerbated the pain in Dan's ankle. He'd been dealing with a dull headache and occasional dizziness ever since he got the concussion. Low atmospheric pressure made both worse, and the combination of ailments put him in a testy mood. It was not a good time to have a serious conversation.

The next morning, Andy arrived on schedule by snowmobile, connected the snowblower attachment to the John Deere in the Quonset hut, and had the driveway cleared by nine. Liss left Andy commiserating with Dan over his injuries to go to her second exercise class. Wearing a comical hand-knit sweater featuring a grinning reindeer and a frustrated-looking elf, she was entertaining him with tales of some of the more outlandish mishaps various New Bostonians had endured over the years, beginning with two stories about hapless victims trapped in the port-o-potty at the roadside rest stop.

It was a few minutes before ten when Liss parked in front of Dance-Ex. Rowena waved to her as she hurried toward the dance studio along a freshly shoveled sidewalk. "How are you faring out there on the farm?" she asked when they met at the entrance.

"Making do." Liss opened the door, and they went in together.

"Did you have a chance to take a closer look at that maze before the storm hit?"

Liss felt her face flame and hoped Rowena would assume her cheeks were bright pink because they'd just come in out of the cold. "I tried making my way to the center, but I chickened out before I got there," she admitted.

Rowena coaxed her into providing more details as they crossed the studio to the changing room. Juliette was stacking floor mats and didn't look up, but several of the other women in the class had already arrived and greeted Liss like an old friend. Sweating together had that effect.

Rowena had only to slip out of her boots, gloves, and hat and hang up her coat, since she was already in her exercise clothes. She and Liss both preferred bare feet to fancy, expensive "aerobics shoes." There were special shoes for almost every sport and discipline. Liss had worn slippers designed for Scottish dancing onstage, but these days she liked to be able to feel the floor with her toes.

"Would it be all right," Rowena asked in a hesitant voice, "if I came out to the farm some day this week to take a look at your maze?"

"I don't know why it wouldn't be." Liss folded her jeans and sweatshirt on top of her coat and smoothed the fabric of her leotard and tights, reflecting that she'd had both since before she "retired." They were loose enough to be baggy, which made them comfortable, but not terribly flattering. Dan must love her very much to find them sexy!

"Simeon wasn't all that clever," Rowena remarked. "I expect he followed the standard practice for creating a maze. That means all you have to do to find your way to the center is keep one hand on the wall."

"That isn't so easy when the wall is made of overgrown balsams instead of hedgerows, but you're welcome to give it a try. And I still have my ball of twine," she added with a self-deprecating grin.

Class proceeded much as it had the previous day, except that now Liss was familiar with Juliette's routines. Only a small part of her mind was occupied with her movements. The rest of her brain busied itself by trying to unravel a small puzzle. As she exercised, she reran every conversation she'd had with Rowena Luckenbill.

When the aerobics session was over, Liss walked with the older woman to All Things Mystical and watched in thoughtful silence as Rowena unlocked the front door and flipped the CLOSED sign to OPEN. The cat, Gozer, once again occupied the spot next to the cash register. He opened one eye, sent a baleful glance their way, and closed it again. Liss, a well-trained cat person, knew her responsibilities. She hurried over and began to stroke his soft fur, murmuring a greeting and an apology for waking him. Gozer's Scottish Fold ears twitched, but in no other way did he acknowledge her presence.

Divesting herself of outerwear as she went, Rowena wound her way through the racks, shelves, and display cabinets and into her office. Liss trailed after her. The entire shop smelled faintly of lavender, the fragrance Rowena used as a perfume. Liss hadn't paid much attention to it on her last visit to the shop, not with all the other herbs present, not to mention the competing aromas of several kinds of incense.

"Did Simeon Snowe get along with Gozer?" Liss asked.

"They tolerated each other." Rowena stopped sorting the mail on her desk, and a short but awkward silence ensued. "Oh, dear," she murmured.

"I hope you don't think I'm prying, but—"

"But you *are* prying. Still, I don't suppose you can help it. Simeon's niece sent you here to go through his things. Of course you'd discover all his secrets."

"I didn't exactly—"

"His secrets and mine." Rowena went on talking as if Liss hadn't spoken. "He was an interesting man. I liked him." She slipped into the tiny adjoining bath. "Excuse me, dear. I have to change."

Liss stared at the closed door. Since the shop had an extremely effective furnace, she took off her hat and gloves and unbuttoned her coat. The office was too small to allow for much movement, especially with several large cardboard cartons labeled CHRISTMAS DECORATIONS stacked on the floor. It wasn't even Thanksgiving yet, but apparently Rowena started the season early. So did many other businesses. Liss had seen a few displays go up as soon as the Halloween decorations came down.

She looked at the closed door again. "I think . . . I think he *more* than liked you, Rowena. I found a poem at the Snowe house."

Rowena made no reply until she emerged, clad once again in her loose, flowing garments and her jangling bracelets. "Did you say a *poem?*"

Liss nodded. "It mentions trees and mazes and love. It occurs to me that he probably built that maze for you.

The first time I met you, you told us you'd always been fascinated by them. Did you tell him that, too?"

"I suppose I must have." The bemused expression on her face touched Liss's heart.

"And the poem?"

Rowena just shook her head. "Poetry? Simeon? That seems so . . . unlikely."

"Perhaps he was inspired."

"Perhaps you'd better tell me exactly what's in this poem."

"I can't recite it, but there was a lot about trees—oaks and apples and rowans."

"Mountain ash," Rowena murmured. "That's the mundane name. Rowans have mystical powers. And Simeon used to call me his sweet apple-cheeked lass." With a laugh, she did a quick little two-step, touching one hand to her face and lightly tapping her backside with the other, before sailing out of the office and into the showroom.

Too much information, Liss thought and went after her.

"What else did he write?" Rowena busied herself setting up the cash register for the day.

"There was only one other line that I remember. 'But some of the apples don't fall quite right.' For some reason, that made me think that the apple tree—you—had a child."

"Oh, I do. A daughter. After we started seeing each other, Simeon took a dislike to her. He never did tell me why."

She looked so sad that Liss hesitated to ask more questions. "It must have been terrible for you when he disappeared."

"You don't know the half of it. We'd kept our relationship quiet, you see, so there was no one I could talk to except my daughter, and she wasn't interested in hearing about it. She didn't care much for him, either."

"The police didn't question you?"

She shook her head. "I'd have said something if I'd known what happened to him, but I didn't." Regret plain in her voice, Rowena sank down onto the stool behind the sales counter and hauled Gozer into her arms, hugging him for comfort.

Although Liss believed her, she also had a strong sense that Rowena was holding something back. "I'm surprised he didn't tell you about the maze. He planted it the spring before he went missing."

"He was a closemouthed cuss." Her fond tone took the sting out of the criticism. "He probably wanted to surprise me when the trees were bigger."

"I'm sorry for your loss, Rowena. Please feel free to come out to the farm anytime. I'll give you the poem, and you can explore the maze. I'm sure Mr. Snowe would eventually have shown both of them to you."

Rowena heaved a deep sigh and returned Gozer to his accustomed place. "The man always did have romantic notions." A reminiscent gleam made her eyes sparkle. "The results weren't always quite what he expected. I imagine he was very bad at writing poetry, but the fact that he attempted to compose verses at all—" Her voice broke, and she sniffled. Tears glistened, unshed.

"He must have loved you very much," Liss said. "Given the length of time it takes trees to grow, it's clear he believed you'd be together for many years."

"Ten, anyway," Rowena said with a watery chuckle.

She seemed about to say more, but she was interrupted by the sound of the shop door opening. A young couple entered, the woman exclaiming over their luck in finding such a unique establishment in tiny New Boston, Maine.

Rowena instantly reverted to her sales persona. When she swooped down on her newly arrived customers, Liss buttoned her coat, popped her knit hat back on her head, donned her warm, lined gloves, and slipped away.

The Dutton house was a one-story ranch-style dwelling of the type built in the 1950s. Liss had no difficulty finding it, since it was right on the road that led to the Christmas tree farm. When she passed the place earlier that morning, she hadn't paid it much attention. She took a moment after she got out of the truck to study the large, carefully lettered sign set out on the snow-covered front lawn. It read WREATHS FOR SALE.

Liss mounted the porch steps and rang the bell. She was curious about Mrs. Dutton, but Andy hustled her away before she caught even a glimpse of the woman who'd hung up on her.

Still pulling on her barn jacket, Andy shouted over her shoulder. "Ma! I'm leaving!"

With that, she grabbed Liss's arm and towed her toward the back of the house. She'd cleared a path around a stand of birches. A few minutes of crunching their way over the thin layer of snow left behind by the plow brought them to a plot of land that covered approximately one acre.

"What do you think?" Andy asked.

"I think," Liss said, "that you're growing your own Christmas trees."

Andy beamed at her. "Isn't it great?"

The fresh coating of snow made everything look pristine and pretty, and Andy's enthusiasm was contagious. "How long till the first crop is big enough to harvest?"

"Four more years. I can hardly wait. This is nowhere near as big an operation as Mr. Snowe had, but I can open a little cut-your-own place. It'll be a success. I'm sure of it."

"And in the meantime you have the boughs you prune to make into wreaths. I wondered where you were getting them."

Andy's smile vanished. "You thought I stole them, didn't you?"

Liss didn't bother to deny the accusation. "I'm sorry if you find that insulting, but look at it from my point of view. Some of Snowe's trees are ready to sell this year— the very ones you took the trouble to shape."

Andy kicked a clump of snow, avoiding Liss's eyes. "So I thought about helping myself. So what? I didn't do it. I decided to grow my own instead."

"Which is why I have a proposition for you, contingent upon convincing Snowe's heir to go along with my suggestions. If she agrees to sell off some of the ten-year-old trees to the local market, are you willing to manage the operation? The last few crops he put in should last until you're ready to sell your own trees. In the meantime, you'll gain hands-on experience and generate a customer base."

Andy's eagerness was tempered by caution. "Do you really think Ms. Snowe will go for that?"

"I don't see why she shouldn't. The only risk is that she'll want to run a small local operation for just one year."

"Yeah. She'd make more money selling all her uncle's trees for pulpwood."

"Even one year would be good experience for you."

"I'm in. What do I have to do?"

"Just like that?"

"Just like that."

Once they shook hands on the deal, Liss outlined the steps they'd need to take.

"First, I have to check with Gina Snowe, to make sure she's on board with the plan. Second, you and I need to discuss specific terms. Don't answer now. Think about whether you want to work on commission or be paid an hourly wage. Third, Gina will have to purchase liability insurance." Liss wondered if policies were available by the month or if Gina would have to pay for an entire year. Either way, that would be the largest single outlay of cash for start-up costs.

Andy was nodding. Liss had a feeling she'd been studying the tree farm business for some time.

"What are Christmas trees selling for this season?" she asked.

"Thirty-five dollars each. At least, that's what other retailers in the state are charging." She frowned. "There's not going to be much profit after the expense of making signs, putting ads in local newspapers, and launching a Web site."

"There will be if we do it right."

With no more ado, Liss pulled out her cell phone and called Gina. Ten minutes later, Snowe's Cut-Your-Own Christmas Trees was in business.

"So, you had a successful day," Dan said after she'd finished giving him a recap.

"Yup."

"Feeling pleased with yourself, are you?"

"I am."

Once again, they were in the kitchen, where Liss had been washing their lunch dishes. When the last of the soapy water drained away, she turned to her husband and planted a smacking kiss on his cheek. She started to move away, but he caught her hand and pulled her toward his lap.

"Dan! Don't! I'll hurt your ankle."

Another tug put her exactly where he wanted her. "Trust me, what I have in mind does not require the use of my ankle."

The very thorough kiss that followed reminded Liss that in five-plus years of marriage, they'd already discovered how inventive two flexible people could be while sharing a chair. But for all Dan's skill with lips and hands, and his obvious enthusiasm for finishing what he'd started, he was still a man recovering from a concussion.

"You're supposed to avoid strenuous exercise," she reminded him when he finally allowed her to come up for air.

"Spoilsport."

Liss pulled back to study his face. He couldn't hide his wince at the sudden movement. "You still have a headache." She ran her fingers along the curve of his jaw. He'd taken the trouble to shave while she'd been out.

"No more than a dull throb. Easy to ignore."

"I don't think so." She disentangled herself and rose, although she went no farther than the adjacent kitchen chair. "Actually, I was hoping for a quiet afternoon so we could talk about a few things."

A look of alarm crossed Dan's face. "We need to talk?

Don't you know those are words that send an icy chill into any man's heart?"

"Only the insecure ones." She didn't believe for a moment that he had any worries about their relationship. "All I meant was that it's time to think about a new five-year plan."

His brow furrowed. "Since when did we have an old one?"

"We made a list of goals before we got married."

"No. *You* did. You must have made twenty gazillion lists before we got married. You make lists for *everything*."

"I'm not *that* bad."

"Yeah, you are, but I love you, anyway."

"Well, then, it's time to make one more list—*together*."

Watching him closely, she saw him catch her drift. Just that quickly, she was the one who felt insecure. Of their own volition, her hands clenched in her lap.

"You want to talk about having kids." It was not a question, but she couldn't read anything else in his voice. His face gave nothing away, either.

Liss nodded. "I think we should, don't you?"

"Have kids?"

Anxiety flashed into panic. "*Talk* about having them."

He cocked his head, and a wry smile lifted the corners of his mouth. "We probably should, but not right this minute. We've got company."

A moment later, she heard what he already had—the sound of a car engine. "That better not be Wyatt Purvey again."

Liss headed for the front door, with Dan following more slowly on his crutches. She was reaching for the doorknob when he stopped at the living room window to peer out at the parking area.

"What are Pete and Sherri doing here?"

"I have no idea."

Framed in the open doorway with Dan standing behind her, Liss watched her friends get out of their car and survey their surroundings. The previous night's snowfall had been steadily melting all day, leaving slushy pavement behind. If the weather stayed fine and the daytime temperatures remained above freezing, they'd be back to bare ground in a day or two.

Pete went around to the trunk and extracted two lightweight duffel bags. Sherri's was fuchsia with purple polka dots. His was dark green.

Catching sight of Liss and Dan as she headed toward the porch, Sherri sang out, "Nursing brigade reporting for duty!"

"Planning to stay awhile?" Dan's voice was neutral, his expression closed, giving Liss no idea how he felt about having their conversation interrupted.

For herself, she had to admit that she was more relieved than annoyed. She knew she couldn't put off the moment of truth forever, but she was happy to postpone it a little while longer.

"We figured your poor wife needed a break from looking after you." Pete sounded jocular, but his eyes cut to Liss, silently asking if Dan knew what she'd shared with Sherri.

Liss gave a negative shake of her head, a movement so slight that Dan never noticed it.

"We've had enough breaks, thanks," he said and lifted his foot to show Pete the plaster cast.

"Nice," Pete said. "I'll have to think of something obnoxious to write on it."

"What are you? Twelve?"

The banter between Pete and Dan got the new arrivals through the door and into the house. Liss grabbed the polka-dot bag away from Pete with one hand and opened the stairwell door with the other.

"Let me show you to your room. Then we can settle in for a good visit."

She was acting as if it had been months since the four of them had last been together instead of less than a week, but if Dan thought her behavior odd, he didn't remark upon it. "I'll make a fresh pot of coffee," he offered as Liss, Sherri, and Pete started up the stairs.

Liss waited until they came out in the second-floor hallway before she said anything. Then she turned to Sherri, half in relief and half in irritation. "What are you *doing* here?"

"We're your backup. You haven't told Dan your suspicions, have you? He has no idea that his fall may not have been an accident."

"Of course I haven't said anything to him. I don't want to worry him." She led the way to Simeon Snowe's bedroom, the one she and Dan had slept in on their first night at the farm. "I'll put you in here. Since Dan can't manage the climb, we're bunking downstairs."

"Nice," Sherri said.

Liss closed the door to the hall and grabbed Sherri's arm, letting the duffel bag fall to the carpet with a plop. "Have you discovered something new? After the last time we talked, I convinced myself that there was nothing to be concerned about. I overreacted . . . didn't I?"

Pete cut in before Sherri could answer. "She had to see for herself that you two were okay. We'll go home in the morning, if that's what you want."

Sherri sent him a look that shot daggers but didn't contradict him.

Liss's gaze went from one to the other. "Okay. Now you're scaring me."

"You had concerns. We're here to check things out." Sherri said. "You're in the hands of professionals. Relax and enjoy it."

"All joking aside," Pete said, "if there was something about Dan's fall that didn't seem right to you, then it's worth investigating. Personally, I think that your theory about someone wanting you out of the house that night makes sense. Sherri and I talked about it on the drive here. We want to go over the place from top to bottom."

"Looking for what?"

"Anything that ties Simeon Snowe to someone on that list of names you sent me, or to the John Doe."

"This place has already been searched by the police, back when Snowe went missing," Liss reminded her. "And I didn't find any trace of an intruder."

"The police could have missed something. You, too."

"We'll have to wait till Dan takes a nap."

Pete looked like he wanted to object but said nothing.

Dan's voice floated up to them. "Coffee's ready, gang! Come and get it!"

They didn't have long to wait before Dan gave in to his throbbing head and retreated to the downstairs bedroom for a little lie down, but the afternoon was already well advanced by then. Liss threw together a casserole and popped it into the oven with four baking potatoes while her friends started their search.

While Pete explored the cellar and checked out the first floor, keeping one ear open for sounds of stirring in the downstairs bedroom, Liss joined Sherri to tackle the upstairs rooms. The results were discouraging. There was nothing beyond the usual clutter one might expect a single, middle-aged man who lived alone to accumulate. Simeon Snowe had read news and sports magazines and Clive Cussler novels, preferred boxers to briefs, and kept a supply of condoms in his nightstand drawer.

They made a brief foray into the dusty, disused attic before returning to the entry hall. By then, the three of them had searched everywhere except the room where Dan still slept.

"I'll take care of that later," Liss whispered, her eyes glued to the closed door.

She'd been happier when she'd been convinced she was imagining things. That conclusion had made staying on in the farmhouse until Dan healed enough to travel comfortably much easier on her. Now she wondered if they shouldn't abandon ship first thing in the morning. Trying to weigh the relative risks was giving her a headache of her own.

Then Sherri voiced the other concern that had been nagging at her.

"You know, you're going to have to tell Dan what's going on. The sooner the better."

"I don't want to worry him."

"He's going to guess that something's not right. This was supposed to be your vacation. You two were going off on your own for a week. He's got to be wondering why Pete and I would intrude on your privacy."

"You heard he was hurt. Isn't that reason enough? Besides, you're leaving tomorrow."

"We *can* leave tomorrow. We don't *have* to. We can stay until Dan's fit to travel."

"You called yourself backup? Did you really mean guard duty?"

"We're your friends. We're allowed to be concerned about you."

"You're terrific friends, but maybe my overactive imagination is contagious. Or we're all so desperate for some excitement in our lives that we're grasping at straws. I found an explanation for the maze. Beatrice Purvey's accusations against Andy turned out to be unfounded. The rest of what happened could be equally innocent."

"Who are you trying to convince?" Sherri asked. "Me or yourself?"

"Both of us?"

"We've got a lot more notes to compare before that happens."

Liss jumped at the sound of the door to the downstairs bedroom creaking open. For one heart-stopping moment she thought that Dan might have overheard the last part of their conversation. Apparently he had not. He hobbled out, looking tousled and sleepy, and barely acknowledged Sherri's presence as he made his slow and ponderous way toward the bathroom.

"No spilling the beans to Dan," Liss whispered to her friend.

"Fine. But first chance we get, we go over your list of suspects."

Supper passed without incident. Afterward, they settled down in the living room to play Monopoly. Pete had found an ancient version of the board game in a drawer in the sideboard. *This will be a nice relaxing evening with friends,* Liss thought. She could almost forget why Sherri and Pete had come to New Boston.

She'd just passed "Go," collected two hundred dollars, and bought a utility when an odd glow in the night sky beyond the living room windows caught her attention.

"Is that the northern lights?" she asked. They did appear in Maine every once in a while, although not as colorfully as she'd heard they did in Alaska.

Sherri got up to take a closer look.

"Oh, my God!" she exclaimed. "Pete, call nine-one-one. The Christmas trees are on fire."

Chapter Nine

Members of the local volunteer fire department responded quickly, but until they arrived, Liss had to watch helplessly from the high ground next to the Quonset hut as flames cut a swath through the balsams.

The maze was fully engulfed. Branches popped and cracked as the fire consumed them. The smell of burning wood, so comforting when it came from a fireplace on a cold winter night, made Liss's stomach heave. Her heart ached for the loss of all those beautiful trees.

"I'm going to see what I can do to help," Pete said when the first fire engine pulled in. He was a volunteer himself with the Moosetookalook Fire Department.

Sherri stayed with Liss and Dan. She tried to hide her fear for Pete's safety, but Liss knew her friend too well to be deceived. Sherri wouldn't breathe easily again until the fire was out.

None of them would.

"Is there a farm pond?" Sherri asked. "Or a river nearby? They'll need more water than what's in the pumper."

"A stream," Liss said, "but it's not very deep."

"Anything will help."

They watched for what seemed like hours as the battle to beat down the flames raged on. Crews and equipment from neighboring towns arrived to assist, using the logging road for access.

"Come back to the house," Dan said when the wind picked up, causing snow to swirl and fingers of fire to shoot even higher. "There's no point in our standing out here in the cold. It may be quite a while yet before they get that blaze under control."

An eddy of cold air caught the hem of Liss's coat and tugged at her wool hat. Out in the field, similar gusts continued to fan the flames. Sparks rose from one area like birds taking flight. They passed over the heads of the men with hoses and settled into the treetops in an adjacent field. Liss fully expected those trees to burst into flame. They flickered, but the fire petered out.

"It's been a wet fall," Sherri said. "And there's snow on the ground. Besides that, Christmas trees are green wood. Full of moisture."

"Then why are some of them burning so fiercely?"

It was a stupid question. Liss realized that as soon as she asked it. Mad as it seemed, she was certain that the maze was on fire because someone had wanted to destroy it. If the entire tree farm burned down along with it, that would be nothing more than collateral damage.

She glanced at Dan. His set face told her he was in pain but was holding on for her sake. As long as she stayed here watching the fire, he'd stick to her like a burr.

She went inside.

Another hour passed before Pete joined them in the farmhouse kitchen. His face was black with soot, and his clothing bore numerous stains, even though it had been covered by borrowed firefighting gear. He brought the New Boston fire chief with him.

Armand Kessler was a big, burly man with the mournful face of a basset hound. In a deep, rumbling voice he confirmed what Liss had already guessed. "I have reason to suspect arson," Kessler said. "I'm not a trained investigator, but I could smell an accelerant."

"It was pretty unmistakable," Pete agreed.

"I've left some of my men to watch for hot spots, but the rest are calling it a night. We have the fire contained." Before Liss could rejoice in that news, Kessler added, "Someone from the fire marshal's office will be coming out here to look things over. Don't try to clean up until after he talks to you."

Shock and exhaustion had taken their toll. Feeling too numb to do more, Liss nodded. As soon as Kessler left, she turned and burrowed into Dan's arms. He stroked one hand across her hair in a soothing motion.

"Who's doing these things?" she whispered against his shoulder. "And why?"

Dan's fingers stilled. "Things?" he repeated. "Plural? What else happened?"

Pete rose from the sofa, where he'd collapsed after introducing the fire chief. "I think I'll turn in. It's been a long evening."

"Why don't you stick around a bit longer?" Dan's tone made it an order, not a suggestion. His voice was dangerously soft. It reminded her of Wyatt Purvey's whisper, but its effect was entirely different. Although Dan rarely lost his temper, he was perilously close to doing so now.

Pete subsided.

Sherri plunked herself down next to her husband and

gestured toward the other chairs in the living room. "Sit down, you two. You may as well be comfortable. No one is going anywhere anytime soon. This time the police *will* investigate."

With a sigh, Liss complied, taking the armchair facing toward the middle room and kitchen.

"This time," Dan echoed.

He stayed on his feet, framed in the archway between the two rooms and leaning heavily on his crutches. He did not look well. His face was haggard. His eyes were bloodshot. But his fulminating glare made it clear he wouldn't stand for any evasions.

No sense beating around the bush, Liss told herself. She took a deep breath and plunged into speech. "Your fall wasn't an accident. I can't prove it, but I think someone deliberately created that slick spot on the ground by the truck. I tried to talk myself out of the idea, but now that someone's started a fire . . ." Her voice trailed off as she caught sight of her husband's face.

"Exactly when were you planning on telling me the truth?"

"Honestly? I don't know."

"Damn it, Liss! You—"

"Don't snarl at me!" She snapped out the words as she sprang to her feet. She was annoyed at Dan but even more irritated with herself. "Yes, I know better than to try to keep secrets from you, but first you were in the hospital. Then you were dealing with the cast and a killer headache. When, exactly, was I supposed to dump a new worry on you?" Toe to toe with him, her glare dared him to tell her she could have handled things any other way.

"Damn it, Liss," he said again, but this time there was much less heat behind the words. He slumped, letting the side of the archway take his weight.

Liss stepped away from him, rubbing her hands over her face. Her eyes felt gritty, and she was all but reeling from lack of sleep.

In a tired voice, Dan asked, "Did you send for Pete and Sherri?"

"We volunteered," Sherri said. "Cut her some slack, Dan."

He ignored her, keeping his focus on his wife. "I still don't understand why it couldn't have been an accident. All kinds of things get spilled in parking lots. I know I didn't slip on ice, but there's motor oil, radiator fluid, antifreeze, windshield-washing solution—"

"Olive oil?"

"What?" Sherri sat up straight and exchanged a startled look with Pete.

"Olive oil." Liss sighed. "I know it sounds wacko, but I recognized the smell. It was definitely olive oil on the ground beside Dan's truck."

"You didn't mention that little detail the first time around."

"Huh," Pete said. "Olive oil. That's certainly . . . different."

"It's preposterous," Liss admitted. "It's also true, and I'm pretty sure the spill wasn't accidental." She explained about the absence of broken glass and the size of the slick.

Dan finally shoved himself away from the archway. After he dropped into the nearest chair, he sent Liss a look of rebuke. "You should have reported your suspicions to Chief Purvey."

Liss snorted. "Like he'd listen."

"And we should have been gone from here long before today."

Liss made an inarticulate sound of frustration. "Oh, sure! Think about that for more than two seconds, okay, Dan? Do you really think you could have faced three hours in the passenger seat of your truck with that cast on your ankle on the day after you fell? There isn't much foot room in the cab to begin with. You griped about that for most of the short drive from the hospital to here."

The floor space on the passenger side of the truck was nearly halved by the hump made by the transfer case for the four-wheel drive. Liss knew exactly how much that limited legroom. She was the one who usually had to sit on that side. The irony of the situation was that they'd normally have used her car for the trip, but it had needed new shocks and Dan had decided that while they were away would be a good time to have the work done.

"She's got a point, Dan," Pete said. "Given that ankle, and your head, you needed a couple of days of rest before you put any kind of strain on yourself."

"I'm doing better," he insisted. "I say we grab a few hours of sleep and leave here as soon as we talk to the fire marshal. I'll ride with Pete in his car. Liss and Sherri can take the truck."

Bone tired herself, Liss said the first thing that came into her head. "What if this saboteur tries to burn the house down next?"

"Highly unlikely," Pete said. "There are still firemen in the field. Besides, the sun will be up in a couple of hours."

"Right," Dan said. "I'm going to go get some shut-eye. Coming, Liss?"

He didn't wait for an answer. Maneuvering awkwardly on his crutches, he got up and crossed the living room to exit through the door to the entry hall.

Absurd as it seemed, especially if someone really was out to get them, Liss felt as if a tremendous burden had been lifted from her shoulders. She no longer had to hide her fears from Dan. And he hadn't been nearly as angry at her as she'd expected him to be. She was pretty sure he'd already forgiven her for keeping secrets.

She said good night to Sherri and Pete, intent on following her husband.

"Hold on, Liss," Sherri called after her. "We need to talk about this. I've got questions."

"Tomorrow," Liss promised. "When I have a working brain."

Dan wasn't in the downstairs bedroom when she got there. He'd detoured into the nearby bathroom. She glanced at the dresser and nightstand, but she was too exhausted to go through with her earlier plan to search the room. It took all her remaining energy to change into a nightgown. She fell into the bed, dragging the covers up to her neck. She heard Dan's crutches thumping along the hallway, heading her way. She meant to apologize to him for keeping secrets, and maybe cuddle a little, but by the time he climbed into bed beside her, she was already asleep.

Wednesday morning dawned clear and bright and warm enough for the remaining snow to continue melting. Liss had little appetite, but she forced herself to get up and make coffee. When Sherri appeared, she didn't want more than cold cereal, but Pete arrived hungry for scrambled eggs. Dan came into the kitchen last and opted for a full breakfast.

When the four of them were gathered around the table, each with a mug of coffee, Liss turned to Sherri. "I'm ready to be interrogated, Officer."

"Good," Dan said, "because there are some things I want to know, too. I still don't buy that my fall wasn't an accident. Why would anyone want me to hurt myself?"

No one answered him. Instead, Sherri asked *him* a question. "You were parked in a busy grocery store lot when it happened, right?"

Dan nodded. "It's shared by a market and a hardware store."

"Describe it."

Liss closed her eyes in an effort to picture the scene as Dan spoke.

"Two rows of parking. Six cars in a row? Maybe eight. I'm not sure. Cars and trucks were pulling in and out. It was late afternoon. People, mostly women, were stopping in to make last-minute purchases before they headed home to cook supper. That's why I chose a spot along the side of the lot, out of the way of all that backing and forthing. There were about a dozen parking slots over under some trees. Maybe more."

Shielded by the trees and with the gathering dusk, Liss remembered, it had been difficult to see well. It would have been easy for someone to lay a trap without being noticed. An enterprising soul might even have backed in next to Dan's truck and poured oil on the pavement without ever getting out of his . . . or her . . . vehicle.

"Liss, are you certain the slick spot was olive oil?" Sherri asked.

"I didn't imagine the smell!"

"But you can't prove it was olive oil, either," Pete pointed out. "It's too late to look for evidence on the blacktop. By now, between the weather and traffic, there won't be anything left to find."

"I knelt in the oil after Dan fell," Liss said. "It's still on my slacks."

Sherri perked up. "A stain on fabric can be tested. Of course, it's still not proof. Even if it is olive oil, who's to say you didn't spatter some on yourself while you were cooking?"

"Who's to say? Me! That's who!" Liss felt herself getting riled up all over again. "Why did you bother coming here if you won't believe me?"

"It's not that we don't believe you, Liss," Pete said. "It's that your theory makes no sense. There's no obvious reason for someone to have pulled such a stunt. And you're short on proof that there was any foul play."

Liss shot out of her chair, taking her empty coffee mug with her. She slammed it down in the sink so hard that it broke on impact. A shard pierced her thumb. She stared at it in confusion.

Sherri was at her side an instant later. "For heaven's sake, Liss! Let me see that."

She forced her friend's hand under cold running water and cleaned the small cut. In short order she'd dabbed it with disinfectant cream and bandaged it. Pete cleared away the broken bits of ceramic.

"I get that you're upset that we doubt you," Sherri said when they were once more seated around the kitchen table, "but you said yourself that you had second thoughts. Let's take this one step at a time. That stain needs to be preserved. I'll send your slacks to the lab to be tested."

"Tell me the truth. If I wasn't your friend, wouldn't you write me off as a nutcase?"

"Maybe," Sherri admitted, "but you are and there's certainly something strange going on. I won't feel easy in my mind until I know what it is."

"We wouldn't have come if we didn't think there was reason to be concerned," Pete said, "but playing devil's advocate is the best way to find any flaws in your logic."

"What's the plan, then?" Dan asked.

"More questions, based on the list of names Liss sent me while you were still in the hospital."

"A list? Why doesn't that surprise me?"

Sherri ignored Dan's rhetorical question and turned to Liss. "You may know more than you realize about some of these people." From the pocket of her jeans she produced the printout, now much folded, that she'd made of Liss's e-mail. "I want your first impression," she instructed, "especially anything that struck you as off-kilter. Dan, feel free to chime in with your observations. Let's start with Andy Dutton."

Liss studied her hands and the bandage that stood out like . . . well, like a sore thumb. "I thought Andy was a guy until she took off her motorcycle helmet." She described their first meeting, then added, "I liked her. But I could tell she wasn't a happy camper when I mentioned that Gina might open up a cut-your-own place. Later, after Mrs. Purvey told me Andy had been in trouble with the law when she was younger, I had to wonder if she might be planning to siphon off some trees to sell on her own. It was a relief when you told me that the juvenile record was only for minor stuff. And, as of yesterday morning, I know what she was really up to, and it's all good."

After Liss had filled them in on that youthful entrepreneur's business plan, Sherri picked another name off the list—the town manager, Steve Wilton.

"No red flags there," Liss said.

"What about Beatrice Purvey?"

Liss made a face. "She'd be my prime suspect if she had anything to gain by it. But there's no way she could have set the fire last night. She's seventy if she's a day and probably older."

"I know a lot of spry older women," Pete said.

"Oh, she can trot pretty fast on solid flooring, but over snow-covered fields in the dark? I don't think so."

"First impressions?" Sherri prompted her.

"At the town office she acted skittish, as if the very name Simeon Snowe spooked her a little. Then, at the grocery store, she was on the defensive, almost angry at us for being critical of her hometown and, more particularly, her son. Then she started dropping hints about Andy's criminal past."

"How did she get onto that topic?"

Liss had to think a moment before she could answer. "I asked her about workers Simeon Snowe might have hired to help harvest his trees. I have those names now. I found them when I went through Snowe's business papers."

"Good. We'll check them out later. For now tell me about Wyatt Purvey."

"I didn't like him."

"Why not?"

"He's the type who'd tell a woman not to worry her

pretty little head about anything, because the big strong man will take care of it. Except that he's not all that big or strong. And I loathe his voice. Words can't describe it. You'll have to hear him speak for yourself."

Sherri gave a low whistle. "You *really* don't like him, do you?"

"Not at all." She paused and reflected. "It really ticked me off that he ignored me and talked only to Dan. He was dismissive when he mentioned Andy, too." She gave them a brief recap of Purvey's visit to the Snowe farm.

"Did he say how he knew Andy Dutton?"

Liss shook her head. "When you get right down to it, he didn't say much at all."

"The first time we met him," Dan interjected, "I got the impression that he didn't *know* much."

"I thought he just didn't *care* what had happened to that John Doe," Liss said. "The unidentified man wasn't anybody local, so he didn't matter to Purvey."

Sherri sighed. "That seven-year-old murder has got to be the key to what's happening now. That's what called attention to Snowe's Christmas tree farm. It was probably the reason Snowe disappeared, too. I wonder if John Doe might have been one of the itinerant laborers Snowe hired."

"In that case, wouldn't Andy have recognized him?" Liss asked.

"That depends. If all they showed the locals was a photograph taken of his face after he was dead, he might not have looked much like himself. I wonder if they also did an artist's reconstruction?"

"I wouldn't mind seeing what he looked like myself," Liss said. "I'm guessing he wasn't a big bruiser. A large man wouldn't have fit through the netter."

"Something to consider," Sherri murmured. "Sometimes size *does* matter. When we're done with first impressions, I'll have you two go through the list and jot down approximate heights and weights for each of these people. Best guess on ages, too. That information may come in handy later. Okay, on to Mike Jennings. I'm guessing he struck you more favorably than Purvey did."

"Definitely." Liss summarized what Jennings had told her and Dan. "About John Doe and the search for Simeon Snowe . . . ," she said before Sherri could go on to the next name on the list. "Do you know any more about the dead guy?"

It was Sherri's turn to make a face. "My hands have been tied because this isn't my case. I didn't have a reason to access official police reports from New York, although I did e-mail some questions to someone I know from a police Listserv. The only good thing about that fire last night is that if it was arson, that may give me some leverage. We'll have to wait and see what the fire marshal says."

"The man in the netter is an unusual case," Pete said, "and not only because of where he was found. Nowadays there's usually something available to base an ID on—fingerprints, DNA, dental records, facial recognition software." He shook his head, as if he had trouble believing what he was saying. "For this guy, they apparently turned up zip. Nada. Nothing. He was a John Doe when they found him, and he's still listed that way."

"That's what Officer Jennings said," Dan agreed, "but I don't understand how someone could be that far off the radar."

"Could be he was just an ordinary guy who never came to anybody's attention," Sherri said. "Or there may *be* records somewhere. Without a name to use to search for them, you're flat out of luck."

"Or he was a very clever criminal who knew how to avoid leaving a record. Oh, don't look at me like that!" Liss accompanied the order with a strained laugh. "Why should we ignore the possibility that the mob is involved? It's no crazier than using olive oil in a booby trap."

Sherri shoved her mug, still half full of coffee, to one side and leaned across the table to take Liss's hands in hers. "I'm not going to ignore anything, no matter how far-fetched. This guy ended up being murdered. Regular joes don't usually get stuffed through a netting machine and shipped out of state."

"The thing that makes the least sense to me is that no one recognized his photo," Liss said. "I don't mean to give him a name," she added quickly, "but because they'd seen him around town."

"No one *admitted* to seeing him," Sherri said. "Isn't that what Mike Jennings told you?" She held up a hand to stop Liss from answering. "Never mind. Forget about the dead guy for now. We've gotten off track. Whoever tried to hurt Dan, it wasn't John Doe." She glanced at the list. "You went to lunch after you talked to Purvey and Jennings, right?"

Liss nodded and made short work of eliminating the next few people on her list as serious suspects. Miranda Madison and her employee and Harlan Woolgar seemed unlikely villains. "The dog's name is Jonas," Liss added. "I don't think he did it, either."

"What about patrons in the café?"

"Any of them could have overheard us talking about the maze," Liss admitted, "but I don't know who they were, and I wouldn't recognize any of them if I tripped over them."

Sherri went on to the next entry. "What about Juliette Cressy?"

"She runs the local dance studio." Liss didn't need to explain to an old friend like Sherri why she'd stopped at Dance-Ex.

"First impression?"

"Rather rude and abrupt for someone whose success depends on attracting and keeping clients. Not as good a teacher as Zara, but not awful."

"So you've taken one of her classes?"

"I've been to aerobics twice. We meet every morning at ten. Rowena Luckenbill is part of the group, too. Oh, and Kitty Sloan. That's the young woman I met on her way into Dance-Ex." She pointed to Kitty's description. "I didn't know her name until Monday." As Liss described their first brief encounter, Sherri wrote Kitty's name on the printout.

"I'll check her out. Now, what about Ms. Luckenbill?"

"She owns the occult shop a few doors down from Dance-Ex. We stopped in there because we'd realized that some of the trees had been planted in the shape of a maze. I bought a book on mazes. Rowena struck me as pleasant but a little strange. I've gotten to know her better since then, since she's in my aerobics class, which is how I discovered that she and Simeon Snowe were an item back in the day. He probably planted that maze as a surprise for her. It's kind of sweet, really. I also found a poem he wrote to her."

Pete snickered. "Be still, my beating heart. Geriatric romance."

"They were only in their fifties at the time," Liss protested, even though she knew he was kidding. "That's hardly over the hill."

"You should be so lucky at that age," Sherri said sotto voce and jabbed him in the ribs with the eraser end of her pencil.

Pete threw his hands into the air in mock surrender.

Ignoring this byplay, Liss reached for the printout and scanned it. "That's everyone we encountered before Dan was hurt, except for the clerk in the grocery store and the old guy in the market's parking lot, the one who was not helpful with directions to the Christmas tree farm, and the woman who suggested we try asking for information at the town office. No one else would have had any idea who we were or why we were in New Boston."

"Except Gina," Sherri said.

"Have you lost your mind?" Liss asked. "Gina's the one who sent us here. Why would she try to scare us off?"

"I wasn't thinking of her for that. I was wondering where she was when her great-uncle disappeared."

"You seriously think *Gina* would go that far on the off chance of inheriting a Christmas tree farm?" Dan asked.

"I think Gina Snowe would bulldoze right over anyone who got in her way to something she wanted. John Doe. Her uncle. Anyone. And we know she was in the area earlier that year."

"Of course she was—for our tenth high school reunion in the summer, months before John Doe turned up in New York and Simeon Snowe vanished."

"All the same, I bet she knows more than she's told you."

Liss opened her mouth to deny it and abruptly shut it

again. "You're probably right. Do you want me to phone her again?"

"Later. First, while Dan writes down height, weight, and age—he's better at guessing that sort of thing than you are—you and I are going to search the downstairs bedroom. Unless you've already done it?"

"Not yet."

They'd barely begun looking for clues when Liss heard the sound of a car engine.

"Oh, goody," she muttered, lifting the curtain to take a look at the parking area. "My favorite cop has turned up again."

Sherri closed a dresser drawer. "Purvey?"

"Who else?"

"How much do you want to tell him?"

"Why should we tell him anything?" Her lips twisted into a rueful smile. "And what, exactly, *can* we tell him that he'll believe? I'm still having a hard time believing it myself. If not for the fire—"

"There's no question that it was deliberately set," Sherri said. "Even if we don't see how that connects to someone using olive oil to cause Dan to fall, the coincidence factor is way too great to discount. Somehow, everything is connected—John Doe's murder and Simeon Snowe's disappearance, too."

"Don't count on Purvey agreeing with that. That man has a mind so tightly closed that a sunbeam couldn't find a way inside."

Liss opened the front door before Purvey could go around to the kitchen entrance and invited him in. The stench of burnt trees still hung in the crisp morning air.

"Your husband around?" asked the chief of police.

"He's in the kitchen," Liss said with forced politeness. "Please go on through." With Sherri beside her, she trailed along after him.

"Chief Purvey!" Pete exclaimed, jumping up and holding out his hand. "Pete Campbell here. I'm a deputy sheriff over to Carrabassett County. I went through the criminal justice academy at the same time as one of your men. Guy named Jennings. Mike, is it?"

As usual, Purvey's expression gave nothing away, but he did agree that Officer Jennings was named Michael.

Putting a great deal of insincere warmth into her voice, Liss offered Purvey a cup of coffee. He shifted his attention away from Dan and Pete long enough to refuse. He had yet to acknowledge Sherri's presence in any way.

Liss wondered if Wyatt Purvey had any inkling how offensive his behavior was to an entire gender. Having met his overprotective mother, she'd have liked to stuff him into a pigeonhole labeled "middle-aged Mama's boy," but people were always more complex than stereotypes. She warned herself not to underestimate him, either. Or tick him off.

"I'm here on official business," Purvey announced in a pompous voice. "That fire of yours last night caused a good deal of damage, and the cost to the town for putting out the blaze will be considerable."

"I'm not sure I know what you're getting at, Chief," Dan said. "Surely you're not blaming my wife and me for the destruction."

"Somebody set that blaze. Is there insurance on this place?"

"Now, wait just a damned minute!" Incensed, Dan started to stand, momentarily forgetting that he had a broken ankle. Pain distorted his features, reminding him to take it easy.

Liss rushed to his side, but he waved her off. She knew better than to fuss over him, but her emotions had been stirred up, too. They needed an outlet. Turning on Wyatt Purvey, a ferocious scowl on her face, Liss spat her words. "We don't have a horse in this race, Chief. No personal connection to this land at all. Why in heaven's name would we want to damage someone else's property?"

Finally, Purvey spoke to her directly. "Maybe that's what you were hired to do by the new owner."

"In case you hadn't noticed, that was a cash crop that went up in flames. The field that was completely destroyed would have been ready to sell in three more years. The other trees that burned, the ones too big to be Christmas trees, had value as pulpwood. Gina Snowe would have to be crazy to want them set on fire."

"The insurance—"

"I doubt there is any," Liss said. "Who do you think would have been paying it all these years? Simeon Snowe?"

For the first time, she saw a trace of a reaction flicker across Purvey's bland countenance. He went so far as to raise his voice by a decibel or two. "You can be sure I'll be checking into that. In the meantime, the fire marshal will be out here to question you. Until he does, none of you are to leave town."

He turned on his heel and strode to the kitchen door. If he was hoping for a dramatic exit, he was foiled by the fact that no one had yet unlocked it. Purvey fumbled with the dead bolt, jerked the door open, and then slammed it shut behind him for emphasis.

"My, my," Sherri said. "How unprofessional."

"I'm surprised you didn't try to spike his guns by telling him what you do for a living. Two chiefs of police.

No waiting." Liss poured herself another mug of coffee and sat down at the table.

Her hands were shaking a little, but suddenly she was ravenous. Seeing that Dan had made himself another batch of toast, she filched a piece from his plate.

"I'm reserving that tidbit," Sherri said. "You never know when the element of surprise will come in handy."

"What an arrogant SOB," Dan groused. "Can he really make us stay here?"

"Not unless he wants to arrest us," Pete said, "but we were going to stick around to talk to the fire marshal, anyway."

"I hope he shows up soon. I want to get this show on the road." Dan snagged the last of the toast an instant before Liss could grab it, then took pity on her and relinquished his prize.

"Moosetookalook is only a few hours away," Sherri reminded them. "And I doubt the fire marshal will have all that many questions. He'll find his answers out in the field."

Still out of sorts, Dan refused to be cheered up. "The way my luck is running, he'll probably agree that we're a bunch of arsonists."

"I don't know what *you're* worried about," Pete drawled. "You'd have to be able-bodied to get out into that field with a can of gas or kerosene or whatever. That lets you off the hook, old buddy. I'm the one who should be worried."

Dan fought a smile but lost. "Cops! You have a warped sense of humor!"

Although Sherri no longer believed there was any point in searching the downstairs bedroom, she was determined to be thorough. Besides, it looked like they were going to be stuck at the Snowe farm for a while longer. She and Liss might as well do *something* to pass the time.

Liss opened the top drawer of the dresser and reached inside. "I did find one thing in here when I opened it before. Sachet. Lavender. Rowena Luckenbill wears this scent." She tossed it back where she'd found it. "But we already know she and Snowe were tight."

She closed that drawer and opened the next one down, while Sherri tackled the nightstand, the only other piece of furniture the small room held, other than the bed.

"Empty," Liss said. "I bet the bottom drawer is, too."

Sherri heard a scrape as Liss opened it and then silence. Having come up empty-handed herself, she glanced over her shoulder in time to see Liss slam the drawer shut in disgust.

"I was right. Not even a stray snapshot."

"That's it, then. Nothing here but what you and Dan brought with you and that sachet." Sherri abandoned the bedroom and headed for the at-home office. "Pete didn't snoop in Snowe's computer. Was there any personal stuff there? Photos? Letters?"

"I didn't find any. The only JPEGs in the pictures file were the ones that came with the software."

"Too bad. It would have been nice if he'd left a pictorial record of his hired men at work."

"I didn't even find any photos of Snowe himself. I have no idea what he looked like."

"There was one with the missing persons report I saw. It looked like it was taken at some kind of fair or picnic. You could see where it was trimmed to cut out the people on either side of him."

"I wonder where the cops found it?" Liss booted up the computer. "If I remember right, the town of New Boston Web site has a photo gallery. I didn't bother to look at it before. I was only after the name of the town manager and the receptionist—sorry, I mean dispatcher—for the police department so I could send them to you to do a background check."

"Speaking of that." While she called up the page and began to scroll down, Sherri explained why she hadn't used official channels to search for information. "I ran up quite a bill," she added.

"Gina's good for it."

"There!" Sherri recognized Snowe's face halfway down the third page of pictures. "The guy with the beard. That's Simeon Snowe."

It was the original of the photograph she'd seen, but it now showed three people. Snowe stood between two women, an arm around each of them. All three were grinning at the camera.

She glanced at Liss, took note of the bemused expression on her face, and poked her in the shoulder. "What?"

Liss pointed a finger at the older of the two women. "That's Rowena Luckenbill."

"Okay. You said they were an item. Why the frown?"

"Because the other one is Juliette Cressy, the woman who owns Dance-Ex. She seems to be on pretty friendly terms with Snowe, wouldn't you say?"

Sherri leaned closer to peer at the screen. "They're having a good time together, certainly. And this bothers you because?"

"The first time I met Juliette, she claimed she didn't

know Simeon Snowe. Why would she lie about something like that?"

"Maybe she thought it was none of your business?"

Liss scowled.

"I agree it's odd. Why don't you ask her why she fibbed when she didn't have to?"

"I doubt I'll see her again. I already missed today's class, and with any luck, I'll be back home in Moosetookalook tonight. Tomorrow I'll work out with Zara. It probably doesn't matter in the long run. I can't picture Juliette bounding through the Christmas tree fields with a gas can."

"At this point, everyone is a suspect," Sherri reminded her. "Especially Wyatt Purvey."

"Why *especially?*"

Sherri filled her in on what Mike Jennings had told Pete when they were both at the criminal justice academy.

"That was a long time ago." Liss sounded dubious.

"It was. But now, while things are quiet, I'm going to do some more digging. If it was Purvey who was chief of police back when Pete was at the academy with Mike Jennings, there are a few other sources I can tap to get the scuttlebutt on what kind of a law enforcement officer he is."

Sherri spent the next few hours searching for information. On one particularly gossipy law enforcement Listserv, she found complaints about Purvey's shortcomings. Included were details of several cases that had been thrown out of court because of botched evidence. Such things happened every once in a while, but the posts left the impression that Purvey was at best incompetent and at worst dirty.

Looking up the names of all the itinerant laborers

Snowe had hired added to Gina's bill but was otherwise unrewarding. Then Sherri typed in "Kitty Sloan" and got a hit.

"Well, well," she said to herself as she read the report. Kitty's criminal record didn't appear to have anything to do with the mysteries surrounding the Christmas tree farm, but it sure was interesting.

Chapter Ten

The fire marshal didn't finish his examination of the scene of the crime until after three that afternoon. Unlike Wyatt Purvey, he didn't imply that someone in the house had set the fire, but he did confirm that it *had* been set. When he asked them what accelerants might have been stored on the property, Liss referred him to Andy Dutton. Once he'd written down their contact information, he left, taking the stale smell of smoke with him.

"He didn't say anything about requiring us to stay in the area." Dan glanced at his watch. "We can be home in a little more than three hours. We might even catch the tail end of the six o'clock news."

But before anyone could make a move toward the bedrooms where their suitcases were waiting, already packed, Liss's cell phone rang. She looked at the caller ID and grimaced. "I've got to take this. I had to make do earlier with leaving Gina a voice mail."

She barely managed to say hello before the other woman burst into speech. Liss held the phone farther away from her ear as Gina unleashed a vituperative reaction to the news of the fire, but she seemed even more upset by the idea that Liss and Dan might abandon the property prematurely.

"You promised to stay for a week," she shrieked. "Who's going to look after the place if you abandon it?"

Dan mouthed "Speaker," and Liss enabled that function, allowing all four of them to hear both sides of the phone conversation. To Gina, she said, "It's not like we had a contract signed in blood."

"We had a binding verbal agreement." The shrill fishwife's voice vanished, replaced by the cold, calculating tones of a highly paid big-city attorney.

"Are you planning to sue me?" Torn between outrage and amusement, Liss gave in to her sense of the ridiculous and laughed. "Give me a break, Gina."

"Well, you can't leave yet." Now she sounded more grumpy than litigious. "I just sent you a package, something I'd forgotten I had. It's a box Dad took from the farm when he went there after his uncle disappeared."

Liss's grip on the phone tightened. "What's in it?"

That Gina took so long to answer a simple question turned speculation into direst suspicion. Liss took note of the skepticism in Sherri's eyes and the exasperation on Dan's face. They were all wondering if Gina had a hidden agenda, after all. Had "forgetting" about the box been an honest oversight, or was this a move calculated to make sure Liss and Dan stayed put?

"There are some personal items in it," Gina said, sounding as if the information was being pried out of her. "Letters and papers and a few snapshots. You'll see for yourself if you stick around. The package is scheduled for delivery tomorrow afternoon."

"We were planning to leave today. In a few minutes, in fact."

Dan muttered something unintelligible under his breath.

"What will one more day matter?" Gina asked.

"I'm not sure we're safe here."

"Nonsense. You've had a run of bad luck. No one's out to get you. Or me, either," Gina added as an after-thought.

"Now you're contradicting yourself," Liss pointed out. "A minute ago, you thought the house needed pro-tecting."

"You misunderstood."

"Did I?"

In her ear, Gina the lawyer blathered on, making her case for them to honor their "contract." Liss barely lis-tened. Would it be dangerous to stay one more night? Whoever had been responsible for the fire was unlikely to try anything else so soon afterward. He or she would have to know that there was an investigation going on and that, even if Liss and Dan wanted to leave, their de-parture might be delayed by a "request" by law enforce-ment officials to stick around.

Of course, that reasoning assumed that the person who'd set the fire wasn't completely bonkers.

Gina was still yammering away when Liss tuned in again. "I'll call you back this evening," Liss said and abruptly broke the connection.

"So now what?" Sherri asked. "Do we go home or stay another night? Pete doesn't have to be back to work until midnight tomorrow, and I'm off for three more days, if that helps any."

"I'd like to see what's in that package," Liss said.

Dan looked as if he wanted to argue, but before a de-bate could ensue, a car pulled into the parking area.

"We ought to charge admission," he muttered, but he had to smile when he saw who it was.

Somehow, Rowena Luckenbill managed to make a winter coat, a knit hat, and heavy boots look as unsubstantial as a fairy's wings. It was quite a trick for a woman who was nowhere near tiny in stature herself. *The power of the mind,* Liss supposed. That Rowena thought of herself as ethereal convinced others that she was.

"I'm so sorry to descend on you without warning," she said after she'd been introduced to Sherri and Pete, "but I heard about the fire and I wanted to make sure the maze was still intact."

"I'm afraid it was the maze that burned," Liss said.

"There's *nothing* left?"

"Charred trees."

Liss glimpsed Sherri's thoughtful expression and frowned. With all that had happened, she'd lost sight of the crucial fact that it hadn't been just any field the arsonist had destroyed. It had been Snowe's maze.

"I'd still like to see it," Rowena said.

"Give me a minute to get my coat and I'll go with you." Maybe seeing the destruction for herself would spark an idea. She hoped so. At the moment she had no clue why anyone would target Simeon Snowe's Christmas tree farm.

Dan said nothing, but Sherri offered to accompany them.

A few minutes later, the three women stood at what had once been the entrance to the maze. The sun was low in the sky, but it had done its job well throughout the day. Patches of brown grass showed here and there, where the snow had completely melted. Where the fire had burned, the ground was bare, well trampled, and black.

"Why would someone do such a thing?" Rowena whispered. "I was so looking forward to seeing Simeon's maze."

There was not much left that resembled one. Here and there, soggy and misshapen stumps thrust up out of a dark scar that covered nearly an acre. An acrid stench hung over the scene, still strong enough to make them cough when they got close. Liss wondered if she'd ever be able to enjoy the smell of a wood fire again.

"Why *this* field?" Sherri asked the question that had already occurred to Liss.

"What do you mean?" Rowena blinked and tore her gaze away from the devastation.

"Was it because of its location? Because the trees were smaller and might be expected to burn more quickly? Or because the maze itself was significant in some way?"

"Hardly anyone knew there *was* a maze here. Did you tell anyone?" Liss asked Rowena. "Or mention you were coming out here to look at it?"

"No, I didn't. But you and I were talking about it at the dance studio. One of the others might have over-heard us. I expect my daughter did. She doesn't miss much."

Rowena had told her that she had a daughter, but for some reason Liss hadn't thought she lived in New Boston. "I didn't realize your daughter was in our aero-bics class."

This surprised a chuckle out of Rowena. "She isn't. She's the teacher."

"Juliette? Juliette Cressy is your daughter?"

"Well, you needn't sound so shocked!"

They moved away from the burned field, slogging back toward the house through slush and a few patches of mud.

"Aside from height and build, you two don't look much alike," Liss said.

"She inherited her father's features," Rowena admitted. "His personality, too, more's the pity, but we muddle along all right."

"You told me Simeon Snowe didn't care for your daughter," Liss ventured. She was remembering the poem Snowe had written, but then she thought of the photograph she'd seen of Rowena and Juliette and Snowe together, all smiles and friendliness. "Did she know you were seeing him?"

"Of course she did." Rowena huffed a bit on the slope below the Quonset hut and paused at the top of the rise to catch her breath.

What Liss really wanted to know was why Juliette had lied to her, claiming she hadn't known Simeon Snowe. Instead she asked, "Would she have found it odd that he planted a maze as a surprise for you?"

"Oh, no. She knew he sometimes had silly, romantic ideas." A reminiscent smile lit Rowena's features. "That's how we met, you know. He was taking ballroom dancing lessons, and I was working late one night and ran into him coming out of the dance studio. Poor man. He was so embarrassed. A lot of men are, you know. They take Juliette up on her offer of private lessons because they think people will make fun of them if they join a class. Most of them, once they get past the first few sessions, discover that they enjoy dancing. Why, one of Juliette's students," Rowena added, a touch of maternal pride in her voice, "Harlan Woolgar, has taken private lessons from her ever since she opened the studio."

On that note, having reached Rowena's car, Liss and Sherri said their good-byes and returned to the farm-house. Liss stepped through the door and sniffed, inhaling the enticing aroma of baking chicken. They found Pete and Dan in the kitchen. Dan was seated at the table, his broken ankle propped up on a second chair. Pete stood before the sink, washing vegetables.

"I take it we're staying another night," Liss said.

"I figured you three would outvote me," Dan said, "so I conceded the election."

"And I started making supper before he could change his mind," Pete remarked, winking at Liss as he said it.

She couldn't help but smile. "Hang on to this one," she told Sherri. "He's one in a million."

"Oh, I know, and I intend to. He cooks. He cleans. And, back when Amber was a baby, he even changed diapers."

Dan gave a theatrical shudder. "Stop making the rest of us look bad," he told Pete. "Real men are supposed to turn green at the first whiff of baby poop."

Liss was turned away from him, hanging up her coat, but she swore she could feel Dan's eyes boring into her. She knew she should turn and smile and make some snappy comeback, but the subject hit a little too close to home. Instead, she took the coward's way out and fled, mumbling something vague about needing to phone Gina again and using the phone in Simeon Snowe's office.

*   *   *

"Any joy from Gina?" Sherri came into the office, bearing a plate of cheese and crackers. "There's wine in the kitchen if you want."

Liss shook her head. She closed the e-mail program and shoved the wheeled chair away from the computer. The monitor reflected her face, disgruntled look and all.

"No joy or no wine?"

"No to both. Gina didn't answer her phone, so I sent her an e-mail. I told her we were going to take things a day at a time." She snagged a slice of sharp cheddar and looked up in time to catch Sherri's expression. "Do you still think she's up to no good?"

"I know it's petty of me, but I'd love to see Gina get her comeuppance one of these days." She held up a hand before Liss could say anything in the other woman's defense. "I know. Get over it. Pete tells me the same thing." With a sigh, she plopped down into the only other chair in the room, an ugly green leather monstrosity patched with silver duct tape, and set the plate on the small table next to it.

"I did catch Zara at home. I asked her if she knows Juliette Cressy. She doesn't. She's never even heard of her or her dance studio, but she said that isn't really surprising. Dance instructors don't exactly have a union." Liss wheeled herself closer to the food.

"No social networking?"

"If they do, Zara didn't mention it. Then again, she doesn't spend much time online. The computer she uses for bookkeeping isn't even hooked up to a modem. She says she doesn't need a high-speed Internet connection, especially not at the monthly fee our one and only local cable company charges."

"You've been in here awhile," Sherri remarked as she

selected a cracker and topped it with a thin slice of cheese. "What else have you been up to?"

"Know me that well, do you?"

"Yup. So give."

"I called Andy. She heard about the fire. Well, she could hardly help it. The fire trucks had to go right past her house, sirens blaring. If it had been daylight, she'd have been able to see the smoke from there."

"I'm surprised she didn't show up here first thing this morning to check out the damage."

"Her mother threw a hissy fit when she tried to leave the house."

"Mrs. Dutton must have loved it when the fire marshal stopped by."

Liss didn't bother concealing her grin. "Andy said that she insisted on sitting in on the interview."

"As if she was afraid he might arrest her baby girl?"

"Who knows? Anyway, Andy told him that there were no accelerants stored on the property, and she says he seemed satisfied with that. She also told me something else you may find interesting. No one ever showed her a picture of our John Doe. So that's what I've been doing the last little while—trying to find one online." After all, it had all started with him.

Sherri didn't comment at once, since she had her mouth full. After she'd swallowed, she held out a hand. "Pass me my laptop." She'd left it on the desk, next to the computer monitor.

Liss nibbled and waited, glad Sherri had resources beyond Google and Bing. A few minutes later, her friend turned the screen around so Liss could see what she'd found.

"There you go. John Doe himself."

"Ugh." The photograph showed a man's face, eyes closed. He looked *very* dead.

"This was probably in the local paper. I'm surprised Andy didn't see it there."

"Her mother must have censored it. Andy was still a teenager at the time."

"Did the police question her at all?"

"I asked her that. Mike Jennings talked to her, but he didn't tell her anything except that Snowe was missing. He didn't say a word about John Doe. She picked that up at school."

Sherri sighed. "Pete says Mike is a nice guy, but there's such a thing as being too considerate of someone's sensibilities. If John Doe spent any time at all at the tree farm before he was murdered, Andy would have been the most likely person to have seen him."

Liss overcame her initial revulsion and studied the photo. The face was long and thin, with a blade of a nose and a scar on one side of a high forehead. The lips were thin and looked cruel—but perhaps that was her imagination working overtime again.

"Quite a piece of work, isn't he?" Sherri asked.

"I can't believe no one recognized him. He ought to have stood out in a crowd." She relinquished the laptop. "A pity you can't see his eyes. What is it they say? The eyes are the mirror of the soul?"

With intense concentration, Sherri began to type. "There's one more thing I can try. My contact in New York may be a little more forthcoming if I tell him about the fire."

Both women jumped when Pete entered the room through the door behind them.

"Chow's ready," he announced. "You two want to eat or what?"

After supper, Sherri returned to Snowe's office alone. As she'd hoped, she had a reply to her e-mail, one that contained an attachment. She opened it to find an artist's sketch of John Doe. The eyes Liss had been curious about were small and set too close together.

He was the victim, she reminded herself. He couldn't help the way he looked. But every feature screamed "Villain" at her.

The e-mail itself also contained a description—height and weight and coloring. As Liss had suspected, he had been a small man, only five-foot-seven and 140 pounds.

It occurred to Sherri that she ought to take a look at a netter for herself. A glance at the clock on the wall told her it was late, but not all *that* late. If Liss asked Andy Dutton to join them in the Quonset hut, she could explain how netters worked and take a good, hard look at the two likenesses of John Doe while she was at it.

A half hour later, Sherri, Liss, and Andy stood in front of the two remaining netters.

"Mr. Snowe had three of these out into the field during the harvest," Andy said. "We stacked the netted trees on pallets until they could be picked up."

Sherri gave the handle of one of the netters an experimental turn. It looked easy enough to operate. There was even a hook to help haul the tree—or the body—into the net. She reached into the pocket of her coat to retrieve the printouts she'd made of the photograph and the sketch. Unfolding both, she handed them over to Andy. "Have you ever seen this man before?"

"No. Who is he?"

"That's the question, isn't it?" Sherri asked.

"He's the man in the netter," Liss said.

"The police should have shown you these pictures seven years ago," Sherri said.

Andy gave a rueful laugh. "My mom would have had kittens. Bad enough she had to let them ask me about Mr. Snowe. She didn't even want me to hear about the guy who got gunned down and put through the netter."

Sherri stared at her. "Gunned down? What are you talking about?"

"You know, shot." Andy put her index finger to her temple and mimed firing a pistol.

"John Doe didn't die from a gunshot wound."

"Yeah, he did," Andy insisted. "That's what everybody at school said."

"Well, everybody got it wrong. No gun. No bullet wound."

Liss had an odd expression on her face. The light fixture in the Quonset hut gave it a greenish cast. "Do I want to know what did kill him?"

"Probably not."

"Well, I do," Andy said.

Sherri's hesitation only made her more determined. Hands fisted on her hips, chin thrust out at an aggressive angle, Andy was a formidable sight. *Strong enough,* Sherri thought, *to have wrestled a man of John Doe's size onto a netter table and through the machine.*

"My contact in New York was pretty cooperative once I told him about the fire, although he's not convinced it has any connection to the murder. He sent that sketch, and he also told me that John Doe was still alive and was probably bleeding from a blow to the head when he was put through the netter. The actual cause of death was suffocation."

Startled, Andy blurted, "You mean the trees—"

"Smothered him. Yes," Sherri said.

"How horrible," Liss whispered.

It was a sickening image. No question about that. But Sherri knew of worse ways to die. She kept her focus on Andy, trying to decide if the young woman knew more about John Doe's death than she was saying. She took back the photo and sketch. "How did you first hear about the dead man?"

Andy didn't even have to think about her answer. "From one of the kids at school. Everybody was talking about it—how he'd been shot and wrapped up like a tree. I was mad because Officer Jennings never said a word about the dead guy when he asked me when I'd last seen Mr. Snowe. Joey Crockett was the one who spread the word. It should have been me."

The surname rang a bell, but Sherri couldn't place it. She glanced at Liss, who seemed equally at sea. "Who's Joey Crockett?"

Andy had eased herself onto one of the sturdy netter tables. Her boot heels thumped rhythmically against the supporting legs. "His mother is the dispatcher at the police department. She knows *everything*." Suddenly she grinned. "Except that she got that wrong, didn't she? He *wasn't* shot."

"Did you help in the search for Simeon Snowe?" Sherri asked.

"Mom wouldn't hear of it. Of course, there wasn't much point in anybody looking for the first day or two, what with the weather and all."

Sherri cocked her head. "Bad, was it?"

With her hands dangling between her legs, Andy seemed perfectly relaxed as she talked about events seven years in the past. She'd unbuttoned her coat, showing off yet another Christmas-themed wool sweater. This one featured a giant Santa Claus face.

"There was a freak October snowstorm," she said. "We got out of school early the day after I talked to Officer Jennings, and everything was closed down the day after that."

By the time the search resumed, any tracks, and any scents for dogs to follow, would have been obliterated. Sherri wondered why Mike Jennings had omitted that little detail when he talked to Liss and Dan.

"Are you going to find out what really happened?" Andy asked.

"Only if we're very lucky. Tell me, has anyone shown an interest in this property, particularly in the field where the fire started?"

"You mean lately?"

"Any time in the past seven years."

"What's so special about that crop?"

"Don't you know?" Sherri shot back.

Andy shrugged. "The trees were planted closer together than usual. It was the last crop Mr. Snowe put in before he disappeared. He fussed over it."

"What do you mean?" Liss asked.

Another shrug was her answer.

"This could be important, Andy," Liss said. "Exactly what did Snowe do that constituted 'fussing'?"

"He kept moving the trees. I don't know why. It was like he was . . . I don't know . . . making tiny adjustments in the way they were arranged. He didn't ever seem to be satisfied. Every time I'd come over, he'd been doing more digging."

"Getting the pattern right," Liss murmured.

"Did you ask him about it?" Sherri asked.

"Sure I did. But he wouldn't answer me."

"Did you ever notice anything that would indicate that someone besides you and Mr. Snowe took an interest in that field?"

Andy shook her head. When she shoved her long hair away from her face, Sherri saw that she looked angry. "It was so *mean* to set that fire. What did those trees ever do to hurt anyone?"

"She doesn't know anything," Liss said after Andy left. "Not even that it was a maze."

"I don't think she does, no. Although I think it's a little strange that she seems to care more about trees than she does about people." Sherri moved closer to the netter. "Help me with something, will you? See if you can lever me up into this thing if I go limp."

Liss made a moue of distaste but admitted that she'd tried to envision the same thing when she'd first seen the netter and heard about John Doe. She was taller and heavier than Sherri and in good physical condition, but she had trouble maneuvering her friend's body into position. When she finally succeeded, she stopped to stare at the hook.

"What am I supposed to attach it to?"

Sherri twisted her head to look behind her. The red netting loomed above her. She took the hook from Liss, noting that it was metal and heavy enough to make a good weapon. Was that how John Doe had been knocked unconscious?

"Maybe he went through feetfirst," Liss suggested. "The hook could go into his shoe."

"I don't think so. Maybe his collar?"

"Creepy, no matter how it happened."

"Don't forget crazy. The netters were out in the field. If he was killed on the spot, he had to have been lured there."

"More likely he was brought. There's a logging road. Knock him out, put him in the bed of a pickup, and back up to the netter. Slide him out. Okay, can we stop hypothesizing now? I'm going to have nightmares as it is."

"Whoever did this was not a small person. Or a weak one," Sherri mused. "And if Snowe himself didn't kill John Doe, then it's a good bet the person who did intended to make it look like he did." She sat up. "So, who had a bone to pick with Simeon Snowe?"

"I haven't heard of anyone who was feuding with him. Mixed reviews as to his personality, but no one seems to have hated his guts."

Sherri joined her at the door. With one last assessing look at the netters, she switched off the light. "The murderer might not have been anyone local."

"Are we back to a mob hit?"

Sherri laughed. "No. This has 'impulse' and 'amateur' written all over it. Actually, I was thinking of Gina or her father. I'll be very interested to see what's in that package she sent you."

Back at the house, Dan had already turned in. Pete was watching the VHS tape of *Ghostbusters* on the ancient television set in the living room.

"Bed for me, too," Liss declared, although it wasn't much past nine.

Sherri sprawled in one of the overstuffed chairs and

tried to enjoy the antics on the screen, but the movie didn't hold her interest. Pete was nodding off on the sofa, but she was wide awake and restless. He woke up with a start when she pushed herself to her feet, grabbed the jacket she'd left on the back of a chair, and headed for the door.

"Whassup?" Pete mumbled in a sleepy voice.

"I'm going to make a quick run into town. See if I can score some Moxie." Since Liss hadn't known they were coming, she hadn't stocked any of Sherri's favorite beverage.

Pete's nose wrinkled. He didn't share her taste for Maine's official soft drink. "It's late. Do you want me to drive you?"

"Thanks for the offer, but you'd probably fall asleep at the wheel. I'll be back before you have time to miss me."

Ten minutes later, she stood in the infamous grocery store parking lot. It was deserted at this time of night, all the stores in the neighborhood closed and locked up tight. Sherri was not surprised. She'd have liked to be able to pick up a bottle or two of Moxie—she really had come to love the taste—but her alleged craving had also provided her with a handy excuse to take a look around. As Pete had predicted when Liss first told them about the olive oil, there was nothing left to see in the area where Dan had parked his truck.

She got back into the car and drove slowly along New Boston's empty streets. Apparently, they rolled up the sidewalks at an early hour on weeknights. Even Commercial Street looked deserted. She pulled in across from Dance-Ex. At All Things Mystical and several other retail shops, dim security lights cast a faint glow behind display windows. Everything else in the neighborhood was dark.

Sherri sat in the car, engine and lights off, staring thoughtfully at the storefronts. She wasn't certain what she expected to see, but when a light flashed briefly—a side entrance opening and closing—she went on alert. A moment later, a furtive figure emerged from the narrow alleyway next to Dance-Ex and scurried away. *A man,* she thought, although it was hard to tell when he kept to the shadows between the widely spaced streetlights.

If he'd been taking one of those private ballroom dance lessons she'd heard about, Sherri thought, it took the phrase "dancing in the dark" to a whole new level. Either that, or Dance-Ex had every window covered with blackout curtains.

She was about to follow the retreating figure when the front door of the studio opened and two women came out. They got into separate cars, both parked across the street from Sherri's vehicle. Sherri had seen photos of each of them online. The blonde was Juliette Cressy. The brunette was Kitty Sloan.

Sherri waited until both women had left the scene and then drove to the New Boston police station. She was hoping to talk to Mike Jennings. Instead, the moment she stepped into the tiny lobby, she came face-to-face with Wyatt Purvey.

This time she introduced herself properly. He asked for proof. She pulled out her ID and badge. He studied both for an insultingly long time.

"What do you want?" The question was his only acknowledgment that he believed she was who she said she was.

When in doubt, Sherri thought, *fudge.* "As you know, my husband and I are friends with the Ruskins, but I have another reason for being in New Boston at this time. What do you know about a young woman named Katherine Sloan? She goes by the nickname Kitty."

"Never heard of her."

"She was arrested a couple of years back for soliciting."

Purvey's thin eyebrows lifted a smidgen. "She's a prostitute?"

"That's what I'm trying to determine."

In court the first time, Kitty had argued that she'd been drunk and accepted a dare. She'd made an indecent proposal to a stranger who'd turned out to be an off-duty police officer. She'd made the whole thing sound like a silly college prank. The judge had been skeptical about her claims but had sentenced her to probation. The second time she'd been charged with soliciting, she'd spent time in jail.

"I don't know what kind of crime you deal with in Moosetookalook," Purvey said, "but we do not tolerate that sort of thing here in New Boston."

"I'm sure you don't, once you know about it. The whole point of an illegal operation is to keep it secret from local law enforcement."

"You're saying there's prostitution in my town?" The tiniest bit of red tinged his cheeks. "And just how would you come to hear about something like that?"

"I'm afraid that's privileged information at present. What I can tell you is that Kitty Sloan spends a lot of her time at the dance studio over on Commercial Street. It's possible she works there. Do you know the place?"

"I've passed by. I've never had occasion to visit the premises."

"Have you ever had any complaints about late-night activities?"

"Certainly not."

"I understand Ms. Cressy does meet some male customers after hours."

"She gives private dance lessons."

Interesting that he knew that, Sherri thought, since he claimed he'd never done anything more than "pass by" Dance-Ex. When she put his evasiveness together with the things Mike Jennings had said to Pete years ago and with the bits of gossip she'd picked up on the police Listservs, she had to struggle to hide her disgust. In her book, there were few things worse than a crooked cop. She had no respect for a chief of police who'd ignore a flagrant violation of the law when it took place right under his nose. If he turned a blind eye when it came to prostitution, what else was he capable of overlooking?

"If this Kitty Sloan has committed a crime in my town, rest assured I will deal with her." Purvey's sibilant whisper made Sherri think of every bad vampire movie she'd ever seen. "Don't you worry your pretty little head about a thing. I promise you, the wrong sort of person doesn't last long in New Boston."

Sherri was so incensed by his condescending manner that she almost missed the implied threat in his words. Everything he said in that whispery voice was creepy, but she was suddenly intensely aware that she was alone with him, late at night, in an otherwise deserted police station.

You're a trained police officer, she reminded herself.

She might be small in stature, but she knew how to defend herself. She'd been taught how to avoid being seriously hurt in a face-off against a belligerent, intoxicated man twice her weight and strength and how to take him down. Pete had added a few more moves to her repertoire, unsanctioned but effective. Sherri wasn't as religious as

Liss was about her physical conditioning, but she wasn't out of shape, either. Purvey was. Unless he pulled a gun on her, she had the advantage, and since they were still in the lobby of the PD, she was only a few steps from the door.

Seeing no sense in taking unnecessary chances, she left.

Chapter Eleven

On Thursday morning, Liss was up early. For a change, she had slept well and, having turned in before ten, had managed more than the eight-hour minimum she needed to function at full capacity. Dan was stirring but was not yet coherent when she slipped her feet into her pull-up boots—she'd forgotten to pack bedroom slippers, and the floors were ice cold—and headed for the downstairs bath.

She hummed off-key as she started the coffee brewing. She was pouring herself the first steaming cup, inhaling the delicious smell and thinking that there was no more perfect drink to start the day, when Sherri joined her in the kitchen.

"You're cheerful this morning," Sherri said.

Liss took a closer look at her friend. "So are you. Is that cat-ate-the-canary smile Pete's doing?"

"Not this time." Sherri chuckled. "In fact, Pete knows nothing about what I was up to last night." She poured herself a glass of juice and sat down next to Liss.

"What did I miss?"

Sherri told her what she'd seen at the dance studio. "I think Juliette's selling sex on the side. And if she's employing Kitty Sloan, then she's a madam, as well as a prostitute."

"That's an awfully big leap."

"Not really. Young Kitty was arrested a couple of years back for soliciting. Looks to me like she's continuing on that same career path."

"If you're right, why haven't they been arrested?"

"My hunch is that Wyatt Purvey doesn't want to know what's going on. It's supposed to be a victimless crime, after all. Some people don't see the harm in it. Purvey may prefer to let her keep on breaking the law rather than put up with the publicity busting her would generate." She took a long swallow of orange juice. "Or she could be paying him to look the other way."

From the jumble of thoughts in her brain, Liss plucked one. "Rowena doesn't know. She thinks Simeon Snowe went to her daughter to learn to dance."

"I don't imagine either Juliette or Snowe wanted her to find out the truth." Sherri leaned a little closer and lowered her voice. "But I haven't gotten to the best part of the story yet. After I saw Juliette and Kitty, I had a little chat with Wyatt Purvey himself. He threatened me."

"And you're *happy* about that?" Liss tried to imagine sitting there, calmly sipping her juice, if she'd been the one in Purvey's sights.

"I thought about it most of the night," Sherri said. "His reaction screams guilty conscience, and I don't just mean over Juliette's sideline. As much as I hate the idea that someone in law enforcement could turn out to be a killer, Wyatt Purvey meets all the requirements. He had motive, means, and opportunity, especially motive, to kill our John Doe."

"What motive?" Bewildered, Liss emptied her cup in three big gulps, but the caffeine didn't help. Sherri's logic still eluded her.

"He's obsessed with keeping what he calls 'the wrong sort of person' out of New Boston. I don't know exactly what threat John Doe posed, but I think Purvey saw him as one and got rid of him."

"Then you ought to be quaking in your boots."

Sherri waved off the warning and got up for a refill.

"Have you been listening to yourself? I don't like Wyatt Purvey any more than you do, but *murder?*"

In the distance, the stairwell door opened and closed. Liss heard Pete's voice and then Dan's. Sherri touched Liss's shoulder. "I'm not ready to share my thinking with Pete yet."

"Fine with me." Talk about dreaming up far-fetched scenarios! Liss wasn't at all sure Sherri was right about Juliette and Kitty, let alone the chief of police.

It wasn't until after breakfast that the two women had another chance to talk in private. On the theory that they'd head home as soon as Gina's package arrived, Liss decided to strip the beds and wash the sheets before they left. She was upstairs, hauling the covers off the bed Sherri and Pete had used, when Sherri joined her.

"I don't know about this theory of yours." Liss tugged the fitted sheet away from the corner of the mattress. "*Maybe* I can see Purvey killing John Doe, but why would he put him through the netter?"

"To muddy the waters. Make it harder to figure out why he was killed." Sherri grabbed a pillow and divested it of its case.

"And Snowe? Did Purvey kill him, too?"

"He must have. Maybe Snowe saw him with the

body. Purvey was in an ideal position to misdirect the search parties. He must have thought he was in the clear until you and Dan turned up."

"All we did was ask a couple of questions." She reached for the other pillow.

"But you're *staying* here. You might have stumbled across . . . something."

"Like a body?"

"Or some incriminating information Snowe hid in the house. Who knows? But Purvey wanted you gone. When causing Dan's fall backfired and you stayed on, he set the fire."

Abandoning the sheets and pillowcases in a pile on the floor, Liss crossed the room to the window that over-looked the Christmas tree farm. The morning sun cast the blackened ruins of the maze in a harsh light. The recent snowfall was only a memory now. Every trace of it had melted away.

"Snow," Liss murmured.

What was it Andy had said? There had been an early snowstorm right after Simeon Snowe disappeared. The search had been suspended until the weather cleared. When it resumed, the ground would have been covered with a blanket of white.

Sherri came up beside her. "What are you thinking?"

Liss shook her head.

"Whatever it is, it can't be any crazier than my theory."

"Well, *that's* true."

Sherri punched her—lightly—on the arm. "Come on. Give."

"What if the reason the search parties didn't find Snowe above ground was that he was already dead and buried?"

Sherri followed the direction of Liss's gaze. "In the maze?"

"Andy told us that Snowe was constantly moving trees around. That would have made it easier to dig in that area and would have helped hide a burial, too. Then add snow on top and who would think to look for him there?"

Now it was Sherri's turn to be skeptical. "If he's buried there, it would be pretty stupid to set fire to the maze. Why call attention to that one section of the tree farm?"

"What if he thought everything would burn, not just the maze?" Liss rubbed her forehead, where an ache was beginning to build. None of this made any real sense.

"I wonder if they used dogs in the search," Sherri mused.

"Rescue dogs?"

"Or cadaver dogs. But I bet they didn't bring in either, especially if someone involved in organizing the search didn't *want* Snowe to be found."

"Wyatt Purvey? Sherri, you're developing a fixation with the man."

Sherri ignored the comment. "It won't do any good to share our suspicions with the local PD, not with Purvey in charge, but I wonder if the fire marshal knew about Snowe's disappearance. Being chief of the Moosetook-alook Police Department may not be all that impressive as far as credentials go, but maybe it will be enough to convince him to give me a few minutes of his time. With any luck, he'll start the ball rolling for someone on the state level to come out here and do some serious excavation." Sherri already had her cell phone out and was punching in numbers. "It's either that or do the digging ourselves."

"You're forgetting that Dan wants to leave this afternoon. And doesn't Pete go on duty at midnight?"

Sherri finished entering the phone number.

Liss left her to it, carrying away the sheets and pillowcases to add to those from the downstairs bedroom. The last thing she wanted was to be the one to find the body.

"I'm not real sure about this," Liss said.

Sherri made an exasperated sound. "You'll be fine."

"I'm still not convinced you're right about Juliette's sideline, but it's going to be awkward to have that possibility in my head and behave normally around Kitty and Juliette and, most of all, Juliette's mother."

"Will you get in there! You're already running late. That should be sufficient reason to explain why you look flustered."

Liss grumbled but got out of Sherri's car and crossed the street to Dance-Ex. Sherri watched until she was inside before setting off on foot.

It had been an interesting morning so far. The fire marshal had not been particularly interested in what she had to say, and when she'd brought Pete up to date, his reaction hadn't been encouraging, either. When Dan reminded Liss of her aerobics class, Sherri had seized on the excuse to go into town.

There was something rotten in New Boston. As long as she was here, anyway, she was determined to dig deeper into Wyatt Purvey's failings as chief of police. The logical place to start seemed to be John Doe's appearance in town a little over seven years earlier, and since Andy Dutton had never been shown the victim's picture, Sherri suspected that there were others who'd missed seeing it, too. Among them there might be someone who had actually encountered the man before he was killed. If she was really lucky, that hypothetical someone had seen John Doe in the company of Wyatt Purvey.

It was a long shot, but since Sherri didn't have any better ideas, she armed herself with a fresh printout of the sketch of John Doe's face and began to canvass the neighborhood.

Across the street and two doors down from Dance-Ex, the owner of a small antiquarian bookshop, Eloise Crandall, was happy to talk to her. "Never saw him before in my life." The elderly woman peered at the sketch through tiny wire-rimmed spectacles. "Cheating on his wife, is he?"

"Not that I know of."

"He looks the sort. Men! Can't trust them as far as you can throw them."

"He was in the area about seven years ago."

"Heeresboro? That's a good eighty miles from here. What was he doing in New Boston?" Despite a prominent hearing aid in each ear, she had apparently missed most of what Sherri said and had put her own interpretation on the rest.

Eloise adjusted her glasses until they perched on the very tip of her snub nose and took another look at the picture of John Doe. "That's the face of a man who'd sneak around in the middle of the night."

Sherri reached for the sketch, but the older woman eluded her with a deftness that belied her age. She carried it to the window, where the light was better.

"Definitely a wrong 'un." She jerked her head in the direction of Dance-Ex. "Is he one of *her* customers?"

Sherri stifled a chuckle. She made sure Eloise was looking at her, then spoke loudly and with careful enunciation. "You tell me."

"Ha! I bet he is."

"But you don't recognize him?"

"How could I? They come and go in the dark. Every half hour some nights. I live above my shop. I've seen them."

"She gives private ballroom dancing lessons."

"Lessons, is it?" Her laugh crackled like old parchment.

"Have you reported these goings-on to the police?" Sherri asked.

"Fleece? What fleece?" The twinkle in her faded blue eyes told Sherri the score. Eloise enjoyed being privy to scandalous goings-on at the dance studio. She had no interest in putting a stop to something so entertaining.

Sherri moved on to the next business on the block. In the course of half an hour, she showed the sketch to a dozen people with no results. When she asked if they'd noticed any unusual nocturnal activities in the area, she sometimes saw a flicker of unease in an expression, but no one admitted to knowing what she was talking about.

Once she turned the corner of Commercial Street onto Main, she no longer had a line of sight that included the dance studio. She continued on, showing the sketch and coming up empty. Only once did someone refuse to talk to her. The proprietor of an old-fashioned barbershop took one glance at John Doe's picture and told Sherri to get out. She felt his gaze follow her all the way to the computer repair shop on the opposite side of Main Street.

The owner was a cheery little man as round as he was tall and as bald as an egg. He introduced himself as Bucky Hogarth—she could guess the reason for his nickname when his broad smile gave her a glimpse of his teeth—but he didn't recognize the man in the sketch.

"He would have visited New Boston about seven years ago," Sherri said.

"Ah, well, I've been here for five. Before that I was running the business out of my house in Doddridge, the next town over. I was barely making ends meet. Now I drive twenty miles each way, but New Boston has a decent population base, enough to keep me in business."

"If you don't live in New Boston, I don't suppose you know your neighbors all that well."

"I beg to differ. I know everybody in the area. They're all computerized these days, aren't they? Who do you think installed those systems for them?"

"So, you know Juliette Cressy?" she asked. "And her mother?" she added as an afterthought. Bucky looked to be more of age with Rowena than her daughter.

"Of course I do. Lovely woman, Rowena. No mystery why she's been married so many times. Five," he added before Sherri could ask.

"*Five* husbands? What did she do to them all?"

He let out a whoop of laughter. "She's no black widow, if that's what you're thinking."

"What happened to her husbands, then? Divorce?"

"First one was a soldier. Killed overseas. Second one was an older guy. Rich, though. Juliette's father. He left money for his kid in a trust fund, and when she was old enough, she used some of it to start her business."

"And the other three husbands?"

"Let me see." Bushy eyebrows knit together as he considered the question. "I have trouble keeping them straight. I think number three was a construction worker. She divorced him. Number four ran a local dry cleaning service. He was sickly—probably all those dry cleaning fumes—and lasted only a year or so before he croaked. That last husband, though . . . I remember him. He was a real stinker, not worthy of her at all. Abandoned the poor woman just because he found out she wasn't as well off as he thought she was when he married her."

"How long ago was that?" Sherri asked. "Do you remember?"

"Of course I do. It was right when Rowena was getting ready to open up her shop. And I'll tell you what else I remember. That girl was furious when she found out what a louse her stepfather was. Told Rowena she should have known the guy was only looking for a meal ticket."

"No boyfriends since?" Rowena had told Liss that she and Simeon Snowe had kept their relationship quiet. Now she had to wonder if that had been more her idea than his. Five times burned would tend to make a woman shy of a sixth disaster.

"None that I know of." Color crept into his face as he leaned across his worktable. "Asked her out myself once, but she turned me down flat."

Sherri glanced at her watch as she left the computer repair shop. It was time to head back to Dance-Ex. If she got a move on, she could show John Doe's picture to the women in Liss's aerobics class before they scattered. She was considering what questions to ask Juliette Cressy and Kitty Sloan when a New Boston police cruiser pulled in at the curb in front of her and a uniformed officer emerged from the car.

Movement in the window of the barbershop caught her eye. Its unfriendly owner was watching her through the plate glass. Dollars to doughnuts, he was the one who'd called the cops.

Sherri shifted her attention back to the officer, her gaze dropping to the small nameplate pinned to his jacket. She bit back a smile. The barber had done her a favor. She was about to make the acquaintance of Pete's old friend Mike Jennings.

The aerobics class was over, but everyone except Josie Underhill was still in the changing room when Sherri turned up. Liss introduced her friend to the others and stood aside, resigned to the inevitable, when Sherri produced the sketch of John Doe.

Hearing one woman after another say she'd never seen him before got old fast. Liss wandered out into the hallway that ran between the changing room and Juliette's office. She didn't intend to snoop, but the office door was open. She was just in time to see Juliette reach into the top drawer of her desk, withdraw a bulging envelope, and hand it over to Josie.

Before either one of them could look her way, Liss hustled on into the studio. Had she really seen what she thought she had? Or had Sherri's speculations colored her perceptions?

She waited until she was buckled into the passenger seat of Sherri's car to tell her friend about the incident. "I can't swear to it," she added, "but it sure looked like there was money inside that envelope."

"Josie? Which one was she?"

"The redhead."

"Is she friends with Kitty Sloan?"

"Friendly enough to kid each other about sex." Liss repeated what she could remember of their exchange the first day she'd gone to aerobics class.

Sherri laughed. "That fits." She turned the key in the ignition but made no move to pull out of their parking space. "None of the women in the class recognized John Doe, but when I showed the picture to Juliette Cressy, she stared at it for a very long time."

"Had she seen him?"

"She said no. But then, she told you she'd never met Simeon Snowe." Sherri set the car in motion, but she drove only as far as Madison's.

"We have coffee at the house," Liss said.

"But this, from what you've told me, is one of New Boston's primo gathering places." Sherri opened the car door. "If you spot Harlan Woolgar, point him out to me."

"You'll notice the dog first—a beautiful golden retriever."

"Like that one?"

Only then did Liss notice that Jonas was tied to the bench in front of Madison's. She scrambled after Sherri as her friend crossed the street. She didn't have to guess what Sherri intended to ask Harlan Woolgar. Rowena had said he was a regular consumer of Juliette's "private lessons." Liss glanced through the window of the café in time to see Woolgar heading straight for them, a bag of freshly ground coffee in one hand.

"Oh, shoot! He's already on his way out."

Sherri reached the door a moment before it opened, the sketch of John Doe at the ready. "Excuse me, sir," she said, blocking his way. "Could you take a look at this, please? Have you ever seen this man?"

Woolgar glanced at the paper and shook his head. "Don't know him. Sorry."

Sherri caught his arm in a firm grip and passed the picture off to Liss. "Why don't you show this around inside while I have a few words with Mr. Woolgar?"

Reluctantly, Liss did as she was told. She kept an eye on Sherri through the plate-glass window and saw that her friend had convinced Woolgar to sit with her on the bench. Heads close together, they engaged in an intense conversation.

Liss made short work of her assignment. In a repeat performance of the scene at the dance studio, no one in the coffee shop recognized the artist's rendering of John Doe. She stepped back outside in time to hear Harlan Woolgar laugh and say, "I don't see what has you so riled up. Lots of folks know what's going on. Nobody much cares."

"Does her mother know?"

"Rowena? Of course not. But then, she lives on another planet. Was born on one, the way she tells it." Still chuckling, Woolgar gave Sherri a polite nod, and he and Jonas ambled away.

Liss sank down next to Sherri. "The mind boggles. Did he actually confirm that Juliette is a prostitute?"

"He did. It gave him the opportunity to brag about his active sex life. He said, and I quote, that he sees 'no harm in paying for services rendered.' "

"And why does he think you showed him John Doe's picture?"

"I've no idea, unless he assumes the dead guy was

also a customer. Who knows? Maybe he was." Sherri hit the button on her key chain to unlock the car as she rose from the bench. "We'd better get going. The boys will be wondering what happened to us."

"What are you going to do next?"

"There's nothing I can do for the moment. I'm way out of my jurisdiction. But there are a couple of ears I intend to drop hints into. And thanks to a conversation I had with Mike Jennings this morning, I think it's safe to say that the authorities will have a spy in the enemy camp if they want one. I may be off base to think Purvey is capable of murder—although the jury's still out on that one—but he's definitely guilty of dereliction of duty."

They made the trip back to the Christmas tree farm in silence. *So many puzzles,* Liss thought, *and so few answers.* Chances were good that they'd never know what had happened to Simeon Snowe or who John Doe really was. Unless Gina's package contained a surprise solution, they'd head home in a few hours, taking those questions with them.

Liss had completed the task Gina had set for her. Andy was better off for their visit to New Boston. But Liss hated the fact that Rowena would inevitably end up being hurt. She liked the older woman. She would be devastated to see her only child disgraced and put on trial.

When they pulled into the parking area at the farm, Liss's thoughts were still on Rowena. She did not look up until Sherri uttered a muffled expletive.

Two state police cruisers and a state police crime-scene trailer were parked next to Dan's truck.

On the verge of panic, Liss's imagination supplied a

dozen horrible scenarios, each more terrifying than the last one. "Dan," she whispered.

"Relax," Sherri said. "Dan and Pete are standing right there on the front porch. They're both fine."

But one of the officers was taking a body bag out of the trunk of his cruiser.

It was some time before Liss and Sherri were allowed into the house. The state police detective in charge had them wait beside the crime-scene trailer while he talked in hushed tones to another trooper. Then they were questioned, not about what was happening in the field, but about who they were and what they were doing at the Snowe farm. Finally, when they'd satisfied the officer that they had a right to be there, he ordered them to go inside and stay put.

Ten minutes later, fresh mugs of coffee in front of them, Liss, Sherri, Pete, and Dan were in their accustomed places around the kitchen table. Liss looked from Dan to Pete. "Busy morning?"

"You could say so. Blame it on my wife. She told me about that cockamamy theory you dreamed up and the fire marshal's reaction to it." There was a sheepish expression on Pete's earnest, square-jawed face. "What can I say? Dreams of treasure buried at the center of the maze danced in my head. I couldn't resist going out there and poking around a little."

"Digging, you mean?"

He nodded. "The remains were pathetically easy to find. He wasn't buried very deep."

The insouciance Liss had been aiming for abruptly collapsed. "Better you than me," she muttered and reached for the coffee, wishing it was something stronger.

"So," Sherri said. "We have a second murder victim, because he certainly didn't bury himself in that field. It's undoubtedly Snowe, although that won't be official for a while yet. Any guess as to cause of death?"

Pete shook his head. "The only thing I could tell was that he'd been dead for a good long while."

Liss didn't want to picture what that meant. Neither did she want to do the next thing on the mental list she was making, but she didn't see that she had much choice in the matter. She retrieved her purse from the floor beside the chair and extracted her cell phone. "I've got to call Gina."

Sherri opened her mouth to object, but Liss cut her off.

"Her property. Her uncle." She thought about retreating to Snowe's office to make the call, but it didn't seem worth the effort.

For a change, Gina answered on the first ring. "Oh, good," she said before Liss could get a word in. "I was just about to contact you. A friend of mine had a great idea for making the farm profitable. What do you think of turning the acreage into a campground? We could leave all those overgrown trees as they are, to provide atmosphere. Our slogan could be 'Wilderness Camping Close to Home.' "

The suggestion left Liss momentarily speechless.

Abruptly, Gina shifted gears and launched into a list of things she thought needed doing in regard to opening the cut-your-own Christmas tree business on the day after Thanksgiving. "You haven't got much time," she added, as if Liss didn't already know that!

"Gina, shut up and listen. They've found your great-uncle."

"What?"

"I said they—"

"I heard what you said. I just don't believe it. Wait a minute. *Found* him? Alive or dead?"

"Dead, of course. Buried in one of his own Christmas tree fields. Probably murdered by the same person who killed that John Doe I told you about."

A lengthy silence ensued. Sherri made a "What?" gesture with both hands. Liss shook her head and waited for whatever Gina might say next.

"Did you get the package I sent you yet?"

Not what she'd expected. "It's barely noon, so I doubt it." She looked at the others, mouthed "Package?" and got a negative shake of the head from Dan. "Why? Is there something in it that—"

"I have no idea. You'll have to go through the letters and papers yourself. I didn't do much more than glance at any of them. Still, there could be something. What was the old buzzard up to?" she added, more to herself than to Liss. "People don't get themselves murdered for no reason." In a more forceful voice, Gina demanded Liss's promise that she'd call when she knew more. Then she hung up.

"That Gina—always such a delight to work with," Sherri said when Liss had summarized the phone conversation.

She might have said more if the state police detective hadn't come to the door. He interviewed each of them separately, in the kitchen, sending the others into the living room to wait their turn. Liss was last. After telling her exactly nothing, except that the area beyond the Quonset hut was off-limits, he took his leave.

The moment the door closed behind him, Sherri bolted into the kitchen and opened the refrigerator. "I'm starving!" she announced. "It's nearly two in the afternoon, and I haven't had a bite to eat since breakfast."

Liss's stomach growled, in full agreement with the idea of food, but before she could join Sherri in foraging for sandwich makings, she heard the sound of another vehicle approaching. "What now?" she grumbled, but she brightened when she saw that it was a FedEx truck that had pulled into the parking area. She went out through the front door to meet the driver, signing for a large padded envelope.

Forgetting about lunch, she took the package directly to Snowe's office and tore it open. The box inside was sealed with tape. She broke a fingernail removing it, but at last she had access to the contents. She cleared a space on the desk and tipped everything out onto the wooden surface.

There were letters, as Gina had said, some of them decades old, but there were also a fair number of photographs. Liss sorted rapidly, making three piles. Letters went into one. The second was for old photographs, including a tintype. Clearly those were family members, some of them ancestors Simeon and Gina shared. One of two of the women bore a strong resemblance to her old friend. In the third pile, Liss put more recent snapshots, mostly pictures of the Christmas tree farm. Among them were photos of some of Snowe's seasonal workers, but she didn't see anyone with John Doe's face.

When the smell of grilled cheese grew too strong to resist, Liss picked up the stack of letters and took it and the mailer with her into the kitchen. Liss, Sherri, Dan, and Pete divided them up to read while they ate.

There was nothing helpful in any of them.

Liss was about to toss the mailer into the recycle bin when she glanced at the label. "Huh! That's odd."

"What is?" Sherri asked.

"Look at the time this was sent. It was *after* I talked to Gina. It went out even later than that, if you consider the time difference. She didn't need us to stay because someone had to be here to collect this package. She hadn't even mailed it yet."

"But why lie about it?" Sherri asked. "Why was it so important that we stick around another day? Gina couldn't have known that would give us time to find her uncle's body. Could she?"

Chapter Twelve

Liss went back to Simeon Snowe's office to make yet another phone call to Gina, but this time there was no answer in Chicago. She was sent straight to voice mail. She didn't bother to leave a message. Instead, she rummaged in Snowe's desk until she came up with a yellow legal pad.

Her habit of making lists had often proven useful. In the present case, Liss hoped that putting everything she knew into a timeline would help her get a handle on what was going on at the Christmas tree farm.

She ran into trouble right off the bat. "Seven years ago" was not exactly a specific date. Liss didn't know any specific dates. That was part of the trouble.

Soldiering on, she wrote, "John Doe murdered and shipped out of state."

Item two was, "Body found in New York City and traced back to Snowe farm."

Liss left a blank next. She didn't know what Simeon Snowe had been doing between the time the body was shipped and the day Mike Jennings had come looking for him. Had someone tipped Snowe off that the body had been found? Or did he know all along that it would inevitably be discovered?

Frustrated, Liss carried the legal pad into the kitchen. Sherri had finished washing the dishes and was wiping down the table.

Once Liss explained the problem, Sherri whipped out her cell phone. A few minutes of conversation with her contact in New York provided one answer.

"Snowe's customer, the one who found John Doe and called the cops, phoned Snowe, too," Sherri reported. "He wanted his money back. He was pretty upset. The police confiscated the entire shipment of trees as evidence."

Liss wrote, "Snowe warned."

"So he knew ahead of time that he was going to be questioned."

"Sounds like it. Unfortunately, that proves nothing."

Liss made a face. "Either he wanted to avoid the police and hid out voluntarily, which suggests that he knew something about the murder, or the killer was worried about what Snowe might tell the cops and decided to make a preemptive strike by getting rid of him, too."

Sherri picked up the legal pad and read what little there was of the timeline. "This is good. Keep going. What else do we know?"

"Not a lot." Liss glanced around. "Where did Dan and Pete disappear to?"

"Dan's lying down." She held up a hand to keep Liss from running off to check on him. "Relax. A little residual headache is normal. Let him rest. And Pete left for Moosetookalook. He has to be at work at midnight, and I suspect he wanted some time with the kids before their bedtime."

"I didn't even hear him leave."

"You were in the office, right? Not surprising. It's at

the back of the house. You'd have noticed eventually, if not that Pete was missing, then that your truck was. He left our car so there would be room for the three of us when we're ready to go home," she added, seeing Liss's confusion.

"You didn't have to stay."

"Wild horses couldn't drag me away."

"We might never find out what really happened, or why."

Sherri handed her the list. "Finish it. Let's see what we do know."

Liss found she could add four more lines: "BOLO issued. Search delayed by freak October snowstorm. Snowe's truck found in field. Search abandoned—no trace found of missing man."

While she was writing, Sherri phoned Mike Jennings. "The manhunt ended eight days after Mike realized Snowe was gone," she said when she disconnected. "And they had the use of a dog for two of those days." Her brow furrowed as she thought over what she'd been told. "That makes it really odd that no one took a closer look at the area where we found the remains. Pete said he wasn't buried very deep."

"You mean he'd . . . smell?"

"Enough that the *dog* should have picked up the scent, even with snow covering the ground. Still, I guess Wyatt Purvey could have steered searchers away from the maze, assuming he was the one who buried Snowe there."

Liss heard the doubt in Sherri's voice. Her friend still thought Purvey was a dishonest cop, but her certainty that he was behind everything else that had happened had begun to erode.

Liss doodled a tombstone on the legal pad, complete with the letters *RIP*. "Maybe Snowe wasn't there yet."

"Explain."

Liss shook her head, uncertain herself what she meant. "If the dog didn't find the body, maybe it was because it wasn't there. I don't know where Snowe could have been, but maybe he wasn't in that grave until after the search was called off. What else did Mike say?"

"That there was nothing suspicious about that field. He remembers it—the one area where the trees were much smaller than any others on the property. The ground didn't seem to have been disturbed."

"But it was covered in snow."

"He said the snow melted pretty fast, the same way the snow from this last storm did. By the time they called a halt to the search, they would have been able to spot signs of a fresh burial."

"Why was the search called off?" Liss asked.

"Why do you think? The police couldn't justify wasting any more of the taxpayers' money. The state police and the police from New York were convinced that Snowe had killed John Doe and was long gone. Most of the local searchers didn't agree, but after they found Snowe's truck, they figured he was dead of natural causes or maybe suicide, somewhere above ground. They expected his body would turn up during hunting season."

"Two deaths and then nothing." Liss drew a line across the middle of the page. Below it she wrote the date she and Dan arrived in New Boston. "What did we do to alarm the killer?"

Sherri's answer was prompt and unequivocal. "You showed an interest in the maze. That has to be it. Who did you mention it to?"

"The subject kept coming up that day—the day Dan was hurt. Outside the police station when we talked to Mike Jennings. In Madison's during lunch. I told you about the acoustics in there. Anyone could have overheard what we said to Miranda."

"Harlan Woolgar was there at the time, right?"

Liss nodded. "But the grapevine in New Boston is in good working order. If someone overheard us talking or was told what we'd said, and if that person knew there was a body buried in the center of the maze, he or she might well have thought we were getting too close for comfort."

"Was anyone in Rowena's shop when you bought that book about mazes?"

"I don't think so. But she could have mentioned it to someone. She was very interested when we told her about it. Well, we know now that Snowe built it for her."

"All that was before Dan's fall. So it could be cause and effect. And then, when you didn't leave, the same person could have set fire to the maze."

"We've been through this before," Liss reminded her. "If the person who buried Snowe wanted to keep us from finding the body, it makes no sense to do something to call attention to that particular field."

"I hate to point this out to you—again!—but *none* of this makes much sense."

Liss sighed and put down her pen. Clarify the situation by making a list? Fat chance! All she'd done was raise more unanswered questions.

Andy Dutton turned up on their doorstep just as dusk started to fall.

"Why didn't you call me?" she demanded the moment Liss opened the door. "You found him, and you didn't *tell* me!"

"I'm sorry. You're right. I should have let you know what was going on."

She'd never given Andy a thought, or Rowena, either, but the New Boston grapevine had apparently been working overtime. When she'd ushered Andy into Simeon Snowe's office and made her sit in the green armchair, Liss decided this was good to know. It was to their advantage that everyone in the county, especially the killer, hear that a body had been found at the center of the maze. That should put an end to attempts to prevent the discovery. There was no longer any reason for anyone to hurt the innocent people staying in Simeon Snowe's house.

"The body hasn't officially been identified yet."

Andy glared at her, hands balled into fists. "Who *else* could it be? It isn't as if people go missing every day of the week around here. You should have called me right away."

"I agree it's a poor excuse, but everything happened very fast." She turned the desk chair around and sat, studying Andy's face. The glint of unshed tears shone in her eyes. "I didn't realize you were so fond of Simeon Snowe."

"He gave me a break. I owed him. Who killed him?"

"I don't know."

Andy leaned forward, her features earnest. "They'll find out, won't they? The police?" She sounded very young.

Liss reached across the short distance between them to place one of her hands over Andy's. "There are lots of people working on the case. And they never give up when the crime is a murder."

"Did *he* do it? The man in that sketch?"

Liss shook her head. "He died first. But the two deaths are connected. They have to be. Simeon Snowe was probably killed because he knew something about the other man's murder. Maybe you can help the police figure out what that was."

"Me? How?" Her anger had faded, leaving bewilderment behind.

"You were here that October. Think back to what you remember."

Andy frowned. "Harvests kind of run together. That was the third year I worked for him. The two years before that, he paid me to help out, even though I was too young for him to hire legally. I worked off the books." She shrugged. "Well, why not? I'd known him all my life. He was our nearest neighbor, after all."

"So you knew him well."

Another shrug. "I guess. I spent a lot of time here. I helped with both planting and harvesting from the time I was big enough to pick up a spade. He tolerated me when I was little. Later he encouraged me to get more interested in Christmas tree farming. He didn't have any kids of his own."

"He never married?"

She shook her head.

"No girlfriends?"

Andy considered this for a moment. "He wouldn't have talked about that to a kid, but I remember there was one woman who came out here once when we were netting trees. Not that last year. The one before, I think." Andy sank lower in the chair. "I wish I could think of something that would help find his killer, but it wasn't like he confided in me."

"Tell me more about the woman you saw. Did she have fluffy white hair?"

Andy shook her head. "No. It wasn't dark hair, but it wasn't white, either. She was tall. Taller than Mr. Snowe. And built." A suggestive gesture at bosom level indicated the relative proportion of that area of the body.

"And you didn't recognize her?"

Andy shrugged. "I don't know a lot of people from town, except for the ones I went to school with. I'm not much of a joiner."

The description was vague, but what there was of it seemed to fit Juliette Cressy.

"Do you think that woman had anything to do with Mr. Snowe's murder?" Andy asked.

"I doubt it." But Liss sincerely hoped the incident had taken place before Snowe started courting Rowena. She didn't like to think he'd been two-timing the mother with the daughter, especially since he'd have had to pay for the daughter's affections.

"Does Ms. Snowe still want to open this place up to cut-your-own customers?" Andy asked in an abrupt change of subject.

"I'm sure she does." Gina would never pass up an opportunity to make a buck or two. "As soon as the police let us back into the fields, we can take a look at the trees that are ready to sell. We need to talk about publicity, too."

"We don't have much time. Thanksgiving is only a week away." Andy got up, starting to button the coat she'd never bothered to remove.

Liss stopped her, catching hold of one lapel and easing the fabric aside to reveal yet another marvel of Christmas kitsch. "What's with the sweaters?"

Looking down at herself and a four-part design that

included the Grinch, a Charlie Brown Christmas tree, the leg lamp from *A Christmas Story,* and Grandma getting run over by a reindeer, Andy heaved a deep sigh. "My mother . . . likes Christmas."

"Ah."

"And when she's not making wreaths, she knits."

And Andy, Liss thought with a smile, instead of stripping off the results the moment she was out of the house, wore her mother's creations. Not every daughter would be such a good sport.

"I'll make a list of what needs to be done," she promised as she showed the young woman to the door.

On Friday, a week to the day after Liss and Dan left Moosetookalook to begin their adventure in New Boston, Liss once again woke up early. Once again, she left Dan sleeping to start the coffee. As she waited for it to brew, she went over the to-do list she'd made the previous evening.

After hearing Andy's description of the woman Snowe had shown around the tree farm, Liss had debated with herself about whether or not to attend the last of her prepaid aerobics classes. If she did, she wouldn't be able to stop wondering if Juliette's intimate relationship with Simeon Snowe had continued after he began seeing her mother. Juliette had known he was involved with Rowena. Rowena had said so.

She shook her head. "Don't think about it."

"Talking to yourself?" Sherri asked as she entered the kitchen. "That's a bad sign." She opened the refrigerator, foraging for juice. "What's your plan for the day?"

"Into town for aerobics. Then a meeting with Andy." Liss tapped the list. "There's a lot to be done before she can open that cut-your-own Christmas tree business. Do you want to come with me?"

Sherri shook her head. "Mike Jennings said he'd come by this morning. I have a few things I want to ask him about."

She reached into the pocket of her jeans for her car keys and tossed them to Liss, then turned the legal pad around so she could read what was on it. Liss put two slices of whole-wheat bread into the toaster and stood beside the kitchen counter, waiting for it to pop.

"Busy, busy," Sherri said, "but I don't see any mention here of driving back to Moosetookalook."

"We left what time we leave here up in the air," Liss reminded her.

"You know Dan wants to hit the road early."

Liss sighed. "I know. I just hate to walk out in the middle of the movie."

Sherri chuckled. "I'd like to find out who dunnit, too. Heck, I'd like to be the one to arrest that sucker. But I expect we'll both have to settle for hearing about it on the six o'clock news, if and when they catch him."

"I guess we *should* both go home and forget all about Simeon Snowe and John Doe and the rest of it."

"Yes, we should."

Sherri downed eight ounces of orange juice, and Liss ate her toast, sipping coffee between bites, each lost in her own thoughts.

As Liss had expected, Rowena had already heard the bare facts about the discovery of the as yet unidentified remains at the Snowe farm. Everyone in the aerobics class had heard something. They peppered Liss with questions the moment she walked in. While they changed into exercise clothes, she shared what few tidbits she knew to be fact with an attentive audience, but she refused to speculate.

"So he was there all along, right on his own property." Rowena looked sad but resigned.

"They can't be one hundred percent sure it's him until they do some tests," Liss said.

"Who else *could* it be? I guess I always knew he'd turn up dead one of these days."

Juliette poked her head into the room. "Isn't anyone going to work out this morning? You aren't going to stay in shape if you do nothing but gossip."

A few of the women looked torn, but they all trooped out into the studio.

"Everybody may have figured he was dead," Josie observed in a carrying voice, "but if someone buried him, doesn't that mean he was murdered?"

Rowena paled at the suggestion.

"Don't look so thrilled, Jo," Kitty snapped. "For all you know, the murderer could be living right next door to you."

"More likely it was some stranger who has long since moved on." Juliette didn't try to hide her irritation as she waited for her students to settle down. She was accustomed to having their full attention during class.

"Wouldn't it be exciting if it turned out to be a *serial* killer?" Josie's eyes went wider, while her smile got bigger. "Old Man Snowe wasn't the first victim, right?" She turned to Liss for confirmation. "That was the guy in the sketch your friend showed us."

"Enough!" Juliette reached for the volume control, cranking up the sound until none of them could be heard above the blaring music. Only after they'd completed the first routine did she lower the decibel level.

Rowena bent close to Liss. "Will you come back to the shop with me after class?"

"Of course."

Juliette's glare stopped her from saying more.

An hour later, Liss followed Rowena into All Things Mystical. Since her last visit, there had been changes, although the cat next to the cash register was the same.

"You've redecorated."

"The magic of Christmas theme," Rowena said as she began the routine of opening her shop. "When you think about it, there are all sorts of paranormal elements—flying reindeer, elves, a fat man who can navigate chimneys without getting burned."

"Or stuck." Liss admired the displays, thinking she really ought to get started on her own Christmas shopping. Books for her nieces and nephews. She'd have to go online and see what was new in mysteries for young people.

Lost in thought, she did not immediately notice that Rowena's usual joie de vivre was conspicuously absent. She'd retreated behind the sales counter to toy with the contents of the tray of jewelry. The jumble of items was in dire need of sorting, but Rowena's efforts were only making the tangle worse. Liss didn't recognize even half the symbols that decorated the amulets and armbands, necklaces and earrings. *Occult stuff,* she supposed. *Or, more likely, pseudo-occult stuff.* A pair of Goth girls, their garish makeup and the unrelieved black of their clothing marginally less jarring in these surroundings than in the rest of New Boston, entered the store and began to browse. Liss wondered if young people in other parts of the country still dressed that way or if rural Maine, as usual, was running a decade or two behind the times.

She was reluctant to broach the subject of Simeon Snowe as long as there were other people within earshot, but Rowena, having worked up her courage, had no such qualms. In a harsh voice, she blurted out the thought that had been haunting her. "It must have been someone local who killed him."

Long, thick hair dyed a flat black shifted as one of the Goth girls turned to stare at the proprietor. "The guy at the Christmas tree farm?" She had a high, fluting voice.

"Ooh, I heard about that," said her shorter, stockier companion. A silver skeleton dangled from one ear. An ear, Liss couldn't help but notice, that was an angry red, as if it had been pierced by an amateur and left to fester.

"Who was he?" the first Goth asked.

"He was probably the gentleman who owned the place." Rowena answered readily enough, but her firm tone of voice discouraged further questions. "Cash or charge?" she asked with a nod toward the rhinestone-studded dog collar the second girl was holding.

The transaction complete, the two young women left. Rowena breathed an audible sigh of relief.

"Are they typical of your customers?" Shopkeeper's curiosity aroused, Liss really wanted to know.

"I have no *typical* customer. I get everything from sweet little old grannies to preteens who wish they attended Monster High." At Liss's blank look, she shook her head. "Never mind. It would be impossible to explain to anyone over twelve. And, of course, I also sell dried herbs for cooking and healing and what have you."

"And crystal balls," Liss said, remembering.

Rowena laughed. "Yes, and crystal balls. A pity I can't really see anything in them."

"Why do you think it was someone local who killed Simeon Snowe?"

"Because I'm not a fool. Nor am I blind. Somehow, you stirred things up when you came to town. That fire was no accident."

"No, but why would Snowe's murderer call attention to the very place where he was buried?"

"Are you certain there's no connection between the two murders and the arson? It seems an awfully big coincidence otherwise."

"I'm not certain about anything," Liss admitted. "That's the problem. Can you think of anything that might help us—I mean, help the *police?* Did anyone visit Snowe at the Christmas tree farm in the months before his death?"

"He didn't encourage visitors."

"Why not?"

"He was a very private person." Rowena's brow furrowed. "No, that's not quite right. He was sociable enough when the occasion called for it. He volunteered his time at civic events and was generous with donations. But he also liked his privacy. That's why he blocked off the driveway." Her lips quirked.

Liss found herself grinning back. "*Snowe* put that sign up? The one that says that trespassers will be shot?"

Rowena nodded. "He wouldn't really have shot anyone, of course. He didn't even own a gun."

"And you, I take it, were always welcome?"

"He never kicked me out of bed." Voice dry, Rowena resumed sorting and untangling the items in the tray. This time, her fingers worked deftly to restore order. "Usually, though, he came here. He hinted that he'd like to make it legal, but of course, marriage was impossible. I'm still married to my fifth husband. He took off on me without a word."

"You could have done something about that, if it had been long enough."

"Have him declared dead, you mean? No point in that now. It isn't as if I can hope to inherit anything. He married me for *my* money."

"I meant divorce him for desertion. Isn't that possible? How long had he been gone when Snowe vanished?" Liss's heart went out to Rowena. She must have thought she'd been abandoned yet again when her lover went missing.

"It had only been a couple of years back then," Rowena said, "and I guess I kept expecting him to turn up again one day—like the proverbial bad penny."

Mike Jennings, as promised, stopped by the Snowe farm in mid-morning. Dan took Sherri's word for it that they had police business to discuss and made himself scarce.

"So," Sherri asked when she and Mike were settled at the kitchen table and he had a mug of freshly brewed coffee in front of him, "what's new?"

Jennings had the grace to look embarrassed. "I have a message for you from the higher-ups. You're to stay strictly out of all aspects of the investigation from now on."

"Which investigation? The one into your chief? The cold case? The arson? Or are they all connected?"

He managed a weak grin. "Sorry. I can't tell you that. I can only assure you that John Doe's murder is being actively reinvestigated, along with the murder of Simeon Snowe and the fire. Anything you try to do to help could jeopardize one or more of those cases. No more showing John Doe's picture to the locals. No more asking questions about Juliette Cressy's sideline, either."

"So someone's looking into that, too?"

"Someone is looking into everything you know about and a few other things besides."

"Like what?"

Jennings shook his head and took a long swallow of coffee.

Sherri wasn't surprised she was being told to butt out. It was standard operating procedure for the state police to take over murder cases. But this time she had a feeling there was more to it. "Are the Feds involved?"

"Sorry. Can't tell you that, either."

"What *can* you tell me? Come on, Mike. You must have some idea what's going on."

He shifted uncomfortably. "There might be an agent involved."

"ATF? FBI?" There were several possibilities.

"I shouldn't have said anything."

"Just promise me that *someone* is taking a long, hard look at Wyatt Purvey. I won't step aside if it means letting a dishonest cop continue to break the law."

"Yes, someone is working on that, but slowly. A rush to put Purvey in jail could mess up the other investigations. Nobody's going to be happy if that happens. Besides, there are a lot of angles to explore. Wyatt Purvey has been chief of police here for a good twenty years."

"Or a bad twenty."

Jennings groaned.

"Sorry. I couldn't resist."

He looked so miserable that Sherri took pity on him. He'd been dealing with suspicions about Purvey for a long time, unable to prove anything against his boss. At least now he'd been able to pass on what little he did know to someone who might actually do something about the situation.

"Did my questions to the chief about Juliette Cressy stir anything up?"

"Purvey's more antsy than usual."

"As he should be if he's been taking kickbacks or bribes."

Jennings wouldn't meet her eyes. "It could be more serious than that."

"*What* more?"

"Maybe embezzlement?"

Sherri gave a low whistle. "I don't suppose they can get him for two murders and a fire while they're at it?"

Jennings choked on his coffee. "He may be a crook, but he's not a monster." Still coughing, he stood. "For what it's worth, I'm in the same boat you are. They want me to steer clear while they gather evidence. We're both out of the loop."

Chapter Thirteen

Liss had arranged to meet Andy in the field full of ten-year-old Christmas trees. She remembered its location from the tour Andy had given them the previous Saturday morning. It wasn't far from the Quonset hut, an easy walk for customers, but it was also fairly close to the field that had burned and they'd have a clear view of the devastation.

She tried to look at the bright side. The wind could have spread the fire, sending their entire cash crop up in flames. And since these trees hadn't been in danger, no firefighters had trampled the area around them. "Pray for more snow," she said aloud, as if starting a new list.

By the time Andy joined her a few minutes later, Liss had her actual list in hand. "How are customers going to get their trees back to their cars?" she asked. "That slope below the Quonset hut isn't terribly steep, but I wouldn't want to carry a six- or seven-foot tree up it."

"Tarps," Andy said. "Bright red ones with ropes attached. You use it like a sled to bring in your tree."

"Where do we get some?"

"Mail order. I'll take care of it if you like."

"It'll have to be a rush order. As you reminded me

yesterday, you open on the day after Thanksgiving—one week from today." Some people put their trees up that early and left them up until after New Year's Day. Liss herself opted for a shorter season, since it left less time for the cats to wreak havoc.

"I've been thinking about that." All business, Andy whipped out a mail-order catalog. "We'll need to send in more than one rush order."

"Let's talk about that back in the house after we're done here. I assume we can order everything online?" When Andy nodded, Liss once again consulted her list. "What do we do about signage?"

"We could order signs, but if I make my own out of wood, they'll be sturdier and I can reuse them. Most will say CHRISTMAS TREES, with an arrow pointing in the direction of the farm, and, in smaller letters, how many miles away it is. For the last mile or so before the turn, I thought I'd make some signs shaped like Christmas trees. They'll give the distance, too. Then the next-to-last one will say ALMOST THERE! and finally there will be a big arrow where customers need to turn into the driveway."

Impressed, Liss checked that item off her list. "Should we place newspaper ads? Does anyone still read newspapers, or is it all online these days?"

"My mom still reads a real newspaper. Our little biweekly. I say we do both."

Why not? Liss thought, especially with Gina footing the bill. Based on what worked this year, Andy would have a better idea what was worth the money and what was not when she went into business for herself.

Back in Simeon Snowe's office, they went through the catalog Andy had brought and Liss placed their order.

After the younger woman left, Liss studied the items on her tree farm list and felt a deep sense of satisfaction. Each and every one had a check mark next to it.

If only she could say the same about her other lists.

While Liss was out in the field with Andy, Sherri left for a quick trip into town. Her yen for Moxie had only been an excuse the other night, but now she found she really did have a craving for the stuff.

The teenager at the cash register fit the description of the young woman who'd waited on Liss and Dan. She was popping gum at a furious rate as she rang up Sherri's purchases.

The small purse Sherri carried was stuffed to overflowing. She had to pull out a few items to free up her wallet and pay for what she'd selected. One of the things she removed and set on the checkout counter was the sketch of John Doe.

The clerk froze, staring at it with her mouth hanging open. "Oh, wow," she said after a moment. "It's the perv."

"The what?"

"Perv. You know, pervert." She stabbed her index finger into John Doe's face. "Who is he? I bet he kidnapped some kid, yeah?"

Sherri studied the young clerk's face. "You're certain you recognize him? It was a long time ago that he was in town. Seven years."

"Well, yeah. That's about right. But, man, did he make an impression!" Earnest as only someone barely out of their teens could be, the young woman hugged herself and rocked back and forth. "I was with a bunch of my friends. You can ask them. We all thought he looked scary. He was trying to get our attention. You know, 'Come here, little girl. I need to ask you a question.' I was the only one brave enough to go talk to him."

"Brave?" Sherri fought the temptation to launch into a safety lecture. "Don't you mean foolish? If you really thought he was up to no good—"

"Hey, my BFFs were right there."

"Was he in a car?"

"Yeah. A big black one. Tinted windows. The whole nine yards." Her eyes gleamed with enjoyment at being the center of attention. "And it turned out he really did have a question. He wanted to know if there was a dojo in town. I didn't even know what a dojo was. Some kind of gym, I guess. He said he needed a workout." Her face twisted into a grimace. "And he said that like it was something . . . you know . . . kinky. Like I said, a real perv."

Sherri returned to the car in a thoughtful frame of mind. She wasn't sure what to make of the young woman's information. It was possible she'd mistaken John Doe for someone else. Then again, maybe not.

She punched in a number on her cell phone. It wasn't as if she'd deliberately gone hunting for information after she'd been warned off. She had a duty to contact the authorities and pass on this new information. If she was lucky, they might feel inclined to let her know if the tip paid off.

The ensuing conversation went about as she'd expected. They thanked her very much and didn't share diddly-squat . . . except for one thing. The detective she talked to let it slip that they thought John Doe had gone to a lot of extra trouble to make sure he couldn't be identified by any of the usual methods.

What, exactly, did that mean? She pondered the question as she drove back to the Snowe farm. Probably that he was connected to organized crime. Maybe he'd burned off his fingerprints with acid. She grimaced. Then her lips twisted into a rueful smile. She wasn't at all sure criminals really did that. It sounded like an urban legend to her.

But if John Doe *was* a gangster, what had drawn him to New Boston? What was there here that could possibly interest the mob? *Drugs,* she decided. Maybe, if a shipment of trees could be used to hide a body, it could be used to conceal other things, as well. Maybe John Doe had been trying to pressure Snowe into helping him smuggle narcotics into New York City.

Did that mean that Snowe had killed him? And that when someone higher up in the mob had found out who was responsible for John Doe's death, he'd decided to retaliate?

"Nah," she said aloud. Aside from sounding like a badly clichéd gangster movie, that theory wouldn't account for burying Snowe in the maze or the haphazard attempts to keep Liss and Dan from discovering the body.

Coincidences do happen, she told herself. *Sometimes accidents are just accidents.*

She wished she could believe it.

Liss's cell phone rang twice while Sherri was out on her Moxie run.

The first call was from Gina, responding to a new message Liss had left on her voice mail. She insisted she hadn't lied about when she'd sent the package.

"I gave it to my secretary to mail and assumed that it

had already been picked up from the office by the time I told you about it. You're lucky it didn't take two days to get there," she added. "That's what 'overnight' usually amounts to when I send something to rural Maine."

"Kind of beside the point, Gina." Liss gave her an update on the plans for the cut-your-own operation and then let her know, in no uncertain terms, that she and Dan were leaving New Boston later that afternoon.

Even as she carried on the phone conversation, she was in the downstairs bedroom, checking to be sure they hadn't forgotten anything. Once again, their bags were packed. The only chores left before they headed out were turning off the furnace and draining the pipes so they wouldn't freeze. Andy would come by later to pick up any food they left behind.

The second call was from Rowena Luckenbill.

"I remembered something after you left the shop," she said when Liss answered. "I have some photos of Simeon, pictures I'd forgotten all about until talking to you reminded me of them."

"What kind of photos?" Liss went to the living room window when she heard a car door slam, but it was only Sherri.

"Snapshots. Not long before he disappeared, he gave me a shoe box full of them. I was supposed to scan them for him as part of a community history project. He wasn't all that enthusiastic about the idea, but I convinced him that he owed it to his hometown to leave a record of the growth of his tree farm business. I was doing the same for my little store and for Juliette's studio. After he vanished . . . well, I didn't have the heart to go through them."

"Are there other people with Snowe in the photos?"

"I'm fairly certain there are in some of them, and I know he wrote on the back of each one—the date and so on. I don't have the pictures here, and my memory is a little fuzzy, but . . . do you think it's possible that man who was murdered is in one of them?"

Although she suspected that the snapshots were duplicates of the ones in Gina's package, the possibility that John Doe might be included, with the added incentive of a name written in Simeon Snowe's own hand to identify him, was too tempting to resist. "Where are they? Do you want me to come take a look at them?"

Dan walked into the room while she was speaking. She ignored his scowl.

"They're in storage." Rowena sounded relieved by the offer. "Do you think you could pick me up and drive me out to the storage lockers? I know it's an imposition, but I don't have a car. I live only a few blocks from the shop, so I walk to work."

"I can be there in fifteen minutes." Liss disconnected and turned to face Dan.

Sherri joined them, carrying a half-empty bottle of Moxie. "What's up?" she asked.

"I need your car keys." Liss plucked them from Sherri's fingers and headed for the kitchen to grab her coat. "I'll be back before you know it."

When Liss pulled up to the curb in front of All Things Mystical, Rowena was coming out of Dance-Ex. She flashed a macramé key chain as she climbed in on the passenger side.

"Perfect timing," she said cheerfully. "Turn right at the intersection. We have to go about five miles out of town."

"Did you stop to tell your daughter where we're going?" Liss asked.

"Why would . . . Oh, because I was in Dance-Ex? No, Juliette is busy with a class. I just popped in to borrow the key. It's her storage locker, you see. I just keep a few things there."

Liss couldn't help wondering what Juliette had stored. Business papers, perhaps? Something that would tie Wyatt Purvey to Juliette's off-the-books second career? A record of payments? She made a mental note to mention the possibility to Sherri when she got back to the Snowe farm.

The turn was marked by a dilapidated sign that read SELF-STORAGE. CLEAN. SECURE. The facility itself, located at the end of a dirt road and hidden from sight by a thick screen of evergreen trees, was a blight on the landscape. Ugly metal units, each fronted by an overhead door, lined both sides of a cul-de-sac. The circular drive was barely wide enough for a U-Haul or a van to pull in to be unloaded. Rowena directed Liss to number eleven.

"I don't remember the place being so run-down," she remarked as she eased herself out of the car, "but then, it's been years since I've been here. I usually give Juliette anything I want stored, and she brings it out here to stash."

"So, you'll have to hunt for Snowe's shoe box?"

"I'm afraid so, but with your help, it shouldn't take long to find it."

And looking for it, Liss realized, would give her an opportunity to snoop through Juliette's possessions. Should she? What if she actually found something incriminating? Then she'd have to call the police, and Rowena would find out how her daughter augmented her income. She would learn the truth eventually, but Liss didn't like the idea that she might be the direct cause of Rowena's distress.

At first the key refused to turn in the lock. After several unsuccessful tries, Rowena motioned for Liss to give it a whirl.

"Maintenance isn't very good here," Liss observed. "The entire door is rusty. It wouldn't take much effort to break in, and I'm guessing there's no burglar alarm."

"It isn't as if anyone has priceless antiques stored out here."

"Haven't you ever watched *Storage Wars* or its clones on television? They always find hidden treasures in abandoned lockers."

Rowena chuckled. "You don't think those reality shows are *real*, do you?"

At last the lock yielded. Liss pushed up the door. It didn't want to stay in place, so she held it with both hands above her head while Rowena found the light switch. To Liss's surprise, it worked.

Carefully, Liss eased the overhead door back down. It was as cold inside as out, and clammy to boot. A single fluorescent light fixture illuminated a space the size of an average one-car garage. There were no windows, so ominous shadows lurked in every corner. There were plenty of those. The entire space was filled with rows of six-foot-high stacks of clear plastic storage bins. Most of them appeared to contain file folders.

Here were Juliette's business records, all right, but the sheer number of bins was daunting. It would take hours, if not days, to go through all of them. Knowing how unlikely it would be that she'd find anything, unless there happened to be a file box labeled BRIBES PAID

TO CHIEF OF POLICE, Liss didn't bother trying to get a closer look at the contents.

Rowena craned her neck, birdlike, for an overall view of the unit. "We'll have to poke around, I guess." She squeezed through a narrow opening between two stacks of storage bins and disappeared.

Liss set off in the opposite direction. A few minutes later, at the back of the unit, she came upon an old freezer chest with several cardboard boxes piled on top. Rowena's name was printed on each of them. One also said TAX RECORDS, another OLD BANK STATEMENTS, and the third INVENTORY.

"I've got something," Liss called.

Rowena popped back into sight. There was a streak of dirt on the end of her nose. "Oh, yes. Those are mine."

Durable plastic for Juliette, Liss thought, but cardboard was good enough for her mother. The boxes already had a musty smell.

Rowena started to shift the cartons, placing each one on the floor beside the freezer until they were stacked in reverse order. Then she opened the top one. Papers rustled as she rifled through them.

"Ah! Here it is. At the bottom of the box, naturally." She hauled out an Old Maine Trotters shoe box held closed with several large rubber bands.

Rowena hastily stuffed the other papers back into the carton and left it sitting on the floor while she placed the shoe box on top of the freezer chest. She tugged at the rubber bands. Two fell apart, dried out with age. As she slid the others off, she frowned. "That's odd."

"What is?"

Rowena cocked her head. "Hear that humming? This freezer is running. Why on earth would Juliette leave it plugged in? What a waste of money." She looked around for an outlet.

"Hadn't you better check inside before you shut it down? Maybe Juliette has a secret stash of ice cream in there." Liss removed the shoe box and reached for the latch.

It stuck at first. Only when Rowena gave her a hand could they open the lid and look inside.

Rowena blinked, backed up a step, and whispered, "Oh, my."

Liss swallowed convulsively.

The body inside was frozen solid.

"Do you know who he is?" Liss whispered. Encased in ice, the man's features were distorted, but he was well preserved.

"Well, of course I do," Rowena said. "That's my fifth husband. The one who abandoned me."

In less than an hour, the storage locker had been sealed off. Official vehicles filled the gravel drive. Farther away, held in check by uniformed officers, news vans had disgorged reporters and camerapersons. They were gathering like vultures, Liss thought, eager to pick over the carrion.

With a sigh, she went back to studying her clenched fists. She was sitting in the back of a police car, forbidden to get out, ordered not to phone anyone. Rowena had been installed in the backseat of a second cruiser and given the same instructions.

With the two of them secured and his officers occupied with guard duty and crowd control, Chief Wyatt Purvey was alone inside Juliette's storage locker.

Liss didn't trust the chief as far as she could throw him. She was certain he was in there destroying evidence. If Sherri was right, he had a vested interest in covering up Juliette's shady business dealings. How far would he go to protect his connection to her?

She felt better when the first state police officer arrived on the scene. He was no more than fifteen minutes behind Purvey and his men. Except in Maine's largest cities, the state police took over from the local constabulary in a case of homicide. The chief of police was allowed to remain, but only as a courtesy. Someone would stop him if he tried to compromise the crime scene.

Another interminable hour passed. Liss squirmed in her seat. It was no longer the mind-numbing boredom of sitting there that made her twitchy. She opened the door and got out.

Instantly, a uniformed officer was at her side. "You need to—"

"What I really, really *need* is to find a powder room!" Liss told him. "Or an outhouse. Or a convenient bush. At this point, I'm not fussy."

He was one of those light-complexioned people who blushed easily. She watched a wave of red climb up his neck and into his face. "Just a minute," he blurted and turned away. Over his shoulder, he flung a command for her to stay put.

She did, but it required the occasional hop from foot to foot. And he thought *he* was embarrassed! She could have cried with relief when the familiar form of Officer Mike Jennings appeared and told her to follow him.

The storage facility had a tiny office that didn't look as if it got much use, but it came with plumbing. The minuscule restroom probably hadn't been cleaned since Lyndon Johnson was president, but Liss held her breath and got on with business. A few minutes later she emerged to find Jennings waiting for her.

"Thanks."

"Not a problem."

"Is anyone ever going to talk to us?"

"You and Rowena?"

She nodded.

"Eventually."

"My husband will be wondering what's happened to me. He'll be worried. I'm surprised he hasn't already called you folks to report me missing."

Jennings fought a grin and lost. "He didn't, but Chief Campbell has been in touch. I've explained to her that you'll be tied up a bit longer to help us with our inquiries."

So much for leaving New Boston today.

Jennings escorted her back to the police cruiser and closed her into the backseat once again. Yet another hour passed before a state police detective joined her there. She didn't know him, but he'd obviously done some checking into her background.

"So, Ms. Ruskin," he said after he introduced himself. "You seem to have a bad habit of stumbling over dead bodies."

She glared at him. "It isn't as if I go looking for them."

"Why were you here?"

"I gave Mrs. Luckenbill a lift so she could look for some photographs she'd stored in that unit. She found them. We were about to leave when she realized that the freezer was running and thought she should shut it off if it was sitting there empty. To conserve electricity."

"Did you open it up, or did she?"

"It took both of us to get the lid up." Liss tried unsuccessfully to repress a shiver at the memory. "And she was as surprised by the discovery as I was. She said he was her runaway husband. Her fifth."

"Who called the police?"

"I did. I had my cell phone."

"And Ms. Luckenbill?"

"She was in shock. I brought her outside, and we waited for the police to arrive."

"You didn't touch anything else?"

"I don't know. We were hunting for Rowena's boxes. I could have run a hand over some of the bins. But I had my gloves on because it was so cold. I don't think I left fingerprints."

"And you didn't know the deceased?"

"Not hardly. If that's the husband who ran out on her, he's been dead for over a decade."

The detective's stern features settled into lines that were even more grim as he wrote her words in his notebook.

"I don't mean to sound callous, but this has nothing to do with me. And nothing to do with the remains found at the farm where I'm staying. Not that I can see."

Nevertheless, he took her through it all again—their reasons for coming to New Boston; the John Doe from seven years back; Snowe's disappearance; Dan's accident; the fire; and, finally, the discovery of a burial in the middle of Simeon Snowe's blackened evergreen maze.

By the end of the recitation, Liss's stomach was in knots and a particularly gruesome possibility had occurred to her. The detective was about to put his notebook away when she added in a very small voice, "I couldn't help but notice that there's room in that freezer for more than one body."

He gave her a sharp look. "Are you suggesting that either John Doe or Simeon Snowe, or each in succession, was stored there temporarily?"

"I don't know what I'm suggesting. I had this mental picture. . . ." As her words trailed off, she shuddered. "Can I leave now? I've told you everything I know."

"We'll want to talk to you again."

"Of course you will." She knew the drill. He, or someone like him, would want her to repeat her story over and over again, until she was ready to tear her hair out in frustration.

He slid out of the vehicle and offered her a hand to help her stand. As she stretched, she saw that the cruiser in which Rowena had been seated was gone.

"Did someone give Ms. Luckenbill a ride home?"

"Don't worry about Ms. Luckenbill. We'll see to her."

His nonanswer stopped her cold. "Whoa. Hold it right there. Are you telling me you've arrested Rowena Luckenbill? On what grounds? I told you, she was as surprised as I was to find that body in the freezer."

"Her husband's body." Taking her arm, he steered her toward Sherri's car.

"Well, yes, but—"

"We'll be in touch, Ms. Ruskin." With one hand he opened the door for her and with the other gave her a none-too-gentle assist inside. Before she could sputter out a protest, he'd walked away. Two other state troopers closed ranks behind him as he strode toward the storage locker.

Liss called Dan. Then she drove to Dance-Ex. Someone had to tell Juliette what had happened. And what about Gozer? Who would take care of Rowena's cat if she was detained by the police?

Juliette was alone in her small office when Liss burst in on her. She blurted out the facts as she knew them. "You need to do something," she added. "The police think your mother murdered her husband."

A flicker of what might have been annoyance showed in Juliette's expression, but it was gone so quickly that Liss couldn't be sure. When she spoke, her voice wasn't just cold, but it was frigid.

"My mother *did* kill him. That's all too obvious. I always knew her tinkering with herbs and potions would end badly."

"What are you saying?" Liss could scarcely believe her ears.

"I'm saying what should be perfectly clear if you think about it for a moment. It grieves me to acknowledge it, but my mother has been living a lie all these years. It's obvious now that she's a seriously disturbed individual. She murdered my stepfather when he tried to leave her. God only knows why she killed that poor man they found in the netter. And then there was Simeon Snowe. I suppose he guessed she'd done it. How many people have access to a netting machine, after all? When he threatened to turn her in to the authorities, she killed him to cover up her earlier crimes."

Appalled, Liss backed away from her. And people thought *she* had an overactive imagination! "She's your *mother*, Juliette! How can you think—"

"I don't think. I *know*." Her thin-lipped smile made Liss sick to her stomach. "And you should consider yourself fortunate. Perhaps we both should. She could just as easily have murdered both of us in some mad attempt to hide what she's done."

Chapter Fourteen

"Well, that's one for the books," Sherri said when Liss had brought them up to date on the events of the afternoon.

She watched her friend down the herbal tea in her coffee mug and refilled it when Liss silently held it out. Dan had said nothing, but the frown on his face spoke volumes. That they were stuck here for another night was the least of what was bothering him.

Sherri patted him on the arm. "Cheer up. I'm sure we'll be allowed to go home tomorrow. If anyone needs to talk to Liss again, they can come to Moosetookalook."

"Juliette sounded like she was rehearsing what she was going to tell the police," Liss said. "She had her facts arranged all neat and orderly. Mom did it. End of story." She set the mug down with a thump that sent tea sloshing onto the tabletop. "I'd find it easier to believe that *Jonas* was the killer!"

Sherri went blank. "Jonas? Jonas who?"

"Jonas the *dog*." Liss sprang to her feet, then stopped, as if she suddenly realized she had no place to go.

Dan caught one of Liss's fisted hands in his and tugged on it. When she was close enough, he wrapped his arm around her waist. Once she was securely in his grasp, he sent a fulminating look in Sherri's direction. "I'll probably regret asking this, but what is it you two are afraid Wyatt Purvey was up to in that storage locker? What does the chief of police have to do with Juliette Cressy or her mother?"

"I was sure I mentioned that I thought he was crooked," Sherri said.

"Hints of police corruption aside," Liss said, "I doubt he put Rowena's husband in cold storage."

"That's not likely, no," Sherri conceded, "but he's guilty of a few other things. I'm certain of it."

"Even if I hadn't believed it of him before," Liss said, "I'd have been convinced by the look of panic on his face when he caught sight of all those records stored in Juliette's unit. And he was in there for a good quarter of an hour before the state police showed up. Who knows what he managed to walk off with?"

"He couldn't have taken much," Sherri said. "If he'd tried to carry away a plastic file box, someone would have noticed and stopped him."

"He could have hidden a manila folder or two under his jacket."

If he had, Sherri thought, there was nothing anyone could do about it now. Still, she was hopeful. Purvey didn't know it, but he was already under investigation. The state police would thoroughly examine every item in that storage locker. If there was anything there that linked the two cases, it would come to light. So long as everyone jumped through the right legal hoops, it would be admissible as evidence against the chief of police.

Liss pulled away from Dan and began to pace. "There's one thing I didn't tell you. Something that really bothers me. Something stupid I said to the detective, except that maybe it wasn't so stupid, after all."

"Cops are used to people saying strange things under stress. They know how to sort out the possible from the truly off-the-wall."

"Thanks, Sherri, but I can't quite let go of this one." She drew in a deep breath and blurted it out. "I told him there was room in that freezer chest for *two* bodies."

Sherri considered that. "Rowena's husband and . . . Snowe?"

"I . . . I don't know. Maybe. But it was true, what I said. There *was* room to store a second body there temporarily. It could have been where Simeon Snowe was while everyone was searching for him. Then, later, when the coast was clear, the killer moved his body, burying it in the field."

"You know that theory makes things look worse for Rowena?" Sherri asked.

Eyes closed, Liss rubbed the bridge of her nose. "I know. But it fits, doesn't it? That sequence of events makes a horrible kind of sense."

"Where's that timeline you made?" Dan asked.

Good idea, Sherri thought.

When Liss had unearthed the page from the legal pad from their luggage and all three of them were seated around the table again, Liss tapped the capped end of her felt-tip pen against her lips, her brow furrowed in thought. "It all starts with the John Doe."

Sherri nodded. "No question about that. Go on."

"After the tree buyer in New York City found the body, he called the police and he also got in touch with his supplier, with Simeon Snowe."

"To complain, if nothing else," Dan said.

"But that same call warned Snowe that the police wanted to talk to him," Sherri said. "So, Snowe was tipped off to the fact that his netter was used in the commission of a crime. What would he do?"

"Doesn't that depend on whether or not he had any idea who was responsible for the murder?" Dan asked.

"Not necessarily." Liss drew two arrows pointing away from the words *Snowe warned*. At the point of one she wrote, "Thinks he was set up"; and next to the other, "Guesses who dunnit."

"Okay," Sherri said. "Assume he thought someone was trying to frame him for John Doe's murder and he had no alibi. In a panic, he might have run away to avoid being questioned. People do stupid things all the time when they're frightened, and even innocent people can have an irrational fear of the police. Where would he go?"

"He'd hide out with his girlfriend," Dan said. "Rowena."

"Not if he suspected she was the one behind John Doe's death."

"Maybe he didn't at first. Maybe something she did, or something he found while he was staying with her, tipped him off. Then she had to kill him, too, to keep him from ratting her out."

"Stop that!" Liss slammed the pen down for emphasis. "You two are worse than I ever was!"

Dan sent a sheepish grin her way. "Sorry. I got a little carried away. But the body you found this afternoon *was* Rowena's husband."

"That doesn't mean she killed him. For goodness' sake! Think about it. If she was the one who murdered him, why would she have led me straight to his body?

Whoever killed him knew he was there. Rowena didn't. There's only one person who could have known. It's Juliette's storage locker. Juliette's freezer. The dead man was Juliette's stepfather."

"And Juliette," Sherri said slowly, wondering why it had taken her so long to see the connection, "had something to hide even back then." She smacked herself on the forehead with the heel of her hand. "Dumb, dumb, dumb! He was asking directions to a place where people exercise. He called it a dojo, but he was really looking for Dance-Ex. He was in New Boston to find Juliette."

"He?" Liss asked in confusion. "He who?"

"It fits. It really does. So long as we make the assumption that Juliette is the one who killed her stepfather and stashed his body in the freezer. There could have been all sorts of reasons why. Domestic violence maybe. That's the most common reason for homicides."

"Go on," Liss said.

"Okay. She's already killed once and gotten away with it. The clerk at the grocery store recognized the sketch of John Doe. She said he was looking for a dojo, but I think he was going on vague information and it was Dance-Ex he wanted. Assume he found Juliette and represented a threat to her business—her *lucrative* business. What would stop her from dealing with it the exact same way? Maybe she even stashed the body in the same place, until she got a better idea. Her mother had been getting awfully cozy with Simeon Snowe, and Snowe knew Juliette's secret. Maybe she was afraid he'd let something slip to her mother. Whatever threat he represented, she decided to kill two birds with one stone, so to speak. She knew how a netter worked and that Snowe left his out in the field, unguarded, overnight. She waited for an opportunity, took the body out to the farm, netted it, and slipped it into a shipment of trees bound out of state. She figured there would be nothing to tie her to the murder, but she could be certain it would cause Snowe a lot of trouble. He might even be arrested and charged with homicide. That would get him out of her mother's life for good."

Dan looked from Sherri to Liss and back again. "What, exactly, is Juliette's big secret? What is it that would drive her to such extremes?"

Sherri laughed. "You tell him, Liss. I've got a couple of phone calls to make."

"What do you think?" Liss asked.

Dan had been shaking his head in astonishment for the past five minutes. "Unbelievable."

Affronted, she glared at him. "I didn't make it up."

"Poor choice of words. I believe you, Liss, but it boggles the mind that she'd be able to stay in business so long without anyone trying to shut her down."

"Police corruption, remember?" Liss was on her feet again, pacing in the limited space between table and door.

"Sherri hasn't let *anyone* forget." He ran his fingers through his hair, as if that would help him order his thoughts. "Prostitution is one of the rackets run by organized crime, right?"

"That's what I've always heard. Drugs and prostitution. From what Sherri was able to find out, the nature of Juliette's second business venture was fairly widely known. It's a miracle her mother never heard a whisper about it," she added as an afterthought.

"Maybe she did," Dan said. "Maybe she ignored or discounted it."

Liss frowned as a snippet of conversation from the dance studio came back to her. Rowena had said something to Juliette along the lines of, "Do what you like. You always do."

"Surely she didn't know Simeon Snowe was one of her daughter's customers. She couldn't have made the connection between those private lessons and sex for hire, although I suppose Juliette would argue that sex is excellent exercise."

Dan gave a snort of amusement. "I haven't met this woman—Juliette. Is she really that cold?"

"I wouldn't be surprised if she's already taken her mother's cat to the animal shelter and started assessing the contents of her shop for a quick sale."

"And you say she has two younger women working for her?"

Liss nodded. "That's what we think."

Another flash of memory confirmed her opinion of Juliette. Kitty had been afraid of her. She'd been falling all over herself to apologize because she was a few minutes late. Late for what, Liss didn't care to contemplate.

"Let me see if I have this straight," Dan said. "John Doe comes to New Boston because he's heard about Juliette's successful operation. Maybe he's planning a hostile takeover?"

"Could be. And she, naturally, doesn't want any part of a merger with the mob. She's a big, strong woman. If he underestimated her, she could easily have attacked him. If she already killed her stepfather and stuffed him into that freezer, she wasn't exactly a stranger to violence."

Dan conceded her point and gestured for her to continue.

"Okay. She's not playing with a full deck, so she

comes up with the idea of framing Snowe. After the body is found, he must have panicked and decided to lay low until he could figure things out. What if he hid out on the second floor above All Things Mystical? Rowena might not have known he was there. She doesn't live there."

"That would also give him a clear view of Juliette's studio." Dan's voice was thoughtful.

"Exactly."

"But I don't see how that would get him killed. He already knew what she was up to."

"Yes, but maybe he'd been trying to get her to quit, for her mother's sake. Rowena claims he was a romantic at heart. He could have been pressuring Juliette to give up her sideline, knowing that if Rowena ever found out about it, it would break her heart. Maybe Juliette told him she had, but from his hiding place he'd have seen that it was business as usual. If he confronted her about it, it would have been a fatal mistake. She couldn't risk letting him live to tell her mother or anyone else."

Dan mimed wiping sweat from his brow.

"I'm serious!"

"I know you are, but you're making some pretty sweeping assumptions. The gaps in your logic are big enough to drive a semi through."

"The gaps are in *Juliette's* logic. She's clearly got issues. But the motive for all the murders looks pretty straightforward to me—in all three cases, she was trying to protect her source of income."

He shook his head. "I thought she killed Snowe to keep Rowena from finding out about the prostitution, which makes no sense when she was so quick to throw her mother to the wolves this afternoon."

"You're right. Snowe might have been worried about breaking an old lady's heart, but Juliette could have cared less." Liss flung herself into the chair beside him. "Mothers and daughters," she muttered, thinking of that photograph of Simeon Snowe with Rowena on one side and Juliette on the other, all of them smiling as if they hadn't a care in the world. "Can you say 'dysfunctional'?"

Dan's arm slid around her shoulders. She inched her chair closer so she could lean against him. The part about killing to protect her income. *That* still made sense.

"Not all mothers and daughters have difficult relationships," Dan murmured into her hair.

"No. Some are lucky." It was a pity she couldn't call any to mind at the moment. Certainly she and her own mother had a . . . complicated relationship.

"You, for instance, would make some lucky girl a terrific mother."

It took Liss a moment to understand Dan's meaning. When she did, she tried to pull away from him. He tightened his grip and kept her tucked in at his side.

"I wouldn't," she protested. "I'd be awful at it."

She felt him draw in a deep breath, the kind that preceded broaching a touchy subject. "No more evasions, Liss. Let's settle this now."

"This is a weird time to have this discussion." With her head on his shoulder, she couldn't see his face, but she could hear his heart beat beneath her ear. It sped up, just as hers had. "Let me up."

He released her, but she didn't go very far. She scooted her chair around so that they were facing each other. For a long moment, both of them hesitated. Then Dan blurted out the question Liss had been dreading.

"Do you want to have kids or not?"

She closed her eyes and crossed her fingers. "Not."

"Me, neither," Dan said.

"What?" Liss's eyes popped open to stare at him.

"You heard me. Now, *listen* to me." He placed his hands on her shoulders, but his touch was gentle. "I have no particular desire to be a father. I have *never* had any particular desire to be a father. I'd have gone along with having children with you if that was what you really wanted, because I love you, but—"

"You idiot," Liss whispered as relief washed over her.

"Well, thanks a lot!" But he was grinning.

"I was trying to talk myself into having a baby just to please *you.*"

The grin widened. "Then it's a good thing we finally had this little chat."

They sealed their new understanding with an enthusiastic kiss and the promise of further celebration when they were back in Moosetookalook.

Dan wouldn't admit it, but he was still feeling the effects of his concussion. He went to bed early. Liss and Sherri stayed up late, watching another old movie on videotape. Neither of them paid much attention to the screen. They'd both seen Indiana Jones go after the Holy Grail many times before.

The day's developments occupied a large portion of Liss's mind. She was kicking herself for not having told Dan sooner how she felt about having children. She should have known they'd see eye to eye on the subject. The only thing of any importance they ever disagreed about was her inability to avoid getting involved in murder investigations.

"I suppose," she said after a while, "that everything in that storage locker has been confiscated, even that shoe box full of snapshots. I wish I'd been able to get a look at them."

"It was a long shot to begin with," Sherri reminded her. "I mean, really, how likely is it that Snowe had his picture taken with the other victim?"

"Not very," Liss conceded.

"Those file boxes are going to put Juliette in jail and make the police think twice about charging her mother with murder." Sherri reached for the bowl of popcorn between them on the sofa. After her conversation with Mike Jennings, she had been able to report that Rowena had not been arrested. She had been questioned for hours but had then been allowed to go home to her cat.

"We can't be sure what those bins contain. All I saw were lots of folders."

"What else could they be but client records?" Sherri sent a sidelong look Liss's way. "You're sure you didn't see any labels?"

Liss shook her head. "Sorry." She munched popcorn, smiling as she watched Harrison Ford and Sean Connery. Tied to chairs, each one thought the evil Elsa was talking to him when she referred to their having made love.

Her thoughts strayed during the next bit. The files in the storage unit might shut down Juliette's illegal sideline. They might even provide proof of Wyatt Purvey's dishonesty. But would they link Juliette to three murders? Theories wouldn't stand up in court without proof. Worse, Rowena could end up being tried on circumstantial evidence and convicted, a handy scapegoat for her uncaring daughter.

The action on the screen diverted her attention. The escape. The chase on the motorcycle. The flight in the zeppelin. Constant danger. A pity no one was guaranteed a happy ending in real life.

"Remember what I said before about walking out in the middle of the picture?" she asked. "I still feel that way. I wish there was some way we could set a trap for Juliette and force her to confess."

Sherri laughed. "Oh, I suppose we could, but that confession wouldn't be admissible as evidence. And you'd probably end up under arrest for—oh, I don't know—kidnapping? Or even assault, if you really got carried away. Let it go, Liss. I've passed on everything we found out. Now we both need to stay out of it. Believe me, that isn't any easier for me than it is for you."

"So, we go home in the morning and forget all about it? All about Rowena?"

"That's right."

Liss reached for another handful of popcorn and tried to follow Sherri's advice.

Two hours later, she was still obsessing about bringing Juliette Cressy to justice. She rolled over in bed and tried to beat her pillow into a more comfortable shape with one fist. Beside her, Dan snored softly, sound asleep. She envied him. He was a champion sleeper. Once he was down for the count, it took an earthquake to wake him.

Good thing, she decided a few minutes later. The way she was tossing and turning, she'd ruin the rest of anyone who was a light sleeper.

The luminous dial of the clock on the bedside table told her it was nearly three in the morning. If she didn't doze off soon, she'd be miserable company on the drive home. Dan and Sherri didn't deserve that.

Thinking that a glass of milk might help, she got out of bed, slid her feet into the boots that had been doubling as slippers during their stay, and felt her way to the door. The room was so small that it was only a few steps away. In the entry hall, a small night-light burned. There was another in the living room and a third in the kitchen, providing plenty of illumination without turning on any of the overhead fixtures.

She was in the middle room, in sight of the kitchen door, when a peculiar odor made her nose wrinkle. She froze. *Imagination,* she told herself. That couldn't be smoke.

Then the first alarm went off. The batteries Dan had replaced a few days earlier had it blaring at full volume.

"Dan!" she screamed and raced back toward the bedroom.

She stumbled in the entry hall but caught herself before she fell. All the while she kept yelling at the top of her lungs, calling out to Dan and to Sherri.

"The house is on fire!" she shouted. "Wake up! Fire! Fire!"

Another smoke alarm went off, this one in the stairwell. Then the lights went out.

"Oh, God!" Temporarily blinded, she felt for the side of the bed.

Dan was stirring. If Sherri was also a heavy sleeper, Liss knew she'd never get them both out, not if the fire was fast moving. She tugged at her husband's arm, shouting right in his ear.

"Move, Dan! Damn it! Get out of bed right this minute!" She threw the covers aside and pulled harder, her agitation increased by the complete and utter blackness all around her.

He wasn't fully awake, and he was too heavy for her to drag all the way out of the house. He had to get up. He had to maneuver the crutches for himself.

The crutches—where were they? Her eyes had started to adjust to the darkness, but not fast enough. She couldn't find them.

For a moment, panic rendered her immobile. He had a broken ankle. How was she going to rescue him when he couldn't walk? What if she *couldn't* get him out of the burning house? In desperation, she gritted her teeth and hauled him toward her.

"What the hell? Ow! Stop it, Liss."

"We've got to get out of the house. It's on fire."

As if he couldn't guess that from the earsplitting sound of the smoke alarms.

"Get yourself out!" he shouted at her.

"Not without you."

"Crutches." He thrashed around, feeling for them. Liss heard the clatter as they fell to the floor.

The stairwell door slammed open, and Sherri burst through. "Pitch black in there," she gasped. "Well, hell! Out here, too."

For a moment, hysterical laughter bubbled up in Liss's throat. Only a week earlier her biggest worry had been that the bulb in that stairwell would burn out while she was going up or down.

The smell of smoke grew stronger. Liss thought she could hear the crackle of flames. "Hurry, Dan!"

"Can't find the damned crutches. They landed somewhere out of reach, and it's too dark to see where they are."

Sherri pushed past Liss into the room. "Put your arm around my shoulders, Dan. Liss, you take his other side."

Together, they got him into the hallway. They were all coughing as smoke tried to engulf them. Liss knew you were supposed to get down on the floor and crawl to safety in a fire, but she didn't think Dan could crawl, and she and Sherri wouldn't be any help to him on their hands and knees.

Shifting Dan's weight more heavily onto Liss, Sherri fought with the dead bolt on the front door. Seconds seemed to stretch into hours, but at last they were through, out onto the porch and stumbling down the steps. Liss gasped in deep breaths of fresh air.

A few more staggering steps took them clear of the house.

Within seconds, the cold made itself felt. Liss had on boots, keeping her feet warm, but her flannel nightgown afforded little protection against a temperature well below freezing. In the dull red glow of the fire behind them, she could see that Sherri wore only a sleep shirt and slippers. Dan was in his underwear, and his feet were bare.

Sherri steered them toward her car. "I've got blankets and woolly socks in the trunk."

She'd also had the presence of mind to grab her purse on the way out of the upstairs bedroom. The small shoulder bag was slung across her chest, leaving her hands free. As soon as she fished out her keys and unlocked the car, she helped Liss settle Dan in the backseat. Then she dug out her cell phone and called for help.

While Liss opened the trunk, Dan scooted on his butt until his legs were stretched out in front of him on the seat. She could hear him rooting around in the pockets on the door and seat backs. Like the good police officers they were, Pete and Sherri would keep plenty of emergency gear handy, especially flashlights.

Her arms full of blankets, Liss froze, staring at the burning building. Flames shot up from the back of the house. The kitchen? She couldn't imagine how the fire had started. They were always careful to turn off the stove. They hadn't been using any space heaters. And surely it couldn't have been the furnace. If that had blown up, she'd have heard the explosion.

She looked away from the conflagration, her eyes stinging. There was no moon, but the light from the fire now illuminated the entire parking area and the side of the Quonset hut. The area beyond was completely dark.

Or was it? The flicker of light came again—a narrow beam moving rapidly away from the Quonset hut toward the acres of Christmas trees and the logging road.

A wooden building burns fast, Liss thought, *but not that fast. Not without help.*

Before she could think better of the impulse, she thrust the armload of blankets into the backseat of Sherri's car with Dan and sprinted after the person who had set the house on fire.

Chapter Fifteen

Liss heard Dan's voice calling her name, then Sherri's, but she paid no attention. If she didn't move fast, Juliette would escape.

Although she hadn't gotten a good look at her quarry, Liss had no doubt about her identity. That Juliette would set fire to the farmhouse with them in it made little sense, but for anyone else to have done so made even less. The memory of how close they'd come to being trapped . . . to being dead . . . pushed Liss onward—right over the edge of reason.

She plunged down the hill behind the Quonset hut and out into Simeon Snowe's Christmas tree farm. Thinking herself safely out of sight of the parking area, Juliette had abandoned stealth in favor of a quick getaway. The light Liss had seen was her flashlight. She was using it to find the most direct route to the logging road, where she must have left her car. Liss saw the beam glint on chrome as Juliette closed in on her goal.

Liss all but flew between the rows of trees. She had no idea how she managed to avoid the hazards underfoot. She didn't trip over any roots or step in any chuckholes, but the snap of twigs and the rustle of branches thrust aside sounded inordinately loud in the still, cold night.

Juliette turned. For a moment her flashlight illuminated her own face. Liss recognized disbelief in her expression, before it gave way to rage.

"Why aren't you dead?" Juliette shrieked and threw her flashlight at Liss's head.

Liss ducked and kept running.

Juliette slid into the driver's seat of her car and turned the key she'd left in the ignition, but Liss caught hold of the top of the car door before her adversary could get it closed. With a strength born of fury, Liss jerked it all the way open, reached inside, and hauled an astonished Juliette out onto the icy ground.

They landed hard, both staggering to keep upright. Liss lost her grip on the other woman's arm. Juliette, enraged, swung around and charged, intent on using her fingernails to claw Liss's face.

Quick reflexes saved her skin, but the sudden jerky movement caused her weak knee to spasm. It buckled under her when she tried to shift out of Juliette's way a second time, and she felt herself falling.

Instinct and years of dance training took over. She landed hard. A rock bit painfully into her hip. But she avoided hitting her head, and she did no serious damage to her limbs. Her bum knee protested even more emphatically when she pushed herself to her feet, but it didn't give out on her again. She gritted her teeth and braced herself for the next attack.

Juliette came at her like a freight train and the force of the impact took them both to the ground. They rolled together down the incline at the side of the logging road and narrowly missed slamming into a tree. The breath knocked out of her, Liss did all she could to protect herself as Juliette struck out, kicking, squirming, punching, and cursing. Her blows landed haphazardly but with bruising force.

Juliette threw another wild punch and overbalanced herself, giving Liss an opening. In an instant, she was on top, pinning her opponent. Juliette bucked, trying to dislodge her. When that failed, she broke Liss's hold on her wrists and grabbed for Liss's hair. Liss evaded the grasping fingers and tightened her knees. For strength, for determination, they were evenly matched. Juliette might be mad, but Liss was *angry*. This woman had tried to burn down a house with them in it. She'd meant to kill Dan and Sherri and Liss herself.

But furious as she was, Liss was rapidly tiring. Being bundled up in warm winter clothing cost Juliette a little mobility, but it also protected her from most of the blows Liss had managed to land. At the same time, what Liss was wearing put her at a disadvantage. She had lost one of her boots, and her flannel nightgown had hiked up. Her bare legs were so numb with cold that she could barely feel them. One more shift in position and Juliette would win.

Liss drew back her arm, made a fist, and put all the force she could muster behind the blow she aimed at Juliette's jaw. They both yelped in pain. An instant later the back of Juliette's head connected with the ground, and she went still.

Liss was still sitting on top of the unconscious Juliette and cradling her injured hand against her chest when Sherri found her.

"Are you okay?"

Liss nodded. "I hurt my thumb."

"You hurt . . . Oh, don't tell me! You had it on the inside of your fingers when you hit her. You made a *girl* fist."

Choking back a laugh, Sherri helped Liss to her feet, then rolled Juliette over and slapped handcuffs on her while she was still too dazed to resist. She jerked her prisoner upright and told her to stay put. She needn't have worried. All the fight had gone out of her.

Liss wondered if Juliette had a concussion, but she didn't much care. She managed to find her other boot with the help of Sherri's flashlight and get it back on her foot, but after that she was shivering so hard that she could barely stay upright. Her thumb was now too cold to throb. Ditto for her knee.

"Sorry it took me so long to follow you," Sherri said. "I had to make sure fire and police were on their way."

"I need a blanket." Liss's teeth were chattering so badly that it was a miracle Sherri understood her.

"With any luck, there's one coming now."

Two bobbing lights moved toward them—men with flashlights. They were no more than shapes at first but soon resolved themselves into Mike Jennings and Wyatt Purvey.

Purvey's face looked ghastly in the uneven lighting. He stared at Juliette as if he'd never seen her before, then turned, briefly, to look back over his shoulder at the fire.

It lit up the sky in that direction. The house was fully engulfed. The parking area was a beehive of activity, full of fire trucks and people rushing about. There was an ambulance, too. Liss hoped someone was looking after Dan.

Jennings draped a heavy gray wool blanket around

her shaking shoulders. Purvey had brought its twin for Sherri.

"Can you make it back under your own steam?" Jennings asked. "The EMTs can bring a stretcher if you need it."

"I'm fine."

"You don't look it," he said bluntly.

Liss wrapped the blanket more tightly around herself. "I'm not going anywhere until you place Juliette Cressy under arrest. She set the fire, and she murdered those men. All three of them."

Wyatt Purvey had moved closer to Juliette, but he didn't touch her or try to speak to her. She ignored him completely.

"And don't you dare leave Juliette in his custody," Liss added. "He'll let her escape."

A sound suspiciously like a sob came from Purvey's direction. "I didn't think she meant it," he whispered. "I couldn't believe—" Unable to go on, he just stood there. His mouth worked, but no sound emerged.

Jennings stepped forward and took charge of the prisoner, helping her to her feet and keeping hold of her arm. He recited the Miranda warning and was met with sullen silence on her part. She wouldn't even nod when he asked her if she understood her rights.

They moved as a unit to return to the parking area, where Dan anxiously waited. The ambulance included crutches in the emergency medical supplies it carried, so he was once again on his feet and mobile, if somewhat hampered by having to huddle in a blanket identical to the ones Liss and Sherri had been given.

"Get back inside the car and keep warm," Liss said after they embraced. "I'm fine."

"You don't sound it."

"Your teeth and hers will be performing a castanet duet if you keep standing around out in the cold," Jennings said. "Get back in the car, Ruskin. Your wife will join you as soon as the paramedics check her over."

Reluctantly, Dan obeyed.

Sherri steered Liss toward the ambulance while Jennings escorted Juliette to his police cruiser and locked her in the back, still handcuffed. Although the delay seemed interminable, it didn't take long for Liss and Sherri to be cleared. Aside from a few scrapes and bruises, skinned knuckles, and a throbbing thumb, Liss had escaped with relatively little damage.

All the while she was being fussed over, Liss kept one eye on Wyatt Purvey. He made no further attempt to approach Juliette, nor did he try to leave. He seemed to be waiting for the other shoe to drop.

Another fire truck, this one from a neighboring town, pulled into the parking area, quickly followed by more volunteer firefighters. The house was gone, but they had to make sure the blaze was completely extinguished. A state police cruiser arrived next. The trooper spoke to Mike Jennings, then to Wyatt Purvey. Mike got into his cruiser, with Juliette still in the back, and drove away.

In the midst of all the confusion, Andy Dutton showed up on her motorcycle. She surveyed the situation without speaking to anyone, although she stared at Liss for a long time. Then she took off again. Fifteen minutes later, she returned, this time carrying dry, warm clothing in a backpack.

A pair of Mrs. Dutton's wool slacks fit Sherri well enough for decency. The flannel-lined jeans she offered Liss were her own. They were too big, but Liss slipped into them gratefully, rolling up the legs so she wouldn't trip over the hems. When she'd added one of the two knit sweaters Andy had brought, she felt almost human again.

While she was dressing, Andy opened up the Quonset hut and turned on a space heater, which Liss hadn't even realized was there. Everyone who wasn't involved in containing the fire trooped gratefully inside. Liss had barely gotten Dan settled on the seat of the John Deere when the state trooper walked up to them.

"Ms. Ruskin?"

She nodded.

"Chief Purvey there . . ." He gestured to the far end of the Quonset hut, where Purvey had been left to stand all alone, shoulders slumped and a resigned look on his face. "He says he's got a statement to make, but he won't make it unless you're a witness to what he has to say."

"Maybe we should wait for the detective handling the Snowe case to get here," Liss suggested.

"Purvey says it has to be now, or he won't talk at all."

Sherri's face wore a worried look. "I get that you want to hear what he has to say, but this is unorthodox."

"Will you be able to use what he says against him?" Liss asked.

"He's been read his rights. I'll record his statement."

Sherri took the trooper aside. After a brief conversation and two quick phone calls, none of which Liss could overhear, they returned.

"We have the go-ahead from the powers that be," Sherri said. "It's okay for you to be the one he talks to."

In the end, Wyatt Purvey had an audience of four—Liss, Dan, Sherri, and the state trooper. He didn't seem to notice. Or, if he did, he didn't mind. All his attention was fixed on Liss.

"All right, Chief Purvey," she said when a digital

recorder had been activated. "What do you have to say to me?"

"I'm sorry."

"For what?"

"For trying to burn down the Christmas tree farm."

For a moment, Liss was at a loss for words. That was not what she'd expected him to say.

"I thought Juliette did that," Dan said. "It seems pretty obvious she was the one who set fire to the house."

"Yes, she did." Purvey hung his head. "That's what she wanted me to do the first time, but I thought burning the house down was going too far. I didn't want anyone to get hurt."

"Why that particular field?" Liss asked.

He sighed, looking even more pathetic. "The trees seemed to be closer together there. I thought they'd burn better. Faster."

Good grief, Liss thought. *Talk about conspirators working at cross-purposes!* By picking that particular field and calling attention to it, he'd accomplished the opposite of what Juliette wanted.

The state trooper interrupted. "Let me get this straight. Ms. Cressy wanted to get rid of the Ruskins? She told you to set fire to the house?"

Purvey nodded. "I thought burning the field would accomplish the same thing—get them gone."

"If you wanted to get rid of us," Dan asked, "why come by the next day and order us not to leave town?"

"Reverse psychology," Sherri murmured. "He knew he couldn't make that order stick."

"I don't understand," Liss said. "Why would you even consider doing something so terrible just because Juliette wanted you to? Was she blackmailing you?"

Purvey gave a short, humorless bark of laughter. "She didn't need to. I was in love with her. All she had to do was say, 'Jump,' and I'd ask, 'How high?' "

"You loved her? Even though she was selling herself to anyone who could meet her price?" Sherri couldn't conceal her incredulity.

Purvey winced. "She didn't. . . . She promised." He drew in a deep breath. "Yes, I knew about her past. That's how we met. I meant to put a stop to what she was doing. I never intended to arrest her, you understand. Hell, no one's getting hurt, right? Not worth making a fuss over. But the next thing I knew, she'd charmed the socks off me."

Along with the rest of his clothes, Liss thought.

"I . . . I thought if I gave her enough money, she'd give up whoring." He stared down at his hands, and Liss saw that they were trembling. "But it was never enough. She said she could make more by keeping her business going. We compromised. She agreed to bring in a couple of girls and to stop seeing customers herself."

"Kitty and Josie," Sherri said.

Purvey nodded. "Those two now. Others before. Some of them were college girls earning tuition money." He made a choked sound. "She used to say she was doing a public service by hiring them."

"So you looked the other way?" Liss asked.

"I thought . . . I thought I'd get to keep her all to myself if I did. She convinced me that she wasn't actually working in the business herself anymore, only supervising. She swore she slept only with me. Probably wrong about that," he muttered. "Seems like I was wrong about everything."

A small sound behind Liss made her turn. The detective she'd talked to after finding the body in the freezer chest had come into the Quonset hut unnoticed. He motioned for the trooper to continue recording and positioned himself out of Wyatt Purvey's line of sight.

"She had me so twisted up that I couldn't tell right from wrong anymore. I lied. I stole. But not murder. Never murder."

"Stole what?" Liss asked.

He didn't look at any of them but rather stared into space. After all the years of keeping his sins secret, Liss had to wonder if he might be finding some kind of relief in confessing.

"I embezzled money from the town to give to Juliette."

"Who caused my husband's accident in the parking lot at the grocery store?" Liss asked.

"Juliette. You stopped by and said you were staying at the farm, and then her mother told her you'd bought a book on mazes. I didn't understand what it was that worried her. I didn't know she'd buried Snowe there."

"What *did* you know?" Liss persisted. "Did you know she'd killed John Doe?"

"I . . . Yes, she told me about him. But she said killing him was an accident. He threatened her. He was a *criminal*. He wanted to bring organized crime into my town."

He said that as if it was okay to kill someone who was connected to the mob. That was how he'd justified Juliette's crime to himself, Liss supposed. "Why did she bring him out here and net him?"

"She was out of her mind with fear."

"More likely, she wanted to frame Simeon Snowe for the murder," Sherri said.

"I believed her when she said she didn't know what happened to Snowe."

"Finding him in that field was proof that she did," Liss said. "That must have been a nasty shock. And then she tried to frame Rowena."

"She's afraid."

"She went off half-cocked, and she doesn't give a tinker's dam who gets hurt or killed as a result." Dan's disgust was obvious. "What about her stepfather? What reason did she have for killing him?"

"I don't know." Purvey seemed to shrink into himself. His voice, never more than a loud whisper, faded away to nothing.

Sherri threw more questions at him. So did the state police detective. Purvey denied that his mother had been involved. He claimed she didn't even know he'd been intimate with Juliette. Then he stopped talking. A short time later, the trooper took him away.

The detective remained behind long enough to tell them that the search for evidence against Rowena had yielded plenty to incriminate Juliette. There had been evidence in the storage locker that would send Wyatt Purvey to prison, too, even without his recorded confession.

"Rowena will be devastated," Liss murmured, "but at least she won't be punished for a crime she didn't commit."

"I could almost feel sorry for Wyatt Purvey if he wasn't such a weakling," Sherri said.

"Do you really think he knew nothing about Snowe's murder?" Dan asked.

"Hard to tell, but I think his disillusionment with Juliette was real. When he belatedly realized that only Juliette could have killed all three men, he had to stop deluding himself. She'd been using him. She never loved him. She probably didn't even enjoy the sex—"

"Too much information," Liss interrupted.

"I have to wonder, though, why Juliette killed her stepfather."

"Maybe he was a customer, too," Dan suggested.

"Or else he found out she was selling herself and tried to get her to stop," Sherri suggested. "Threatened to tell Rowena, maybe. Or threatened to turn her in to the cops."

"So she, what?" Dan asked. "Killed him, shoved him in the freezer, and forgot about him?"

"Hardly. She knew he was there. By the time she was on her third victim, she had no qualms about giving him a temporary freezer mate. From the sound of it, she was willing to dispose of anyone she saw as a threat, including us."

"So you think Snowe was giving her a hard time, trying to get her to give up her sideline for her mother's sake?" Dan was shaking his head in disbelief.

"Maybe. Talk about déjà vu!"

Almost all the emergency vehicles had dispersed by the time they left the Quonset hut. There was nothing left in the ruins of the house to salvage, and now that they had answers to most of their questions, Liss wanted nothing more than to go home. Exhaustion was taking its toll, but she had one more obligation to fulfill before she could leave.

She borrowed Sherri's cell phone and called Gina Snowe.

Once she'd brought the property's owner up to date on the latest developments, she cut short a barrage of questions with one of her own. "Why did you send us here, Gina?"

"To find out what really happened, of course, but I

didn't expect I'd have to lose the house in order to get answers."

"You expected me to snoop."

"Well, it's what you *do*." Gina chuckled. "You keep denying it, but you're the closest thing to Miss Marple that Moosetookalook has. Why shouldn't I take advantage of that?"

Liss resisted the urge to hang up on her "old friend." Gina *owed* her.

It took some fast talking, and a threat or two, but in the end Gina agreed to let Andy go ahead with her plans for the holiday season, bankrolling any additional expense involved in cleaning up after the fire. Satisfied, Liss disconnected.

Dawn was breaking as they drove away from the Christmas tree farm, Liss and Sherri dressed in their borrowed clothing and Dan still wrapped in a blanket.

Two weeks later, in early December, Liss, Dan, Sherri, and Pete drove back to New Boston. Liss had been in touch with Andy almost daily, but she was still astonished to see the progress the young woman had made in her absence. Neighbors had helped clear away the debris from the house fire and cover over the cellar hole. A fresh coat of snow now blanketed what had once been an ugly scar on the landscape.

"This is amazing!" Liss exclaimed as Andy led them past the burned field. Dan and Pete each carried a bright red plastic tarp, while Sherri had charge of two handsaws. "That was such an eyesore, and now you can't even tell where the charred tree stumps were."

There was already a family—parents and two children under the age of six—searching for the perfect tree in the lot. The little girl wore a cap with antlers on it. The boy had on a Santa hat. Their delighted laughter filled the crisp winter air.

"We should have brought the kids," Sherri said.

"Next year," Pete promised. "Amber will be old enough to appreciate the experience by then. And the long drive won't be as likely to make her cranky."

"We'll see," Sherri said, and she and Pete exchanged sappy smiles.

Liss felt a moment's guilt at depriving her friends of the fun that other family was enjoying, but she'd encouraged them to leave Adam and Amber behind. The conversation she intended to have with Andy was likely to contain material unfit for young ears.

"Any new developments?" she asked in what she hoped was a casual voice.

With four avid listeners surrounding her, Andy turtled her head, suddenly self-conscious. "A few," she mumbled.

Liss sent her an encouraging smile. She could well imagine what the local gossips had been saying about Juliette's arrest, especially when Kitty and Josie had been taken into custody right afterward. The local paper would have reported the nature of their alleged crimes, and it wouldn't have taken a rocket scientist to figure out their connection to Dance-Ex.

Andy shrugged. "You probably know more than I do."

"We've had a few updates," Sherri admitted. "The last time I checked, Kitty and Josie were out on bail, but Juliette, with three counts of homicide against her, will have to remain in jail, awaiting trial. As for Wyatt Purvey, I understand he's had a complete mental breakdown. He's in the hospital, being evaluated."

Andy was nodding. "It didn't help that his mother had a heart attack when she heard he'd been arrested. He thought she was dying. She isn't. She's driving the nurses at the hospital crazy because she insists that her son was framed."

"Mother love," Liss murmured, although she had more sympathy for the other mother in the case, Rowena Luckenbill.

"Anything else?" Dan asked.

"Well, Mike Jennings got a crappy deal."

Sherri stiffened. "What are you talking about? He was instrumental in uncovering Purvey's other crimes."

"We figured he'd be acting chief of police by now," Pete remarked.

But Andy was shaking her head. "The town manager didn't take kindly to losing both his administrative assistant and his chief of police."

"Not to mention he was probably a tad embarrassed because he never noticed that Purvey had embezzled from the town coffers," Liss muttered. She wondered if Beatrice Purvey had stuck her finger in that pie, helping to cover up what her son had done.

"The board of selectmen was some put out, too," Andy said. "They had a meeting last week and fired the entire police force, including Mike Jennings."

"Idiots," Pete said.

The expression "throwing out the baby with the bathwater" came to mind, but Liss couldn't get a word in edgewise to voice it. Between Sherri's pithy comments and the expletives Pete showered on New Boston's town fathers, the air around them came very close to turning blue.

These were all delivered in low voices, in deference to

the family coming toward them with their Christmas tree.

"Do you have to take care of them?" Liss asked.

"Mom can do it. She knows I wanted the chance to talk with you."

Liss's eyebrows shot up. "Mom?"

Andy shrugged. "Did you really think I could stop her from volunteering?"

Pete and Sherri wandered off in search of their own Christmas tree. At Dan's urging, he and Liss followed suit, but at a slower pace. Dan was still on crutches.

Although Liss had spent a fair amount of time looking at the trees before this, everything seemed different now that her agenda had changed. Which one would look best in their living room? Was that one too tall? Too full? Not full enough? And was she going to have to go out and buy more ornaments and lights? Some of the joy she'd felt as a child on a similar mission reasserted itself as they spread out.

Dan, ever practical, used one of the crutches to make little Xs in the snow beside each tree that he thought was a possibility. When they'd been through the entire lot, they circled back, taking a second look at each candidate before making a final decision.

"You're going to have to cut it down." Dan offered her the saw.

"If you kneel on the tarp, you'll stay dry." Andy made the suggestion with the air of one who had given the same advice dozens of times during the past week.

It was a good idea, especially since achieving the correct angle from which to use the saw required not only kneeling, but also lying down full length on the ground. The tree toppled over with a minimum of effort after that and, once positioned on the tarp, was ready to be dragged back to the Quonset hut for netting.

Following a trail of cute hand-lettered signs, they reached the overhead door at the far end of the Quonset hut. It had been left open to give customers access to the two netters, but nothing else inside was as Liss expected. Gone were the John Deere tractor and the piles of miscellaneous junk.

Christmas music from hidden speakers greeted her first, along with a profusion of Christmas decorations. They led the eye not toward the netters, but rather to a section of the interior that had been partitioned off. It had its own door, with a sign above it that said SANTA'S GIFT SHOP. Smaller signs told customers that it was heated inside—welcome news after spending time out in the cold, hunting for a tree—and that there was free hot cocoa available.

"Go ahead in," Andy said. "Mom will take your money and give you a receipt while I put your trees through the netter. If you had little kids with you, I'd let them turn the crank. They get a huge charge out of that."

The small gift shop was a revelation. A sales counter on wheels was to her right as Liss walked in, a smiling Mrs. Dutton—the embodiment of Mrs. Claus—seated on a stool behind it. On top were an iPad with a PayPal attachment, a receipt book, a pocket calculator, and a display of maple syrup bottles in various sizes, all provided by a local farm.

"Help yourself to hot chocolate," Mrs. Dutton invited Liss, gesturing to a small table that held a hot-water dispenser, packets of cocoa, a stack of Styrofoam cups, a mug full of wooden stirrers, and a roll of paper towels to mop up spills.

Liss had expected to see wreaths for sale, but she was unprepared for the wide variety of stock displayed in such a relatively small space. There *were* wreaths, but there were other Christmas decorations, as well, and they were not the boxes of colorful balls of the sort found in any store during this season. Each one was unique, made by a local craftsperson. With a low whistle of appreciation, Dan went to inspect them more closely.

Autographed copies of children's books by a Maine author were nicely arranged on a second small table, the one title with a Christmas theme displayed so that the front cover rather than the spine faced out. Colorful knitted throws, hats, and scarves filled the rest of the shelf and table space, all of them for sale. Sweaters, it appeared, were reserved for Andy.

That young woman joined them after netting the trees, humming along with Bing Crosby's rendition of "White Christmas."

"Where's Pete?" Sherri asked.

"He's tying the trees to the rack on top of his car. I'm not allowed to do that for customers. Gina says it gets tricky legally if a tree falls off. If the customer does it, though, anything that happens is his own fault."

"I am seriously impressed by everything you've accomplished here," Liss told her young protégé. "If Gina isn't able to sell the place right away, I'll lobby her to let you continue to sell trees here until your own crop is ready."

"Already talked to her," Andy said. "She said she'll consider it if the profits are good."

Liss jumped when a Klaxon sounded.

"That's the alarm for the driveway," Andy explained. "A customer's about to drive into the parking area. Gotta go."

Mrs. Dutton watched her daughter leave, a smug expression on her face. "She rigged that up herself," she announced with pride. "And when someone walks in front of the sensor on the corner of this building, coming back with a tree, we get another signal. That one sounds like sleigh bells."

"Clever." Liss couldn't get over the change in Mrs. Dutton's attitude. As she pulled out her wallet to pay for her tree, she risked a question. "How come you used to be so opposed to having Andy help out here?"

Her shrug was an exact duplicate of her daughter's. "Seemed like that Ms. Snowe was taking advantage of her. Oh, she gave her money to stock the house with groceries, and she kept to the bargain her father made with Andy to look after the place, but she never said one word about a raise. Wouldn't you think that after seven years my girl would be entitled to one?"

"Yes. Yes, I do," Liss told her, "but it sounds as if Andy has figured out how to deal with Gina Snowe. Maybe better than I ever have."

A short time later, they were in the car and headed home. Liss was feeling rather pleased with the way things had worked out for Andy. She tried not to think of the other, less happy outcomes.

"Damn shame about Mike Jennings," Dan said.

From the backseat, where she and Sherri sat, Liss saw Pete meet his wife's eyes in the rearview mirror. He gave a slight nod. Liss turned in time to see Sherri's lips curve into a small, satisfied smile.

"What?"

It was Pete who answered. "I phoned Mike after I finished getting the Christmas trees tied down. There's a job opening up in Carrabassett County. One of the old guard is about to retire, and we'll need to hire a new deputy. Mike's definitely interested. It seems his attachment to his old hometown isn't quite as strong as it used to be. He's not only willing to move, but he's also eager."

"Good to know." Sherri's smile turned into a grin. "Because if the county job doesn't pan out, there might just be an opening for another police officer in Moosetookalook. This time around, I'm planning to take a nice long maternity leave."